Nick Earls is the author of twelve novels and two collections of short stories. He is the winner of a Betty Trask Award (UK) and a Children's Book Council of Australia Book of the Year Award. *48 Shades of Brown* and *Perfect Skin* have been adapted into feature films, and five of his novels, including *The True Story of Butterfish* and *Zigzag Street*, have become stage plays.

T0359216

THE
FIX
NICK
EARLS

VINTAGE BOOKS
Australia

A Vintage book
Published by Random House Australia Pty Ltd
Level 3, 100 Pacific Highway, North Sydney NSW 2060
www.randomhouse.com.au

First published by Vintage in 2011
This edition published by Vintage in 2012

Addresses for companies within the Random House Group can be found at
www.randomhouse.com.au/offices

National Library of Australia
Cataloguing-in-Publication Entry

National Library of Australia
Cataloguing-in-Publication Entry

Earls, Nick, 1963–.
The fix / Nick Earls.

ISBN 978 1 86471 151 6 (pbk.)

A823.3

Cover photograph by Scott Rudkin, courtesy of Flickr via Getty Images
Cover design by Peter Long
Internal design by Midland Typesetters, Australia
Typeset in Bembo by Midland Typesetters, Australia
Printed and bound by Griffin Press, an accredited ISO AS/NZS 14001:2004
Environmental Management System printer

Random House Australia uses papers that are natural, renewable and recyclable
products and made from wood grown in sustainable forests. The logging
and manufacturing processes are expected to conform to the environmental
regulations of the country of origin..

BEN HARKIN'S FATHER DIED when his coronary arteries closed over while he windsurfed at Club Med Bora Bora on his honeymoon with his energetic, third and youngest wife. By then the worst of his crimes – all of the white-collar variety and very much of their time – had long before been found out and subsequently prosecuted with results sufficiently mixed that he could still find money somewhere to spend on the business of looking prosperous.

He hit the water dead, more than likely, and, despite his young wife's strong swimming stroke and her quick progress to his body, he was gone and that was all there was to it. Everything had until then been perfect about the day, but there he was with his luck changed in a moment, floating facedown, breath gliding out of him for the final time, gazing dead-eyed at the coral and the clown fish and the anemones and a world that went on.

The day the Courier-Mail ran four paragraphs about his father's death, they also covered the announcement that Ben was to be awarded the Star of Courage.

The stories fell several pages apart and I wondered if anyone but me would think to link them. Kerry

Benson Harkin senior – corporate rogue, dead with the last of his creditors left in his wake and never to be satisfied. Kerry Benson Harkin junior – lawyer, hero. They shared a name, but Ben was always Ben and never Kerry. It put at least a small distance between them, as did the fact that Ben looked more Japanese than European.

Ben Harkin had been out of my life for years by then, and I had wrongly assumed that he would never be back.

★ ★ ★

TWO MONTHS LATER, as the worst of the Brisbane summer heat ebbed, I caught the CityCat from the back of West End into town. Two European back-packers with sandals cut from tyres and skin the colour of hazelnut sat on the back deck with their legs stuck out into the sun, while I kept to a nearby arc of shade and braced myself to be grateful to my brother.

My brother's PR company had done well while I had been out of the country, and he had booked me in for a week or two on his coat-tails, covering a job for a staff member who was away. From our phone call the weekend before, that was all I knew. No, I also knew that the person I was filling in for was skiing in Aspen.

In families, if things are not set in stone, they are set in something close to it that most days feels no easier to negotiate. Families make up their minds early about who is a big mouth and who is a keeper of secrets, who is reliable and who is a fuck-up. About every minute characteristic. And then, too often, we do things that reinforce their worst expectations.

Eight years before, when I was twenty and Brett was yet to have staff who skied in the other hemisphere, I had MC'd his wedding. I had heard my father telling him I should be best man, and Brett saying that I'd be shit at it and Dad knew that. I waited for our father to stand up for me, to tell him he couldn't be more wrong, to insist that he ask me. There was a pause, and then our father's voice said, 'Well, you could at least make him MC.'

So, when the big day came, I had too much to drink and, as the best man simpered his way through a wasteful speech that denounced none of Brett's foibles, I sat making snide remarks to the bridesmaids, in the hope that it might improve the odds of some of that ill-considered wedding sex people talk about. While the best man went on about true friendship, I simulated gagging and decided somebody had to achieve some balance. I made notes on my place card, but the ink smudged on the way to the microphone and, with a hundred and forty faces turned my way, I blurted out – for the first and only time in my life – something about the teenage crush I'd had on the woman who happened to be the bride.

Francesca was a model, and spectacular as a bride in a way that I had been trying all day not to mention to people. At the podium I owned up to keeping a Bras 'n' Things catalogue in which she had featured hidden on my bookshelf. It was in the middle of a copy of The Catcher in the Rye. I had been thirteen at the time, though I omitted to mention that, and probably made it sound as if the catalogue was still there. Still a visual prompt for my lonely carnal acts in the very week she was marrying my brother.

'Has everyone read The Catcher in the Rye?' I heard myself saying, in case that fixed it, as the large hands of the best man took my shoulders and turned me without a fight away from the microphone. He was reading emails as I left the marquee to throw up in a nearby bin.

'Meeting Francesca,' the note on the place card said above the smudge where I had wiped my palm across it. I had meant to talk about Brett meeting Francesca. It was a story in which he came out looking mildly foolish.

I could recall one catalogue picture in particular, in which she was on a bed in a black G-string and camisole, the dusky shapes of her nipples clear through the flimsy fabric. Had I talked about that? I hoped not.

The next day we had a breakfast at a hotel with the newlyweds, and I slunk in late and sat next to a deaf great-uncle for whom the speeches of the day before had been as safe as a mime. My mother found me at the buffet, looked disapprovingly at the large pile of bacon on my plate and said, wryly, 'Josh, you always wear your heart on your sleeve, don't you?' She told me she had thought about it, and that was the best thing she could offer.

My father sat with his back to me in a booth at the far end of the room. He was boring Francesca's bird-like mother, who picked at a small glass bowl of low-fat yoghurt with a spoon. I was mustering up the courage to go over there when I saw the corkboard photo montage of the reception. There were pictures of the speeches, the bouquet in the air, and bad dancing by people who were respectably drunk. The montage had started in the middle of the board and grown out from there, a bloom of images overlapping at their edges and corners. Except for one. All by itself, in the bottom right corner, was a picture of the MC, his head in a bin, chucking his guts up.

My father didn't speak to me for weeks. Brett and Francesca never mentioned it.

Months later, when he was angry with me about something unrelated, Brett said, 'You realise Francesca doesn't ever want to be alone in a room with you?' I could only think it had something to do with my brief speech about our catalogue days. Perhaps I had talked about her nipples after all.

As the CityCat slid in towards the Riverside stop, I looked up at the towering buildings above – their blue and bronze glass and concrete, and their blunt geometry – and it felt as if I might be anywhere. I had been called into buildings just like them before, in British cities. I had worked from one in London for two years until, one day, I didn't.

Somewhere, here in one of them, someone had an issue about to pop. Someone was about to need perception management. An issue needed fixing, and I was to be the fixer.

I hoped it was bad news. I was better with bad news. Good news meant a new product or a new deal, and all the effort went into persuading the media to buy into someone showing off. With bad news, I would walk in to the rank smell of fear and I would usually discover that the clients had already fantasised about the most dire outcomes, and all I had to do was shore up the sky and stop it falling as they took their pain and surprised themselves by coming out the other side intact. They had often hidden something, or bluffed their way through with a half-truth that was starting to unravel. They would want to lie, ambitiously, and had bought me as armour. But, in the job's only moral moment, I would tell them we would start with the truth, and build the fix from there. And I would explain in detail how their lives would be in the days and weeks ahead. They would wear some bruises but, after it was all done, they would find themselves only a few deep breaths away from feeling that they had integrity back within reach.

Brett was sitting at a white plastic table outside the coffee shop where we had agreed to meet. He was wearing a dark suit and, when I got closer, I could see that it had fine pinstripes. He was ignoring his coffee and scrolling through a document on his BlackBerry. For the first time, I noticed that his sandy hair was thinning on top. He looked up as I pulled another chair away from the table and its legs scraped on the tiles.

'Do you have a tie?' he said. He looked as if he had been about to smile, but it didn't happen.

'Hello.' I paused to allow him time to get reacquainted with the word. 'With me right now, or at all?'

He thought about it. 'Either.'

'No.' I had ties, somewhere. In a box.

'How does anyone not have a tie?'

I was a barbarian who had, out of nowhere, appeared on the wrong side of the battlements.

'I had a couple,' I told him. 'They never came back from England. Maybe you could get over it.' He was looking at my shirt by then. 'And before you ask the question "Do you have an iron?" let me just say, "Don't." I already have a mother for that shit, and if we needed a wardrobe session for this meeting you should have told me.'

This whole conversation should have been, in a word, nicer. He should have started with hello, instead of behaving like a housemaster noting a uniform indiscretion.

He looked past me, at Kangaroo Point and the final downward sweep of the grey girders of the Story Bridge. He seemed for a moment to be focusing on the bridge hard enough to count individual rivets.

'Let me just check one thing,' he said. 'You are able to fit this in, aren't you? Your diary is clear until next Monday?'

'Pretty much clear.'

'And if I hadn't called about this job, how would it be?'

Pretty much clear. 'Flexible,' I said instead. 'That's one of the perks. That's the beauty of my present arrangements.' It came out sounding as contrived as it was. 'I have some out-of-town commitments for a couple of days from late next Monday, but I'm fine till then.' I added it so belatedly that it probably seemed made up. 'That's for an article.'

'Okay,' he said. He gave his coffee a perfunctory stir, and took a mouthful of it. 'I've read the blog you do. That's going well. And Mum said you'd had a few pieces in magazines.'

He had flecks of latte froth on his gingernut-coloured moustache. He licked at it, sensing the froth was there but missing it. He'd had the moustache for close to twenty years, and grew it in the first place to hide the jagged scar on his upper lip from the time he went over his bike handlebars as a kid. Of course, the scar itself couldn't grow anything, so the rest of it had to be extra bushy to make up for it. It was a mo the Marlboro Man would have been proud of, had he not died of product-related cancer when working for the one industry the Western world could no longer spin. In an attempted concession to the times, Brett's Marlboro Man mo was now paired with a flavour-saver below his lower lip. It missed the mark, and he looked like a ginger cavalier.

'So, tell me about the job,' I said. He had work for me and I needed it.

He picked up a slim salmon-coloured zip-up document satchel that had been leaning against the leg of his chair.

'Have you seen these before?' he said. 'It's made from an old vinyl billboard skin.'

He showed me the tiny picture of the billboard that was stuck on there. The satchel had been cut from a salmon-coloured exclamation mark. Brett had greened up while I had been out of the country, and the satchel was another green credential. I still wasn't sure if the conversion was sincere or just the right look for the firm.

'Here's the job,' he said, pulling a printout of a scanned newspaper article from the satchel and setting it on the table in front of me. 'It's helping a law firm through this, the highlighted bits, the medal. Getting it some tasteful attention, making it a plus.'

He said something more, but I had stopped listening. He was showing me the article I had read two months before, about Ben Harkin and the medal.

Ben Harkin, his two paragraphs covered in yellow highlighter pen, was the job.

The words had been crunched a little by the scanning, but I knew them anyway. Brett's tone changed. He was asking me a question. He wanted to know what I thought.

'Did you know his father died?' I said. 'It was in the paper the same day.'

'So you're already onto this? Did I talk about this before? The details of the job?' He leaned across to check the page. 'I didn't know his father had died.'

'We have a past. Ben Harkin and I.' It was the simplest way to put it, even if it sounded more dramatic than I wanted it to. 'And I read a lot of papers. I'm forever scouting for blog material.' I needed to focus. I needed to put a different thought in my head. The thought of Ben Harkin as a siege hero, as my new job.

The picture was of one of the other award recipients, a pilot who had climbed onto the fuselage to save a skydiver caught on the way out. Both the pilot and the skydiver were leaning against the opened door of a small plane, one of them holding a parachute as a prop. They were laughing. Their story was the first six paragraphs. Ben's Star of Courage, for jumping a gunman in a siege, was paragraphs seven and eight.

'So why did the pilot get most of the article for the Bravery Medal when it says that Ben's Star of Courage is actually a bigger deal? Is it just that two people and a plane make a better picture?'

'Good question,' he said. 'I don't know. What kind of past do you have?'

'We know each other.' Knew each other.

'Oh. Well, that's a bonus.' He rotated the sheet of paper on the table so that we could both read it easily.

'Yeah, the Star of Courage is the higher category. Maybe their last PR people weren't on the ball. We've only had Randall Hood Beckett as a client for a month or so. The medal presentation's next Monday. What do you think you can do in a week?'

'A week? Depends if you want quality or quantity. Depends on the story, and what he's like at telling it. A week is fine, though, particularly if he's okay talent. It counts as news on Monday, and news isn't big on lead times. As you know.' My hand was on Ben's two yellow paragraphs, both mentions of his name covered. It was easier to think that way. 'Even beyond the news angle, Monday's the day we've got to hang it on. We'll land it on the news and spin it out of there.' It was jargon I had picked up somewhere. I had once thought it sounded good, but maybe it didn't. Maybe it sounded false. 'We should be fine, unless there are bigger heroes around that we don't know about.'

'We should get you a coffee,' he said, struck by the thought for the first time and glancing around half-heartedly for staff. 'Except we're going to have to head off soon. You could get it takeaway.' He reached into his pocket for some coins.

'I'm okay. Thanks.'

He opened the document satchel again, and pulled out another sheet of paper. 'There's some background,' he said. 'Some more on the story. They sent through this article from when it happened. Late September the year before last.'

'Are you planning to give it all to me one page at a time?'

'I didn't want to overwhelm your Gen Y concentration span.' It was a longstanding joke making a comeback.

We were a clear half-generation apart in age, and it mostly felt like one of those halves that rounded up. We hadn't had enough common ground to work the way brothers were supposed to, but on our better days we had still connected in some ways – the music he brought home, mainly, and movies. And I had of course spent my teenage years in a relationship with a photo of the woman he later met and married.

'Somewhere out there is a demographer I want to slap over all that Gen Y stuff,' I told him, 'but I'm too distractable to find out who.'

He laughed. 'I'd give you more, but that's all I've got. Just those articles. I'm sure the firm'll have more.'

The older article had more details of the siege, though it hadn't really been a siege, not in the way it was conceived or carried out. Perhaps the word siege had come along early in the coverage, and stuck. The gunman was an aggrieved or troubled client. He had taken Ben and the managing partner, Frank Ainsworth, hostage and blocked the exits. Ben had saved the day but, in the struggle, the man had been fatally shot by his own weapon. I got the impression it hadn't lasted long enough to become a siege.

'So, Ben Harkin's a friend of yours?' Brett was saying.

I didn't look up. There was a photo of Ben being led to an ambulance, and an older man – Frank Ainsworth – on a stretcher with a bandage wrapped around his head. 'Well, I'd happily never see him again, but don't let that bother you.'

Brett picked at his nails. It was a habit that had always irritated me.

'But you're okay with this?' he said, as nonchalantly as he could manage. 'I've told them it'll be you doing the job. I've pitched you based on what you did in the UK.'

'I'm okay with it.' I straightened the two sheets of paper out in front of me, one on top of the other. 'I'm a professional. Watch me. I can be the most professional guy you've ever seen without a tie.'

'Remember that job you did with the contaminated water in the UK? That went really well. You'll be great with this. And it's easy. In and out in a week or so.'

'I did practically nothing on that. The contaminated water job.' I had already said I was okay. I didn't need to be persuaded. 'I was really junior then.'

'Maybe, but it was a tough sell. This is good news. The water story shows you know how to find the angles to play. It's a good example.' It wasn't any kind of example, but I was going to take the work, even if Ben Harkin was to be right at the centre of it. 'And there was more, right? Privatisations? A toll road through some piece of unspoiled wilderness?'

'It wasn't exactly unspoiled wilderness. It was the Midlands. But, yeah, I ran interference on that kind of stuff. Spun it till its eyes popped, if I had to. A good-news story like this looks like a gift in comparison. I'm your man, Brett. So stop pitching. At least stop pitching me to me. Or to you.'

'Just talking things through. You'll be great.' He looked at his watch, then straightened it on his wrist. 'Mum said you picked up the camp stove from her a week ago.'

'Yeah. My oven kind of conked out.'

So this was where it all came together – my oven, the visit to my parents, the out-of-the-blue call from Brett offering work. Not so out of the blue, as it turned out. Aspen now sounded too obvious, a cliché. I wondered if the job was complete charity. I took a long slow breath, and I sucked it up.

I was tucked under the overhang of a mortgage, I had money coming in but only in fits and starts, and Randall Hood Beckett was to be my oven job. The camp stove was a very temporary solution. It had to be. It was no more sophisticated than a Bunsen burner.

'I want to make the right choice with the new oven,' I told him. 'I don't want to rush it. It might be smarter to do the rest of the kitchen at the same time. Renovate the lot.' I had no plans for that, but it sounded like an adult thing to say. 'The camp stove'll be fine in the meantime.'

'Sure,' he said. 'And there's always salads. Most of us don't eat enough salads.'

The job was charity. I was sure of it then.

He checked that I didn't want the takeaway coffee, took the last mouthful of his latte and led me out of the coffee shop in the direction of the nearby office towers, and Randall Hood Beckett.

As we waited for the traffic lights to change, I realised that the news photo had been taken from exactly the spot where we were standing. I could see where the ambulance had parked. I could see the jacaranda trees that had framed Ben's exit from the building.

'Does he know it's me?' It was the building diagonally across the intersection. He was up there now, somewhere, high up behind the gold glass, waiting.

'Who? Ben Harkin?' Brett glanced at me just as the green walk sign came on. The woman to his right bumped his elbow as she stepped out onto the road. 'Yeah. I guess so. I'm sure he does. I sent them that CV you emailed. They said he'd be glad to know it was someone with the right experience.'

Like most respectable CVs, the facts – the dates and places – were true enough, but I read better than I was. Since my job was spin, though, there would have been a kind of negligence involved, surely, if I hadn't applied just a little steady torque to my own story.

We crossed the street and the granite forecourt, and cool air rode out of the open glass doors ahead of us as we approached the building. In the foyer, the granite floor was polished and people in dark suits – men and women – crisscrossed between the lift wells and the doors. It looked almost choreographed, like the opening ceremony of a lawyers' Olympics. In two places, a pair of camel-coloured leather sofas had been arranged as if for conversation, in an L-shape with a potted rubber tree where they met. The Ls were mirror images of each other, and the rubber trees nearly identical. The sofas were empty.

Mid-foyer, Brett stopped. 'Ben wasn't the one with Eloise, was he?'

'Yeah. He was the one with Eloise.' It was the one question I had wanted him not to ask. 'This has always been, and remains, a small town.' A small town, and I had come back to it, come back and stuck myself to my past like a moth to a pantry moth trap. Eloise was in my head, vividly. I tried to force the image of her to pixelate, to erase. I had worked my way clear of all that, almost clear.

Brett was looking at me, measuring up what this might do. I could tell he was expecting flight – gutless little-brotherly flight – and already planning for its consequences.

'That was then and this is now,' I said. I realised I could live with the camp stove, pretty much indefinitely. It wasn't the point after all. 'I'm not walking away in the foyer of the building on the way to the meeting. You've pitched me. They're expecting me. And you know I can do this job.'

'Okay.' He had something big-brotherly that he wanted to tell me, some toxic platitude or perhaps an update on the benefits of salad, but he held it back. It's a rare moment when a family member works out in time that every single thing they want to say would be wrong. 'I think it's on thirty-seven. Reception.'

Half of the lifts, I noticed, went only to twenty, while the others serviced the upper floors. We stepped into one as the doors were closing.

'As good-news stories go,' I said to Brett, 'this one should be easier to work with than most. At least it's got a good story. A real story.'

'Yeah, right,' he said, too positively. It was as if he had held his breath since he'd mentioned Eloise, and now he could let it out. 'Yeah. And I don't think they've done much with it yet at all.'

At thirty-seven, the lift doors opened to a curved white marble reception desk and, behind it, a broad painting of the city at night. It was an aerial view, with the vigour of the brushwork on show and picking up all the colour and mess of the lights without being gaudy. On the front of the desk, fixed by steel rods to the marble, the names Randall, Hood and Beckett had somehow been worked into a wave of bluish glass. I wanted a tie. I should have looked harder for one, back at the flat. I should have thought it through.

'They're expecting you on thirty-eight,' the receptionist said when Brett signed us in. 'Let me sort that out for you.' She took a pass on a lanyard from her drawer and led us back to the lift. When the doors opened, she stepped in, waved the pass in front of a sensor and pushed the button for the next floor. 'For Mister Ainsworth's office, you turn left out of the lift, then keep going to the end. I'll let him know you're on your way.'

She was leaving the lift as she spoke, but she kept her hand on the doors to stop them closing on us as we got in.

'Security,' Brett said as soon as it was just the two of us. 'I think that's since the incident. I heard they'd had a security revamp.'

'But wasn't it a client? Wouldn't he have got in anyway?' I was trying to work it out, not trying to pick a fight.

'I just heard,' he said. He cleared his throat, and watched the thirty-seven change to a thirty-eight on the liquid crystal display. 'I think if a client turned up on thirty-seven with a gun and looking kind of crazy, it'd be a hint that you wouldn't take them to thirty-eight.'

'Good point. Here's hoping I'll do all my work on thirty-eight then.'

The lift doors opened to a corridor of glass-fronted offices. We stepped out onto a dark blue carpet with a recurring green motif, and just enough give to underline its quality.

Frank Ainsworth stood as we arrived at the open door to his corner office.

'Brett, come in,' he said, his voice a little louder than it needed to be. 'And you must be Joshua.'

Through the windows behind him, the office blocks paraded down Charlotte Street, the afternoon sun flaring from their glass faces. I could only see the middles of most buildings and the tops of some, and couldn't tell between them. One or two of them might even have been built while I was away. I recognised the street less than I expected to. Maybe it wasn't Charlotte Street, but one of the other queen streets instead.

Of the two walls without windows, one had a dot painting that at a guess would have cost ten grand, and the other had shelves full of the kind of books that make a classic lawyer backdrop in TV interviews. I had never seen them close up, and wondered if they were legislation, or textbooks, or something you bought by the metre – a kind of office dressing from the age of encyclopaedias.

Frank came around his desk to meet me with a bone-crushing handshake, a wave of manly sandalwood aftershave straight out of the eighties and his pale blue eyes working me over, summing me up, already checking whether or not I was up to the job. He was not someone to be sucked in by a well-massaged CV. He wore a crisp white shirt and a club tie and could have been any other hard-edged, no-nonsense man in business, had it not been for the pink scar on his tanned bald scalp, zigzagging back from his forehead.

'Don't worry,' he said, tapping the scar with his left index finger. 'I've heard it all before. Harry Potter at fifty.' He gave a bark of a laugh and then quickly said, 'Sit down, sit down,' motioning towards the two seats on the opposite side of the desk to his. 'I'm only forty-eight anyway. Just a bit weather-beaten.' He took his own seat, straightened his tie in a way that looked like a habit and said, 'You're going to be an asset to us over the next week, Joshua.'

He looked well over fifty, with his sun-leathered skin. He had deep frown lines etched into his forehead. The backs of his hands were mottled, and the veins and tendons stood out as his fingers tapped on his desk. But he looked as if the years had toughened him, not worn him out.

There was a family photo in a simple silver frame on the desk. It was black-and-white, a formal portrait, Frank with a smile as comfortable as an ill-fitting suit, his wife, two dark-haired teenage daughters.

'It was dreadful in the days afterwards,' he said. 'Particularly for Ben.' He looked across to Brett, and then back to me. 'We offered him counselling, but he said no. He had time off. When his medal was announced a couple of months ago – it was in the papers, we might have sent that one to you, I think – he couldn't do the interviews. We had to say he was in Japan on business.'

'But there's no escape at the investiture, and you want him to be ready.' Already I had the answer about the skydiver story in the paper.

'That's right,' he said. 'More than that. We want it to be the positive experience, and the recognition, that he deserves. Part of the healing process.' He seemed to choose the words carefully. They had the sound of a prepared statement.

The phone on his desk rang, and the noise seemed to surprise him. He grabbed the handset.

'Did I tell you I wanted to be interrupted?' There was no hello, no start to a conversation. 'No. No, I didn't think so.' On the other end of the line, a woman hurried to explain herself. 'Later. We can deal with that later. Let's have no more calls unless there's a fire, or somebody wants to shoot me. Right?' He tried to smile but it was the smile of the photo or one quite like it. It was for Brett and me, not the caller.

He put the phone down.

'Do people often want to shoot you?'

Brett gave me a look when I said it. Frank laughed, but not convincingly. 'Just the one so far.' He wanted to keep things light, or make it seem as though the conversation was light by nature. He wanted his outburst erased. 'I'm hoping it stays that way. Anyway, it's Ben who's the story now, and we've persuaded him he needs some backup, someone like you to manage the media side of it and get him ready. Take that stress off him, at least.'

'That's Josh's thing,' Brett said quickly. 'This is going to work out well.'

He was trying to fix my crass comment.

'Okay, here's how it looks to me.' It was time to demonstrate my thing. Time to sell Frank to himself, and file the incident away. 'This is a firm people can rely on. It's dependable, it's efficient and it will deliver. It doesn't cut corners. It has substance.' It was a message everyone liked hearing about themselves, particularly the people who had spent money on carpets and art. 'It doesn't make a lot of noise. It's a firm you can trust.' I watched him on 'trust', but I saw nothing. 'What Ben did fits with that. This is a firm where the lawyers would throw themselves at a gunman to save a life, and seek no glory for it afterwards. He's a genuine hero, but a reluctant one, and I think that's a good place to start.'

'That's us,' Frank said. He was picturing how it would look in the papers. 'It's Ben, and it's the firm. That's it.'

'So tell me who you want to reach with this. There'll be quite a bit of media interest on the day, when it's news, but the best way to secure something more, so that it isn't just a news item, would be for me to get to work contacting the right people this week. Selecting a few that'd be a good fit and locking them in, while at the same time working with Ben and you and anyone else to get a handle on the best way of telling the story.' Frank was nodding while I was speaking. He had his pen in his hand, as if he might make notes. 'Maybe you could also tell me about media coverage you've been getting for other things – anyone who's taken an interest in the firm and might be up for a follow-up, or anyone who doesn't like you.'

'I can't imagine why anyone wouldn't like us.' Frank smiled again, as if the three of us were in on a joke. 'We're all about helping the little guy. But I suppose there's always someone who doesn't like you. Someone who remembers one time when you had to knock a few heads together.' He said it as if all reasonable people were in the business of knocking heads. 'Not the media, though – they don't take much of a look at us. We buy some ad space in the papers for the crash-and-bash and family bits of the firm, but that's about it. My work's particularly with SMEs – small-to-medium business enterprises. Some of them are big enough to make the papers. We want to reach them, I suppose.' He stopped, to give it some thought. 'When regular people – by which I particularly mean cashed-up regular people with six to fifty staff – have legal needs, we want to be one of the names they think of.'

'Good.' Regular people. By Frank's definition I knew only one, and he was sitting next to me with a bad mo and a salmon-coloured satchel. 'If you're thinking of linking any kind of ad spend to this, my advice is don't. This needs to run down purely editorial channels, or you'll undermine it, and undermine Ben. If you routinely do run ads in any of the publications we get him into, or radio stations we get him on, I think you should pull them for a few days. By all means, bring them in after that, once we've put the firm's name out there, but it's too ugly to look like you're commercialising something like this. People won't like it.'

'Right,' he said. 'Excellent.' This time he reached for a pad and made a note. 'I don't know if anyone's thinking that way, but I'll stop them if they are.' He drew a box around the note, which I couldn't read. 'Maybe it's time to drop in on Ben.'

His face made it seem as if it might have been a question, but he was already standing. Brett looked my way. I thought he was about to speak, but instead he nodded and then checked his watch. I had imagined Ben Harkin over the years, on and off, and now I was about to see him again.

Frank led us along a corridor that passed glass-fronted offices on one side, and a storeroom and a bay of work stations on the other. A woman sat typing in the first cubicle, her gaze fixed on the screen, a line of Simpsons figurines along the top of her computer and a Dilbert mug half-full of tea or coffee beside her. Pinned up on her divider was a sheet of A4 paper with a message that read, 'Workplaces are to be kept neat and tidy, and without personal adornments. Please feel free to express yourself on your fridge at home.' It looked like it had come from an email, but it had been bumped up to eighteen point and covered with glitter and a chain of coloured paperclips.

Next to her, I could see the back of another woman who was on the phone and saying, 'I just wanted to check that the courier had got there . . .'

Frank had stopped at the third office down the corridor and was tapping on the glass.

Ben Harkin stood in his tailored suit as we walked in, and he met me with a steady handshake. It was the first time we'd ever shaken hands. His black hair had a sheen to it and his shirt cuffs had gold cufflinks, not buttons. He looked like a Vogue magazine-shoot version of a lawyer, but he also looked at ease there, not like a model brought in to pose. He looked to me like a lawyer other lawyers might envy.

'Josh,' he said. 'Joshua Lang. Riding in like the cavalry. You've done a lot these past few years, from what I've heard. Over in London. Though you did cross over to the dark side . . .' He was smiling, as if we were back right away at a place where he could make a joke about my old ambitions. He knew I'd gone overseas hoping to write features, to work in investigative journalism and break stories people needed to know about. 'Lucky for us,' he said. 'Lucky for me.'

He seemed to have forgotten that we had stopped being friends, and for a moment had me doubting my own memory of it. I was smiling back. I could feel it, the smile opening up on my face. He had me missing the better times we'd had. I couldn't speak, and I was sure my smile had fixed itself into a stupid grin.

'Ben, we've had a bit of a chat,' Frank said, his hands on the back of a chair. 'But I thought we'd hold off on the detail until we came in to you.' He turned to Brett, and then looked past Brett to include me. 'I think we just want people to know that we're proud to have someone of Ben's calibre at this firm.'

It came out stiffly, like a distant father trying to manage a hug. Ben looked down at his desk, and moved his pen. It was Mont Blanc, or something similar.

'You're going to have to stop feeling awkward about that,' I told him. 'There'll be pride everywhere on Monday.' He put on a shudder, for effect. He wanted to be sure there was no pretence of willingness. 'I'm going to have to get to know your version of what happened inside out.'

'Ben, we've got to do justice to the story this time,' Frank said. 'You've got to get your due.' He looked at Ben long enough to make sure that the message was getting through, and then he turned to me. 'It's hard to imagine what it was like. I really didn't think I'd get out of it alive.'

'Rob Mueller was a very disturbed man,' Ben said. More words that felt rehearsed, or at least spoken before, perhaps worked out when the siege was fresh and Ben was made to tell and retell his story to police, workmates, whoever he came across.

'There was no reasoning with him,' Frank said. 'He was deluded. Hearing voices. He said he was on a mission from God. He was going to shoot me and anyone who stood in his way.'

I needed it from Ben, so I turned back to him. 'And you . . .'

'Ben jumped him.' It was Frank again. 'He'd already hit me in the head. There was blood everywhere. He was about to shoot me.'

'Okay.' I kept my eyes on Ben. 'Well, I'm going to have to hear it from you too. We can't do all the interviews with Frank's hand up the back of your shirt. The media aren't much into ventriloquism.' It was supposed to be a joke, but it came out sounding hard. 'You and I are going to have to talk it through. The siege and anything else that might come up. Your father, for example. He's probably going to come up if we do any profile pieces. I was really sorry to read about him.'

Ben nodded, but his face told me nothing. 'It's okay. You know we weren't close.'

'Yeah. I was sorry to hear it, though. It can't be easy for you. And I think we've got to expect that it might come up. Not so much in the news stuff, but if there are any feature articles or any longer TV pieces, like Australian Story.' There was something ugly about getting down to business, when this bit of business was his father's death. 'We can't have it in the back of your mind any time someone's interviewing you. You'll feel better if we have a plan.' Some of his hair had fallen across his forehead, making him look even more like a model. 'The best way to deal with any difficult issue is to be ready to tell the truth. Be up-front about your version of the truth. Own it first. So, we're open about your father. I think we have to be. And most of the time he won't be mentioned. This is a hero story, a tragic event that will be remembered for one person's courage. I haven't been called in to fix a problem. This isn't a question of spin.'

'Exactly,' Frank said, hearing something that sounded right to him. 'It's not a question of spin. It's about heroism. And you're here to get Ben through it.'

'And look at it from the media's point of view. They need stories, and this is a good one. So you need to be able to tell it. This is a story that says that in a troubled world there are good guys out there, and good does not go unrecognised. These people are picking up bad-news stories from the wires all the time, and they want something positive. And plenty of the good-news stories they get pitched to them are crap, people flogging gadgets that the world just doesn't need – internet-enabled fridges, multi-articulating tooth-brushes, four-blade razors. They'll want this, your story. So we need to work out how to let some light in on the instant when a city lawyer decided to be a hero. That's the key to it. And I can help you get there.'

In one way, it had been easier with the toll road in the Midlands, the organic grocers, the bottled water. There was no siege victim to push into the glare then. I wasn't sure if this was for Ben at all or just good pub-licity, the firm's unspecial name going out there, hitched to an act of bravery. It felt as if I had left Brisbane as Anakin and come back as Darth, rebuilt into something infinitely cynical and talking amorally about heroes in my breathy metallic voice.

Ben blinked a couple of times, and then smiled. 'I think we have five-blade razors now.'

I almost told him I was glad we had that covered, but then decided not to take the bait.

'So can you tell me what happened?' I needed to know that I could get him to the point. 'Your version of it?'

'It's just like Frank said. The guy lost it. Hit Frank in the head with the gun. Was going to shoot him. What else could I do, really?' He left it there, the roughest of pencil sketches of what had gone on. He shrugged. That was it. He looked down at his phone. He reached out and touched the digital time display with his fingertip. 'I'm actually expecting a call from Osaka any minute.'

'Okay, but there's got to be more.' The self-assured Vogue lawyer who had shaken my hand had backed away, without a story to tell. 'We need to find a more detailed version of it that you're comfortable putting out there.'

'I know.' He waited for the phone to ring, but it didn't. 'Your vowels have changed, Josh. There's something English about them.'

'Knock, knock,' a voice said in the doorway. It sounded upbeat, out of step with the mood.

'Max,' Frank said. 'This is Brett and Joshua Lang. Max Visser. Max is the partner Ben reports to. Josh will be working with Ben, and the rest of us, around the public side of Ben's medal presentation.'

'Josh Lang,' Max Visser said with unnecessary emphasis, reaching his hand out for me to shake. He was forty-ish, sandy-haired. He was like a better-looking version of Brett, minus the lip thatch. He stepped past Brett on his way into the room and left him standing there like a before photo. 'Tell me, you are the Josh Lang I read in the Brisbane Times? Of course you are. I know it from the photo.' His accent was South African. He pumped my hand as if I might spout water. 'That blog on photocopiers was hilarious. That one with the repair guy. Totally hilarious.'

Ben's phone rang. 'That'll be Osaka,' he said.

'We'll talk tomorrow,' I told him, and he nodded without looking my way.

His hand was already reaching for the phone, but he checked his move and said, 'Actually, Wednesday. I'm in Cairns for the day tomorrow.' And he took the Osaka call without letting me say a thing more.

'Sorry about that,' Frank said once we were in the corridor. 'I asked Ben to put some time aside today, but sometimes the clients aren't too accommodating. Tomorrow too, from the sound of it.' He was looking back through the glass at Ben, who was talking, nodding, scrolling through a document on screen. 'Things come up. But you'll want some time to familiarise yourself with the file anyway, and then you can hit the ground running with Ben first thing Wednesday. I'll make damn sure that works, don't worry.' He said it in a way that left me in no doubt. 'I'll leave you in Max's capable hands and he can let you know what's what.'

'Come with me,' Max said. 'I've got something to show you.'

As he led me further down the corridor, I could hear Frank's voice receding in the other direction. He was taking Brett back to his office, or to the lift. 'We're practically carbon-neutral now,' he said. 'That could be a story, once this is done.'

I heard the word 'satchel' from Brett, and then Max said, 'In here, in here.' He ushered me into a room with a large copier/printer and shelves of toner and paper. In its own quiet way, it looked like a carbon crime in progress. Perhaps, in some wild place, Randall Hood Beckett paid for a forest to grow with this room's name on it.

'Take a look at that,' he said. He was pointing to my photocopier blog, which had been zoomed, printed and stuck on the wall above the open copier lid. 'Did you really follow the repairman around?'

'Yeah, I did. It was one of my first blogs. I hadn't worked out then how much you could cover without stepping away from Google.'

Max was reading it, and not really listening to me. 'Hilarious.' He pointed to a part he had gone over with a highlighter pen. I knew which bit it would be.

December was the worst time of year for office photocopiers and, prospecting for blog topics, I attached myself for a morning to the surliest repair guy in the business. As the city geared up for Christmas, he came upon the tinselled offices as some kind of anti-Santa, an Ebeneezer Scrooge turned up a century or so later as a malcontent mechanic, cursed by the frivolity of the season. So why was December the worst month of his year? There are two crucial pieces of copier info every responsible office should circulate in the weeks before the Christmas party: the maximum weight the glass can bear is fifty-five kilos and the temperature of the light is 170 degrees. He made it plain that scorched body parts were not his problem, and he drove a vanful of replacement glass around every December.

A few hours of his grouchiness and I had myself a blog, and a place on the wall in this windowless room at Randall Hood Beckett. At the bottom of the printout there was a note in blue pen that read, 'RHB accepts no responsibility for buttock or other trauma due to misuse of this copier, whether the owner of said buttocks (or other body parts) weighs above or below 55kg. MV'.

'What I think is great,' he said, 'is that, even now, when everyone could do it, it's not the same to take a photo of your arse and email it.' My blog seemed to mean we were already mid-conversation, and the topic was arse imaging. 'Technology may have moved on, but there's still something special about pale butt cheeks pressed onto hot glass. What is that?'

People would warm to Max. The media, audiences. He would be good interview talent, if I could keep the lid on. Frank was focused and he could tell his story, but not in a way that would make people like him. There was a hardness to Frank, made harder by the scar.

'Your office,' Max said, when no more great buttock thoughts would come. 'I should show you your office.'

It was two doors down the corridor, on the internal side. Its three off-white walls had empty hooks for art to hang on, and boxes were piled high in one corner. There was a desk with a computer, and a whiteboard with a half-finished game of noughts and crosses smeared across it, but no sign of marker pens.

'We figured you'd need to be close to Ben and the rest of the unit while you're getting this sorted out. I'm down at the end.' He looked around the office, as if he wanted it to be better. 'We thought you might need a whiteboard.' Through the glass wall, something in the corridor distracted him. 'Selina, Selina.'

Selina stopped in the doorway. She was maybe late thirties, with bordello cleavage that wasn't easy to look away from, and pewter knick-knacks on chains around her neck. She was the owner of the Dilbert mug and the Simpsons toys, and she was giving Max a wary look, probably not for the first time.

'Selina's our admin person,' Max was saying. 'She keeps us all on track. We'd be a shambles without her. Well, I would be. It *is* him, Selina. I was right. *The* Josh Lang, the one who does the blogs.'

'Great,' she said, as though it wasn't. 'Max was hoping. Well, I'm pleased to meet you anyway. And I hope your personal life improves.'

'So do I,' Max said. 'Hilarious.'

★ ★ ★

HILARIOUS. UNLESS IT'S YOUR own life. In which case, not so hilarious. The version of me in the blogs wasn't quite my life, though it did make its way in there, remixed for comic effect. The guy in the blogs took the pratfalls I mostly managed to avoid, but that was the job.

I told my mother she shouldn't read them and, if she did, she shouldn't believe them. 'But it's in the paper,' she said, as if there had to be an editor checking that I had truly eaten a stock cube thinking it was fudge, or been dropped by a girlfriend in a particular way.

30

I had, in fact, got my hopes up about the stock cube, but worked it out in time. The girlfriend blog had been mostly true, but that was beside the point.

I went home on the CityCat with a file of documents and DVDs that Selina had given me about the siege. It was a Monday, so I had five hundred words due, and now I had Ben Harkin to wonder about.

I had cast my net wide when I returned home a few months before, and the Brisbane Times was the one regular thing I had snagged. I was to be their new Gen Y guy, blogging about life, the universe and not much, each time posing some kind of question or point of interaction. We had talked through names, and they had wanted to stamp my generation all over it and call the blog 'Y Indeed' or 'Y Us' or 'Y Exactly', until I told them that sounded like a very baby boomer thing to do. It ended up being called 'Random', since that was what I was hired to be.

It ran with a photo of me in a tie and surprised hair. That created the illusion that I had a job, that I went out somewhere to a workplace that had certain stand-ards, when really it was all styled at the shoot. They had borrowed shirts from some boutiques with the promise of a photo credit, but they had sourced them all in large, so I ended up with a row of bulldog clips down my back. By then their hopes about aesthetics were on the slide, and the stylist lassoed me with the first tie to come to hand and there I was, your best idea of the perky office junior, blogging subversively from a cubicle right near you.

It was a fraction of a job, though, so that saw me whoring myself around anywhere that might take a few words on anything, or fund me to subject myself to any mildly degrading experience that might have a story in it. I had found myself living at a time when trivia had been elevated to high status, and it turned out I could make myself far more trivial than I had ever imagined, when there was money on offer. But it was journalism of a kind, not PR, and I had come back determined to work in journalism. I had been telling myself it was a start. I had so far broken no bones, I had vomited only once and it was a start. Randall Hood Beckett was, if not a cave-in, the first sign of subsidence.

The 'out-of-town commitments' I had mentioned to Brett amounted to as many games of mini-golf as I could fit in over several days at the Gold Coast. I had a travel magazine waiting for thirteen hundred words on that, plus pics. 'Everyone writes about golf tourism,' I had said to them in the pitch. 'But what about mini-golf tourism?'

It was not quite the life I'd had in mind when I was at uni with Ben Harkin. We first met in a tute group in a small windowless room in Arts. Back then he seemed to be doing Law on the side, as if it was expected of him. It was two months before I found out who his father was, before he could trust me enough to tell me. Kerry Harkin, like several others, had been high on other people's money in the eighties and come unstuck quite spectacularly late in the decade. A decade or so later, he was back and showing off a tin of Mozambique diamonds, a suite of Angolan oil exploration permits and one or two other traps for the unwary. He was promising returns of twenty percent plus, but it all turned out to be a Ponzi scheme, with new investors funding the dividends of old, and little business conducted other than that. There were no diamonds beyond those in the tin, and the oil permits had been pock-marked by other people's dry dusters before being written off and sold to Kerry Harkin for next to nothing.

Those were almost certainly the facts, but they proved very hard to pin down, as Kerry had built a paper labyrinth around them and had a story of well-intentioned failure ready to tell. Still, he was charged and it made the front pages as the semester ended. His passport was taken when the court discovered he had booked a ticket on a flight to Spain. Ben told me he couldn't work out whether it would be better to be the son of a fugitive or someone soon to be a criminal.

'At least I've got my disguise,' he said. 'Thank God for my Japanese mother. Though a place to crash on the Costa del Sol mightn't have been so bad.' But we both knew he would never have seen it. His father was gone from his life by then.

It seemed that Ben's main ambition that year was to become someone other than his father's son. Mine, as he had recalled, was investigative journalism. Brett had shown me Robert Redford and Dustin Hoffman in All the President's Men when I was twelve, and I wanted to be that kind of guy. Mainly the Robert Redford version of that kind of guy, because he looked like the one who might also score a girl occasionally. I wanted to live lives like theirs, to put stories together from discarded bits of paper, terse phone calls and ballsy truth-chasing. They lived in mess and they looked scrappy. Even when they found ties, their collars would stay open and their top buttons undone. But they were smart and determined and right, and they shook the system.

I went to London wanting to be them, but London cast me in another role, as one of the people in the shadows changing the story's shape, keeping it from being caught. Not that my job was ever about outright lies – it was about picking the right bits of the truth and casting the right light on them, while the other side picked different bits and tried to do the same. I had gone there to break the truth, and instead ended up bending it. That was a skill too, I told myself, but so was juggling toasters. When All the President's Men came on TV one night, I watched it for a few minutes and then changed channels.

★ ★ ★

I OPENED THE DOOR to a flat full of boxed-in warm air and the sound of my upstairs neighbour vacuuming. The aluminium frames of the kitchen windows screeched when I pulled on them, but a cool breeze came in right away.

I had got used to walking around the boxes, I realised. I had yet to feel the impetus to unpack most of them. 'Make sure you label the contents of every one,' my mother had said in yet another nagging email to me in London, so I hadn't. I had eventually located most of the things crucial to everyday life, and then run out of steam. And then blogged about it. Five hundred words on the subject 'Packing and Un'. Most reader feedback on my side, one suggesting I could consider unpacking my head from my arse for a change. Fair enough.

A copy of Cooking with Asterix was open on the kitchen counter. It had been a childhood Christmas present that, back then, had resulted mostly in fried cheese sandwiches. As if my London boxes weren't enough, my parents had a rule that, every time I visited them, I had to leave with more of the junk I had burdened them with for too many years. Snow domes, board games, smooth stones or chunks of petrified wood picked up on a beach somewhere. My childhood bedroom was a museum being sacked one cardboard box load at a time. I had copped a box on the night I borrowed the camp stove, and Cooking with Asterix had been on top. My mother told me it might inspire me to great feats with the camp stove.

Despite that, rather than because of it, on the night of my first Randall Hood Beckett meeting, I turned to page twenty-four. I took my domestic Bunsen burner, made myself a potful of Gergovian meatballs and set my sights, inevitably, on five hundred words. I could already quote Obelix, facedown in a basin on the same page as the recipe declaring the meal 'shuper shen-shastional'. The meatballs he was eating, though, were a rich cinnamony brown in colour and neatly arranged on a bed of peas, while mine ended up more like grey fists of beef in a pea swamp. But they held together, and they tasted pretty good. I could report a genuine partial success.

I started typing. 'It turns out the last village in ancient Gaul to hold out against the Romans wasn't powered by only magic potion and fried cheese sandwiches . . .' Twenty-five words. Easy.

My phone rang on the table. It was Brett. Four

hundred and seventy-five words fell straight out of my head, I was sure of it.

'Just calling to see that everything's okay after the meeting today,' he said when I answered.

'All fine from my point of view.' Except for the greatest ever blog about Asterix cuisine, now a stub twenty-five words long. 'Are you worried about something?'

'No.' He paused. I waited it out. 'I thought it went really well. It's just that you're, um, you're on my team this week. This is a team call. Standard practice. Just checking that there's nothing you need.'

'I think everything's okay.' Standard practice. Useful code for non-patronising. 'I haven't cracked Ben yet as far as the siege story goes. There's work to do there. I think they should have pushed harder with the therapy, maybe.'

I could imagine the conversation Brett would have had with our parents when they made him offer me work. 'But what about when you made me have him as wedding MC?' Brett would have said, in the whinier version of his voice that none of us liked. And our parents would have stayed silent, and the silence would have broken him.

'Maybe. But you'll get him there.' There was some static on the line now. I couldn't be certain if it was a statement or a question. I wondered if he was in his car. 'Frank's got it all ready to go.'

'Yeah, I think he might have.' Frank had certainly had it ready for us. 'People aren't usually that prepared.'

'You'll probably find he did interviews back when it all happened,' Brett said. It was a good point.

'Do you trust him?'

There was a silence, or a rasping metal space when he said nothing. I wondered if the call had dropped out.

'I don't really know him,' he said eventually. 'It's an unusual question. Why would I not trust him?'

'No reason.' I didn't have enough. In that second there wasn't one doubt big enough to put a finger on. 'These stories are often complicated. Not that I do a lot of medals, but you know what I mean. It's also a client-with-a-gun story. Not all good news. And you don't usually get the full story straight up. People have got too used to telling it. They settle on a version that sounds right – often to themselves as well as everyone else – but it isn't always. I've got to unpick a bit yet, that's all.'

'Okay,' he said, but I couldn't tell what kind of okay it was. 'Okay, that's good.' Something had distracted him. He had arrived somewhere, or another call had come through. 'Well, you let me know if you need anything.'

Once I'd put the phone down, I bashed out a version of the blog. It was good enough, but not great. It was a draft, and it would be better. I saved it, backed it up and stepped away.

I had a post-it note on my laptop to remind me to do neck and back exercises frequently. I had been taught them by a physio in London when I had seized up after some long working hours. He told me I risked ending up with the posture of a medieval monk who had spent his entire life illuminating manuscripts. So the note regularly gave me Name of the Rose flashbacks, and not to the good bits. Name of the Rose summary: young supple guy has sex with hot girl, old manuscript illuminators get hunchy, bitter and die. Those were the key points anyway. Though they were absolutely no help in remembering the back and neck exercises, which I had completely forgotten, other than that a broom handle was involved, or could be.

So, no sex with hot girls then, and I faced a hunchy bitter death. I had read somewhere – during some idle googling, no doubt – that five minutes an hour away from the keyboard was good for something, and I tried to live by that as a substitute for the exercises. Perhaps that had put me in some kind of Name of the Rose middle ground, where I was round-shouldered and somewhat misanthropic, and had a real chance of sex with an average girl with low standards whose recent luck hadn't been good and whose vodka goggles were firmly in place.

I stretched, I looked up to the ceiling and something in my neck cracked like a starting pistol. If the average girl didn't show up soon, I would be ordering gold leaf, or a neurosurgeon.

There were boxes to deal with, a meal to clean up after, and the substantial Randall Hood Beckett siege file was waiting for my attention on the kitchen counter, all of which meant it was time for a walk.

Outside, the cool breeze had picked up and blown away the last signs that the day had been a warm one. I had come back to a summer hot enough that in City News the prostitutes had headlined their advertisements 'busty, discreet, air conditioning'. I got the impression that a Brisbane prostitute without air conditioning watched a lot of TV in January and February while she waited for the phone to ring. I figured that made the air conditioning a legitimate business expense, and tax deductible, and there was surely blog potential lurking in there somewhere. It needed an interview, though. And if she charged me for her time, would that be a legitimate business expense for me? And if she was charging me all that money, and I was there anyway, well, it had been a while . . .

And then I would blog about it, my mother would read it, and another family dinner would take a turn for the worse.

So I called the ATO instead. People give the ATO money all the time, and practically none of us has sex with them in the process, so that seemed safe enough. And, yes, a work-from-home prostitute's air conditioning is tax deductible. In fact, the unit itself can be depreciated, while running costs are tax deductible. As long as the business premises has a separate entrance. Cue Benny Hill double entendre music.

'We just treat it like any other home office,' the ATO guy said. 'Accountant, writer, prostitute – it's all pretty much the same to us.' Blog done, and I had a lot less to explain to my mother.

I walked up the hill and turned into Hardgrave Road. The sky was clear and the stars were sharp, and that was unlike the way London had been, most of the time. There was a scent in the air. It might have been jasmine. Something was flowering, but I couldn't see it.

Two joggers in serious running gear ran by, and I fell in behind a group of walkers who were breaking in new Kathmandu hiking boots, clumping along as if their feet had been bricked in and trying to convince themselves that the boots would soften up soon.

I walked past a Vietnamese medical practice and restaurants, the laundromat and a thrift shop where you could buy the fifties at close to fifties prices. Outside Café Checocho, the feral-styled kids of Labor lawyers clattered their skateboards against the kerb while men in hats hunched over chessboards.

After three or four months of these sights on a near daily basis, they still made the neighbourhood for me. West End had poets who lived like poets, and graffiti that meant something, and eateries that proved you could take the gluten out of anything if you were so inclined. All soft targets for five hundred crass words and yet, for me, unbloggable. To mock them might be to change them, just slightly, at least in my own mind, and that was a risk I couldn't take.

I turned left after Mick's Nuts, then right, and I walked past building sites and new high-end apartment blocks that were going up in places where light industry had given way. Red lights blinked on top of cranes against the night sky. The wind kicked through the huge Moreton Bay figs at the edge of Davies Park and the plants of the community garden, and it felt as if it was here that the two kinds of West End stared each other down. On one side of the street, herbs and vegetables indistinct in the dark and unfenced. On the other, screened off by the long vinyl sleeves of advertisements promising a better life, future underground car parks punched their way into bedrock.

The ad sleeves featured rainforest and falling water and Greek columns, and they talked about tranquillity. On a huge billboard above, a woman about my age, blonde and almost inconceivably beautiful, trailed her hand through the water and looked off into the distance. She was dressed for business, a serious professional just home from the city and back in paradise.

She could have been the other half of the Vogue lawyer photo with Ben Harkin. I wondered how many of the buyers of the apartments were twenty-eight, how many were beautiful, how many had perfect lives of a kind that could lead them to only this spot.

Not so many years before, Francesca would have been the woman in that ad.

Brett didn't deserve her. That's what I had felt at the start, and the feeling had not completely gone away. Even as the real Francesca hadn't quite lived up to the fantasy, she had come close enough. Every time a conversation moved on without her I let myself believe, or at least hope, that she kept her best thoughts in her head, if only to honour my adolescent catalogue fantasies in which she had been clever, as well as lingerie-clad, on my bed and ecstatic at the prospect of the hottest sex of her life with a pasty thirteen-year-old virgin.

A detached corner of the vinyl banner flapped in the breeze, a corner of rainforest lifting and then slapping back down against the wire mesh of the fence. I could imagine it as Brett's next document satchel, the green spikes of the leaves of its generic forest undergrowth fanning out, Brett talking it up.

I wondered when I last gave my brother credit for anything. For giving me work when I could really do with it, for instance.

Brett met Francesca on a shoot while he was working for one of the big advertising agencies. Her face was everywhere then, and her body. She was on the list for premieres, she never paid a cover charge, and every club in town dropped its velvet rope as she approached the door. Brett must have met her when her guard was down. If our family put on a version of The Name of the Rose, we could cast him only as Christian Slater's Adso of Melk, the young guy who gets to play entirely out of his league when the hot chick disrobes, jumps him and nails him. In the midst of it, the movie has a fleeting close-up of his face, a mixture of bafflement and beatitude as he surely thinks he has died and gone to heaven and then realises his luck is even better. He is not dead, and heaven has come to earth, and specifically to him.

Brett ended up riding his luck way better than Adso of Melk. He kept the girl and at the same time started his own business and turned it into some kind of success. Francesca now worked only when she chose to, taking on the occasional yummy-mummy modelling job for fun and to catch up with old friends. Most of the time she redecorated, and taxied Darius and Aphrodite around to their many extracurricular activities.

Perhaps the only part of my life about which I had no ambivalence at all was my nephew and niece. I had missed the start of their lives when I had been in London, and I was determined to make up for it now. I was the reckless tree-climbing ice-cream-buying wastrel of an uncle who undermined any piece of discipline their parents put forward, and they had quickly decided they loved me for it.

I heard a late CityCat surging along the Regatta Reach of the river, just beyond the end of the street, and I turned for home.

The flat still had a damp boiled-mince smell about it, so I opened the sliding door to the balcony. I stood at the kitchen counter with a new box of fortune cookies telling myself only two, only two. I took only two, and stepped away. I had become attached to their sweet wheaty flavour, and now they were my standard dessert. It tended to go one of two ways. Either I helped myself to a finite number at the counter and had some chance of sticking to it, or I took the box to my beanbag – another piece of detritus from my childhood bedroom, recently re-beaned by my mother – and woke up hours later covered in shrapnel and fortunes.

'Food and conversation in a box', I had written down once with a blog in mind before backing away from suggesting to the world that I was quite that sad.

I dragged the beanbag over to the balcony door, turned the TV on and the lights off and sat with my two cookies. I cracked them open, and waited for a daylight scene so that I could read them.

★ ★ ★

SOMETIMES I BREAKFASTED at Café Checocho to prove I could, to prove that every morning didn't start when it became too warm to sleep, that every day wouldn't be spent in only boxer shorts until well into the afternoon. Convention dictated that a meal out required more than one item of clothing. It required shoes, interaction. Some days that was a lot to ask, but the upside was caffeine in quality form and a kickstart to the day, plus a chance to read the paper in the old way, and every detail of it, rather than just staring at the screen at home, soaking up the pixels.

The morning after the meeting at Randall Hood Beckett began like my other days, though, facedown in a messy forgettable dream. I missed the call from Selina that came through around nine and went to voicemail.

'Just checking to see that you've got the media file on the incident,' her message said when I picked the phone up from the table an hour later. I had been about to charge it when I noticed someone had actually called. 'I'm not sure if you're aware that files don't leave the office without high-level approval.' There was a pause there, as though I might want to make excuses to her recorded voice. 'I've marked it down as checked out to you. Not that I'm high-level or anything,' she said, 'but consider your arse covered, new boy.'

My toast popped, half-done as always.

I called Selina back right away, worried that my arse was even in play, and she said, 'It's probably my fault you didn't know the score. Anyway, Max okayed it just now. And it's not like it's a legal file. So, enjoy.'

I gave my toast its second go through, Vegemited it, and thought about having fortune cookies instead.

I opened the file and took my first good look at the photocopy of Ben's medal nomination. It had been submitted in Frank's name, and he had signed the covering page. The form asked the nominator to attach photographs and statements from eyewitnesses, and Frank's covering letter itemised a dozen or more. It was a lawyer's letter, making a case and making it robustly. I couldn't imagine him doing it any other way.

I read through his own report of the incident and some of the material he had included to support it. Rob Mueller had appeared psychotic, deranged, crazy. Different people put it in different ways, and some said only that he was angry. He had been a client of the firm once, though in a minor way. Another lawyer who mentioned that made it seem like nothing, just routine business.

It was Frank's letter I kept coming back to. It had the story. 'My head wound was bleeding profusely. By this time Mueller was even more agitated. It was clear he was going to shoot me. I was on the floor when Ben rushed him. In the struggle, the gun discharged.'

Ben in his sharp suit and his neat hair, rushing, struggling, with a loaded gun as part of the fight.

I could hardly imagine what it would be like to be tested that way. Perhaps none of us could know how we might respond. I wasn't planning to flatter myself by thinking I would do the same.

Ben was a hero and I was building a solid fraction of my next career on pieces that began with lines like, 'Whoever invented shiny toilet paper anyway?' He was owed a good investiture, and I would put the past aside to give him that.

When I had left for London I had assumed that I would be home one day, but I had imagined arriving if not in triumph then at least in something – some state that said my time away had amounted to time well spent. Perhaps buying the flat was proof of that.

I had big ideas about what my deposit would get me, but then I converted my hoarded sterling into dollars and saw what had happened to Brisbane real estate prices while I had been away. The Venn diagram of my first weekend driving around open houses would have had one circle for places in which I would have liked to live, one for places I could have afforded and no intersection. My expectations duly got beaten down. I gave up city views for city glimpses, and city glimpses for a balcony that opened out to the next block of flats. I gave up character for something solid. I gave up fully renovated for workable, or thought I did. I found my box of a flat and told myself it was four times the size of anything I could have bought in London, and I signed on the dotted line.

After the shortest possible settlement period, I unlocked the door on the hot afternoon when they gave me the keys and I walked in to a stale smell, as though people had sat there too long and failed to live up to their own lowest expectations.

It was mine, though. And it was a start.

I had been on contract in London, rather than being an employee. That had been my choice, since it let me believe I was a serious journalist killing time as a fixer until the right offer came along. But the GFC crashed the party, and I was among the first to go. The contract made it easy for them, but plenty of employed staff went too. 'Things look a lot less bad in Australia,' my director said to me, in an apologetic tone he was about to become accustomed to. 'You'll probably end up one of the lucky ones.'

So I took a box, the first box I could find, and I filled it with my stuff. I wanted to get out before people could look at me, before anyone knew. On the previous Saturday, my girlfriend Emily had decided we weren't working out. I had already been packing boxes.

As I caught the lift to ground, I wasn't aware that two banks with head offices in the building were in the process of collapsing. When the doors opened I saw TV cameras, a scrum of media, and they saw me. They caught me, trapped me there. They asked which bank I'd worked for and I told them it hardly mattered now. They asked who I was and I faked a name. It was only when I saw the news that night that I noticed how they had framed the picture. I was carrying a Billecart-Salmon box, Grand Cuvée.

I was that day's perfect picture of the hard landing of greed, even though the picture was all wrong. I was no banker, I had no idea where the box had come from, and greed never landed hard in the end anyway. It was the engine of that machine.

* * *

ON WEDNESDAY I WENT back in to Randall Hood Beckett. Ben was out at a meeting with a client, but due in by ten, and Frank had commandeered his diary after that for me. Through the glass wall of Ben's office, mid-screen on his sleeping laptop, I could see the post-it note on which Frank had written in bold black pen '10am – Josh. No excuses. F'. The laptop was turned around, putting the note on show, and I couldn't know if Ben had left it at that angle, or Frank had turned it.

I had put the siege file aside the day before without going through all of it. I had yet to watch any of the DVDs. I had realised that time was short and that I needed to make some calls, so I had gone through my media guide and pasted together a list of targets and their details.

When I turned up at the office there were red and blue marker pens on my desk, so I drew a grid on my whiteboard and wrote up my pitch list. Surely rule number one when spinning anything was to spin yourself first, and my big visible list said I meant business, I had a plan. I wasn't just the guy in the room with the boxes.

My first call was to QWeekend at the Courier-Mail. They heard me out and said, 'You know, it's close. Normally we'd probably take it but we've run a few hero stories lately. And his dad rates as a bit of a white-shoe villain, but there were worse. I'm sure we'll do it in news, though. If he's getting the big gong on Monday, news'll give him a run on Tuesday. We'd have a photographer and reporter going along.'

I left messages on voicemail at the Weekend Australian and Financial Review magazines and, since Frank wanted a broad reach, I also called Who Weekly. I didn't know what line of work his six-to-fifty-staff clients were in but, if they had anywhere for customers to wait, chances were they would have Who Weekly. I had looked through some recent issues at Café Checocho and I asked for Aimee Duroux. On the strength of a couple of her stories, she looked like a good fit.

'I think we might be up for this,' she said, once I had styled Ben as a self-effacing hero who had looked death in the eye. 'If we can get some kind of exclusive. What else are you looking at doing?'

'Well, it'll be news,' I told her, 'so there'll be some coverage from the dailies. We could look at a magazine feature exclusive, maybe. If you're up for a feature. Like, if you wanted to give it say, three or four pages and really flesh it out. I could email you some background stuff. He's got a good story to tell.'

'Okay. Well, I think we might be interested.' Something distracted her then. 'If you could send me the stuff, that'd be great. I think we're probably up for it, if it's all ours. I'll put it to the editorial team and get back to you. But send the stuff, yeah.'

I hung up, took my red marker pen and wrote 'PROB FEATURE' on the whiteboard. I took a look at my radio targets and decided to start with the talk formats, feed the content hungry.

When I got to Ben's door at exactly ten, an itinerary was already beginning to come together. He was standing crumpling the post-it note from Frank in one hand and realigning his laptop on the desk with the other.

'I've started to book in some interviews,' I told him. 'We're going to need to spend some time together to get all this clear. I need to get a sense of the story you'll be telling.'

He threw the note towards the bin, but it hit the edge and fell to the floor.

'It's not a story,' he said.

'You know what I mean. We did media subjects together. You know what I mean by story.'

He nodded, and smiled in a way that said he was resigned to his fate. 'Yeah.'

'Are you avoiding this? Or avoiding me?' I couldn't read him yet. The new Ben had even made my memories of the old Ben slippery, less distinct. As he stood in front of me, he looked like someone who had once played the role of Ben Harkin, but in a less than convincing amateur production. I could place someone like him in my past, but not this man, who seemed elegantly wounded.

He laughed, but not convincingly. 'Not for a second. I'd be happy to put this in the past – the medal was definitely not my idea – but I'm not avoiding anything. It turns out the world doesn't stop because they start handing out medals. That's all.'

'And after next week you *can* put it in the past. I've read the nomination paperwork. You deserve this, and people want you to get it. It might not feel like what you need right now, but maybe it'll help put it in the past, once it's done.' This was not unfamiliar territory, this mixture of cajoling and therapy, though it felt more contrived than usual telling it to Ben. 'You're going to have to drop your guard, or look like you're dropping your guard. You're going to have to let something out, and I'm here to make that as painless as possible. To help you find a version of what happened that you can tell.'

'Yeah,' he said. 'I know.' He looked at me. He half-smiled again but his guard was up. 'How weird that it's you, doing this.'

Behind me, there was a knock on the door. 'Josh,' Selina's voice said as I turned. 'Phone call for you. ABC TV, Australian Story.'

'You're avoiding me, Josh,' Ben called out as I left. 'Why are you avoiding me?'

I turned back, and he threw a ball of paper at me. It bounced off the glass and landed in the corner, near a filing cabinet. It was a forced gesture, a fake, and we both knew it.

Selina put the call through as I got to the door of my office.

'I've looked at everything you've sent us and it looks like our kind of thing,' the producer said. I hadn't caught her name. 'I'm happy to go to a production meeting with it. Who else can you get us apart from the medallist? Could we get other people who were involved? Maybe some family? A mentor?'

Yes, always yes. Keep them on the hook. 'We've got plenty to choose from. I can line them up for you. There's people at the firm for a start. A couple of the partners. I can get you the partner Ben reports to, who was in the building at the time. And the one who got hit on the head. He's still got a scar.'

'A visible scar?'

'Sure. He's got practically no hair.'

'Excellent.'

'Harry Potter at fifty. That's what people have said. It's a jagged sort of scar going back from his forehead.'

'We like that,' she said.

By the end of the call, I had another 'PROBABLE' to write up on the whiteboard. I turned in my seat to write it, then swivelled back around to find Max Visser in my doorway in sky-blue lycra bike shorts, genitals like a pressed pigeon.

'Hey, good work,' he said, looking at the board, the stink of exertion starting to infiltrate the room. Sweat ran from his chin and his elbows and dripped onto the carpet. 'Australian Story, hey? That's the TV show?'

'That's the one.' I pushed and rolled my chair back behind my desk and away from his anatomically correct crotch. 'If it works out they'll probably want you and Frank, so maybe we could have a talk. Once you're . . . ready.'

'Ready? Oh, yeah.' He looked down at the vibrant Gatorade shirt that stuck damply to his stomach, pink flesh showing through the white parts of the lycra. 'One of my kids is sick, so I started off the day at home. There's a shower at the other end of the floor. Did they tell you that?'

'No. Well, I don't want to keep you from it.'

'Yeah, right. There's a place near here where they make great coffee. Why don't we go there once I'm decent and I've checked there aren't any fires needing putting out?' He retreated, leaving a dark damp patch on the floor.

Ben was still the issue. I could line up all the interviews and prep Max and the others without a fuss but, without getting Ben worked out, I had only trouble ahead. I put the cap on the pen, held back from the next call.

Selina was waving her hand in front of her face as I approached her work station.

'Phew, man sweat,' she said, as if it was still coming back at her, like a disturbed hive of bees. 'How is it that it's okay to wear that stuff, just because there's a bike involved? Allegedly. Sometimes I turn round and, there it is, a face full of package. I swear he sneaks up on me. How do men think that, just because it's got the name of some European bank across it, it's acceptable? Blog about that some day, would you? He's also got a totally white pair. Is anything more wrong than white lycra? Does anyone look good in white lycra? Brazilian dancers don't look good in white lycra.'

'You should see my floor where he sweated. It's like I just got a puppy.'

She laughed. She pushed her chair away from her keyboard, and turned so that she was facing me. She had three photos on her desk, two of fluffy white cats and one featuring her, probably drunk, hugging a man with a shaved head and thrusting her hand towards the camera to show off an engagement ring with a splinter of diamond. The thrust put her hand out of focus, and the diamond was mostly a dot of white light.

'Is there any chance I could see some of Rob Mueller's legal file?' I said to her. 'In case there's anything in it that would help me get Ben ready for next week. I'm not expecting that there will be, but I want to cover all the bases. I don't know what's confidential and what's not, though, so if I can't that's fine. No big deal.'

'I'll give it a go,' she said. 'It's probably not one to take home with you, though.'

'No, I'd figured that.'

She wrote herself a note. 'Now do you want me to fumigate your room if the Tour de Max has been in there? I have spray.'

★ ★ ★

IT WAS AN ALTOGETHER more presentable Max Visser who met me soon after for coffee. I had tried again with Ben in the meantime, but he was out of his office. He seemed to be nowhere on the floor. He had got past us somehow.

Max took me to a coffee shop around the corner where they knew him by name and beverage. It was dark inside, and wood-panelled, and we took a booth up the back, beneath a black-and-white image of one of the market stalls that had been near the site a century before. The stallholder was gaunt, with a moustache like Henry Lawson and cheekbones that cast shadows. He was selling knives, and meeting the camera with a fixed unsmiling stare.

Max sat back in his seat and leaned his head against the wall behind him.

'Sleepless night at our place,' he said. 'My youngest daughter's not well. She finally got to sleep around six, by which time I couldn't, so I started work instead.' He glanced over to the counter, where they were making our coffees. 'So, Australian Story. I like that show. I like the way they get a bunch of people on, and you really feel like you're getting the detail behind the story. From the horses' mouths.'

'Exactly. So I think it could be good for this. And I think you'd make a good horse. I'd want to steer them towards you because I think you can humanise the story, and because Ben reports to you. We could cast you in a kind of mentoring role.'

'I don't know that Ben looks for a lot of mentoring.' He smiled wryly. I could remember the Ben who knew it all, and perhaps he hadn't gone away.

'No, but you know what I mean. I'm sure we can make it work.'

He thought about it for a while.

'I think you'd come up very well on TV,' I said. 'And you do work with Ben.'

'Yeah, I do.' He had a sachet of sugar in his hand and he was tapping one end of it on the table. 'And we'll be working into the night tonight. We've got a dinner with a client and some Koreans he's trying to tie a deal up with.' He noticed he was tapping the sugar sachet, and he set it down. 'I don't know about Ben. There's plenty I can say about him, but it's all pretty impersonal. I can't say that I know much about him outside Randalls. I don't think he's even got a photo on his desk. Some people, you get to know their whole lives inside out in the first five minutes. But not Ben. I can talk about him at work, though. And I can talk about the incident. About how it played out anyway.'

'So, tell me a bit about that. What could you tell Australian Story?'

'Okay.' He stopped to think it through. 'I was on the edges of it, really. It seemed to be pretty much out of the blue. The guy was a client of Frank's, an importer. Teak furniture from Indonesia, I think. I was in a meeting room on the floor below, but there was mayhem when it happened, so all of a sudden people were pouring out of the fire stairs. The meeting room's quite near the door. They were pretty shaken up.'

'Apparently Rob Mueller turned up saying he was on some kind of mission from God.'

'I heard that. But later, afterwards. Not from the people who got out. That stuff really only came out when he had them trapped in there – Frank and Ben. Before then he was obviously disturbed, by all accounts, but not in that kind of way. It went bad pretty quickly. The gun came out, he herded people out of there, barricaded the three of them in.' He stopped as our coffees were put down in front of us, and waited until we were alone again. His latte had a sweeping cursive M drawn into its foam, mine had a fern. He didn't seem to notice. 'We were all just waiting for the shots, frankly. And then Ben saved the day. It was still quite a while before we knew that it was Rob Mueller himself who'd been hit. I was trying to get the building evacuated. You plan for that, supposedly. It's a black alert, a code black. I found that out afterwards as well.' He paused, stuck in his recollection of it. 'We want to do a lunch at the firm. Did Frank tell you that? For Ben, when he gets the medal. It hasn't been right yet.'

'In what way not right?'

He poured sugar onto his drip-etched initial and plunged his spoon through it. 'Not right for Ben. Not right because someone died. It was a big adjustment for Ben. He killed a man. He's a wheeler-dealer who gets his suits tailor-made. He's a damn good lawyer, but you know what I mean. A life-and-death struggle involving a shotgun is not part of his world. Or anyone's obviously. Not in this country. But he's coming good now, don't you think?'

He stirred his coffee. I didn't have an answer.

'He told me about the band you guys were in,' Max said. 'Tokyo Speed Ponies.'

'It wasn't much of a band.' I couldn't believe Ben had chosen to keep his life outside Randalls to himself, but had mentioned Tokyo Speed Ponies.

'I looked at the website,' he said insistently, as if I was unjustly playing it down. 'I tried to download the screen saver, but it didn't work. There was chat in the chat room. I don't know from when, though. There are people waiting for the next album.'

'Please try not to sound like you're one of them. It's not going to happen.'

He laughed. 'I haven't been able to track down the first one yet.'

★ ★ ★

IT THREW ME, the reference to the band. The 'band'. Inverted commas definitely necessary. There was no band. Not in the usual sense of the word, that being people getting together and playing instruments.

Back in my office at Randall Hood Beckett – and for the first time in years – I googled Tokyo Speed Ponies.

It made no sense that there had been chat room activity, but there it was, people raving about the album and comparing rumours about the follow-up.

But there had been no album, just as there had been no band. I stared at the screen, at the evidence, at the facts. It looked as real as my own hands, as the chair I was sitting on.

At the time when the law had turned on Kerry Harkin, Ben became preoccupied that the family stain would seep through to him, no matter what he did.

'They won't touch me,' he said. 'The law firms'll never touch me.' He said it like a rebel, but he felt it like an outcast.

Then he decided it wasn't what he wanted anyway. He wanted to live a different life, to create things. Music, art. He decided to learn how to put websites together, and that he would work with bands and artists. So, for the brief course of this fantasy and for the purpose of showcasing his skills, he came up with Tokyo Speed Ponies. Other people might have chosen something real, a friend's band that was on the rise, and offered to do their site for nothing, but not Ben.

He was into Japanese punk, particularly Japanese girl pop punk like Shonen Knife, and he decided Tokyo Speed Ponies would be that kind of band. He said the name had come from something he had seen written on a shirt while visiting his mother's family in Japan, though I had never been sure that was true.

He took my photo with a borrowed bass guitar, and I became the bass player. He found a picture of a hot Eurasian model in a magazine, and he photoshopped her top half in as the drummer. Ben was the guitarist and lead singer. I took those photos, and I took plenty before he was happy. He was aiming for a particular look, and said he would know it when he saw it.

He had always had an interest in anime and manga and got himself some animation software. He made a start on a video, but I didn't think he had done much with it.

'You're the writer,' he said, when we were most swept up by the idea and wondering how far we could take it. 'You should write articles about the band. Do some gig and album reviews.' So I did. Then he dared me to try to have them published, to send them out to magazines. I did that too, under another name. A couple were even picked up by street press, and Ben scanned them once they were published and put them on the website's media section.

He called our album Tangerine Coloured Hot Spot, which he admitted meant nothing but insisted was just right for the genre.

He started talking about the band as if it was real.

Then it stopped. I thought it stopped. We fell out, I left the country and in our last conversations we had no reason to turn to Tokyo Speed Ponies. But the website was still there. It was linked to nothing, and I could hardly believe it was still afloat at all. In the vast ocean of the internet, it sailed on like the Marie Celeste. Abandoned, a shell of a journey, a ghost of a band. Dreamt up for practice, but pushed out into the world with enough belief that, years later, it looked as real as anything.

'I hear the next album's a step on from Tangerine,' someone called pinknantucket wrote in the chat section. 'Same cranked up bpm and choppy guitars, but even more so. Can't wait!!!'

I told myself to stop looking, and clicked my way to Google.

My back and neck felt stiff, so I stood up and stretched them, in an imprecise way that would make no physio proud. I needed a break from the keyboard, the requisite five unstiffening minutes, and it seemed as good a time as any to go to the bathroom.

I wondered who pinknantucket was, who any of them were. Where was the parallel universe in which this band was a real thing? I could just manage to suppress the fear that it might have been real after all, and I had buried it somewhere.

I was about to open the cubicle door to leave when I heard someone come into the bathroom. It was Frank, and he was on the phone.

'No, don't go softly with this one,' he said. There was a pause. He had stopped in the middle of the room while the other person spoke. 'Like a ton of fucking bricks. We've been waiting for this, and it's a clear breach if they've used another supplier. Make it clear, eloquently clear, that if they don't remedy it right away – and that will include damages – we'll screw them. We won't stop till they've used their tea lady's super to pay their legal bills and we've got locksmiths coming round to change their locks.' He listened to the reply. I could hear his shoes on the tiles as he paced. 'That's it, Justin. Good.'

He ended the call there, and I sat out his time at the trough and several more minutes before going back to my office.

My phone was ringing before I got to the door. It was a radio producer returning my call. She wanted Ben for Monday. He was turning out to be an easy sell. The siege had made three consecutive front pages when it happened, and no one had forgotten it.

'What's he like as talent?' she said.

'He'll be okay. It's not the easiest thing for him to talk about but, you know, that's real. It works. I don't think we want to lose all that.'

I was writing 'CONFIRMED' on the whiteboard when Max Visser stopped in my doorway.

'Just checking,' he said. 'You're coming tonight, right? It'll be a good insight into the kind of work we do. The non-boring part, anyway. And who knows what kind of blog material you could get? Oh God, the karaoke stories I could tell you from trips to Shanghai. I can just imagine Mister Park tonight putting his heart and soul into I've Never Been to Me or Wind Beneath My Wings. It's really not to be missed.'

He was keen, more than keen. He was my biggest and possibly only fan in the world. I couldn't remember him suggesting before that I might be part of dinner, but it wasn't an Asterix re-heat on a camp stove. I wasn't going to say no.

★ ★ ★

BEN WAS ALONE at Terroir when I got there. I had gone home to put in some more work on a blog, and arrived back in the city at close to seven-thirty.

'I'm just bagging the table,' he said, sitting there lazily, low in his seat with his legs stretched out. 'Max and Vincent have gone to pick the Korean guys up in a cab at the Stamford Plaza.' He seemed to want to show me that he was blasé about the surroundings, about the whole occasion. He sat with his back to the windows – full of the lights of the Story Bridge – and ignored his water glass, which was frosted with condensation. I assumed Vincent was the client.

'But that's only a few blocks away, the Stamford Plaza.'

'Well, it's not as if we can make our guests walk . . .' There was sarcasm in the way he said it, though I wasn't sure if it was directed at the expectations of the guests or my ignorance of how they should be treated. 'Not brilliant for our green credentials, is it? Maybe we'll get the cab company to plant a tree. We're so full of shit sometimes. You've probably noticed that already.' It wasn't a game I planned to be sucked into playing, not yet anyway. He smiled when I didn't respond.

'Ha. You have noticed, obviously. We should get you a drink. You *are* drinking, I assume? I'm expecting the Koreans to get shit-faced on Scotch, but maybe that's a racist stereotype.'

He explained that this was the firm's first Korean project, or at least the first time one of the firm's clients had a real chance to do some serious business with Korea. The client created software for toll roads.

'I could explain how it works,' he said, 'but both of our lives are far too short for that, and I'd be grateful if you didn't even pretend to give a shit.'

'I think I can manage that.'

'We'd like to do something in Korea,' he said, making it sound as if he called the shots, and possibly from a jacuzzi somewhere amidships on the corporate jet. 'We can cover Japan and Max speaks passable Chinese, but we don't have a Korean speaker. Luckily, this time one of the Koreans, the junior one, speaks pretty good English.'

He had forgotten about my drink already, but I didn't need it.

I mentioned that Max had suggested karaoke was likely later, and he said, 'Max is always hoping someone'll suggest fucking karaoke.' Then, in a Japanese accent, he corrected himself. 'Karaoke. Half my genes gave the world that artform.'

'Oh, be proud. It's a great leveller, bringing down statesmen and businesspeople across Asia and beyond. I hope you're up for it tonight.'

'You know me. I couldn't carry a tune unless it was strapped to my back.' He was still lounging in the seat, like someone watching TV.

'And yet somehow you managed to have your own band. What possessed you to tell Max Visser about Tokyo Speed Ponies?'

'He asked about our past.' Ben shrugged. 'It seemed like one of the better bits.' He was smiling, as if we could be okay about the less good bits now.

'But it was made up. It only existed because you were teaching yourself to build websites back when you were pretending you weren't going to be a lawyer. The whole thing was a fake.'

'Hey, the evidence is there to support it. You wrote some great fake articles. Not even fake articles. You got them published.' He pretended to look around the room, as if the wrong people might be listening. 'You might have even accepted some cash for it. So don't go holier-than-thou on me. Anyway, it was a good website.'

'I don't remember any cash.'

'Convenient.'

There had been no cash.

'Max Visser is trawling music vendors across the electronic universe trying to track down an album called Tangerine Coloured Hot Spot that never existed. *Never existed.*' I had put on a tone of exasperation, but it was hard not to laugh at the prospect of it. 'If he starts featuring you, me and your anime fantasy chick as his screen saver I don't want to know about it.'

'I've still got that screen saver, probably. A version of it. I could sneak it onto his computer one day while he's riding in to work.'

'Don't even think about it. Stop thinking about it. And what is going on with the chat part of the site? It had me thinking I'd actually been in a band. I felt like one of those Days of Our Lives characters coming back after years of amnesia.'

He laughed. 'Sorry. I would have told you. In different circumstances. That was just me, a couple of years ago. I got bored for five minutes. I went looking for the site, figuring it wouldn't be there, and there it was. Pristine. I don't know how. It's not like I pay anything for it. It must have slipped into some accounting wormhole or something, some warp in the space–time continuum. So, I played around a bit. Without even the intention of messing with your head. That's just a bonus. I wish I'd been there when you read it.'

'Arsehole. I've had second album pressure all afternoon. I mean, how do you follow up Tangerine Coloured Hot Spot? Particularly now that I've seen at least one person call it a classic.' In the low light of the restaurant he looked more like himself, more like the way he used to. Only the suit was different. 'And where would Frank Ainsworth be if you'd been bunkered down in a studio with me and the top half of your anime fantasy chick trying to knock out album number two?'

It had been a joke, but it kind of crumpled.

'Yeah, well,' he said. 'No second album since there wasn't a first, I guess. And I never did find that girl a good bottom half.'

'Is Frank different since the siege?' It was supposed to come out sounding like conversation, but it probably didn't.

'How do you mean "different"?' He straightened one of his cufflinks.

'I mean not the same.' It shouldn't have been a hard question. 'Is he more irritable, more likely to react to things? Is the way he deals with people different?'

'Oh, right.' He laughed. 'They book you to get me through the interviews, and as some kind of bonus you diagnose Frank's PTSD? Or is that part of the service?' He waited for me to say something. At the bar behind him, a waiter was lighting tea-light candles and dropping each one into its own small glass bowl. 'No. He's just the same. Frank is Frank.'

'When I was in his office on Monday, the phone rang and he went nuts at whoever called. Then today I overheard him talking about coming down on someone like a ton of fucking bricks.'

Ben started to say something, but then held it back. 'He's not known for being indirect.'

'Does it ever have consequences?'

'Consequences? It gets the job done. That's a consequence.' He seemed to be losing patience with me. 'It cuts through the crap.'

'What about negative consequences? Was it a factor with Rob Mueller?'

He pushed back in his seat, and bumped his knives with his forearm. 'I don't know what you've seen. But I'd be pretty sure it's nothing. Just the kind of thing that goes on in any workplace with more than one person. You probably need to get over it. It really won't help us with Monday, with next week.'

He put his hand out to straighten the knives, lining them up in parallel again. A champagne cork fizzed discreetly from a bottle at a nearby table and he looked over that way, distracted by the noise.

'You should take a look at the menu,' he said. 'This place is good for steak. Some would say the best. I don't know if you've worked those things out since you got back. It hasn't been that long, has it? They showed me your CV. They said our new PR company had this great guy who'd be just the thing. You'd got all kinds of fucked-up people ready for the media. They handed it to me and I just kept seeing Joshua Lang, Joshua Lang, Joshua Lang. And thinking, he's never going to take it. But you did.' He laughed, as if the world – or perhaps the stupid people who lived on it – could still surprise him. 'When did you know it was me? The job?'

'After I'd said yes to it. After my oven failed and needed replacing. After I'd told Brett I'd do it. Monday. About twenty minutes before I got to your office.' So, we knew where we stood. Or I thought we did. I believed him. I believed his response to being handed my CV, and he had given it to me without needing to. I would need that directness from him, and the best way to get it was to give an honest answer in return. 'Most of these jobs aren't like this. Most of the time, someone's hiding something. Even when the job isn't bad news. Even if it's just to make the story neater. But usually someone got screwed somewhere along the line, or there's a slightly dirty secret or two, ticking away. And I've got to find them and see if I can cut the wire. I don't do a lot of heroes.'

'And do they feed you?' he said. 'Those people whose wires you're cutting? I'd recommend the steak. Any time someone else is buying this steak, you should say yes.' He handed me his open menu. 'Of course, don't feel you need to take my advice.'

The more wires I had to cut and the dirtier the secrets, the better they fed me. That was how I remembered it. I looked at the two pages open in front of me. Each dish was named in bold and then described by a further paragraph of text. Most of the dishes had detailed paddock-to-plate stories about their meat. Ben watched me read it, and then looked away, towards the door.

'What is it with menus since I went away?' I hadn't meant it to, but it came out sounding like a comedian's set-up, like a line from someone who had watched too much Seinfeld. 'I've known less about women at the end of a second date than they tell you about the beef now.'

'I know. That's what the women you date say too.' He laughed, a little too loudly. The line was fair enough, though, there for the taking. 'No, it's crazy, isn't it? It's great beef here, but for some reason restaurants all got in the habit of giving you the bio. Or maybe the obit'd be more correct. I assume that, in the days when they told us nothing and sold it to us for a lot less, the cattle used to live on the same romantic undulating grasslands they've been inhabiting more recently.' He picked up another menu and opened it. 'You could write this copy. You were always good at that kind of stuff at uni.'

'Well, I do think the present version could do with a little more work. The months in the feedlot are a huge missed opportunity. I'm seeing something along the lines of "handfed luscious golden grains by fair Swiss maidens". That's just before the bit where they have the backs of their heads punched in and they get slung up on a hook. That's the part of the happy cow bio that's the real test of spin.' Did the cows ever wonder, as one week of an exceptionally lucky life stretched into another, and food became only more plentiful? Or was there no greater narrative than the grass and the grain?

'And despite that image,' he said, 'I'm still going to eat it, because it's just too damn good. Anyway, there's plenty of choices on other pages for those of a more delicate disposition. The Koreans will go for a big lump of bloody Black Angus, though, so that's why we're here. Otherwise we'd probably have updated things a bit and gone somewhere molecular. Or post molecular, depending on how much wank was called for. Granita of clarified mussel broth with coriander flower puree smoked over organic olive pits,' he said in his best wanker voice, 'dusted with dehydrated saltbush and served on a coffee soil. I'm sure you saw all that in London. Foam it, burn it, turn it into dust.'

The restaurant door swung open, just as he was gathering momentum. Max noticed us and seemed to nod. The lighting was too subdued for me to see the others clearly.

'It sounds like you're describing something you found in a bin,' I said, but Ben was standing, and not listening.

Max handled the introductions, talking slowly about my brief role with the firm, and its link to Ben's hero status. The larger, older Korean, Mister Park, looked surprised and did a gun-cocking mime to Mister Kim who nodded and clarified.

Everyone ordered steak, of one kind or another. Bottles of red wine arrived. Both countries were toasted, and remarks were made about working together and mutual prosperity. Mister Kim translated as quickly as he could, but the pauses made each sentence of the toasts seem even more stilted and more formal. Vincent talked about what a pleasure it had been to meet Mister Park on a trade mission to Seoul, and what a pleasure it was now to have the chance to show him some of Queensland.

Mister Park ate his steak ravenously, and drank the wine as if it was water, nodding as Mister Kim translated and offering in return succinct asides through mouthfuls of partially chewed Black Angus. Mister Kim made these into polite, even gracious, sentences and watched his own meal go cold. He talked about how pleased Mister Park was with his meetings in Queensland, and with the beef. He talked about the great future of toll roads, and their automation. He talked about golf, Mister Park's liking for golf, and for shooting things, especially large animals. He said Mister Park liked Alaska, and moose hunting.

'He always wants to do more business with Alaska,' he said. 'But Australia is good too. Queensland is good. We have met – Mister Park and I – some Australian businessmen before. One night in Manila. They know how to have a good time.'

He turned to Mister Park and said a few words. Mister Park gave a laugh, put his cutlery down and gave the nation two thumbs up. 'Aussie, Aussie, Aussie,' he said, and Mister Kim added, 'They said that, the Australians. They often said that. And oi, oi, oi.'

'Oi, oi, oi,' Mister Park reminisced, and he laughed again.

'Mister Park liked those Australians. He had a good night. There was very fine entertainment for Mister Park in Manila.'

Max turned my way and said, 'What did I tell you?' He leaned forward and caught Mister Kim's attention. 'Mister Kim, could you please tell Mister Park we like entertainment too?'

He sat back and hummed, badly, a bar or two of I've Never Been to Me. Mister Kim translated his remark about entertainment and Mister Park smiled a fat, knowing smile. He cleared his throat, as if he was about to make another toast.

'Bring her over and rub her with butter,' Mister Park appeared to say then, in halting English and like a man talking through a mouthful of marbles. He laughed uproariously.

The rest of us laughed too, the way people with guns to their heads laugh if their captors tell them to. Had he really said it? Butter? Bring her over and rub her with butter? Max Visser, stuck in his humming somewhere around the word 'paradise', stared at Mister Kim.

'That is a phrase he picked up somewhere on his travels,' Mister Kim said hesitantly. 'Mister Park likes to pick up things on his travels. That's just a phrase. He understands it also to be Australian. I was not with him on that journey.'

★ ★ ★

SO IT WASN'T KARAOKE. It was never going to be, as far as Mister Park was concerned. Max Visser's evening plans vaporised before we had even climbed into the two cabs that took us to the Silver Spur.

'Jesus,' he said to me as we pulled out from the kerb.

'I really don't know . . . This isn't for blogging, okay? Ben, Ben, did you think this is how he'd take it when I mentioned liking entertainment?'

'Well, crass Australians in Manila . . .' Ben was in the front seat. 'Sounds like titty bar to me. Maybe even ping-pong balls.'

'Oh god, not ping-pong balls.' Max seemed to flinch at the thought. 'There's no way I can go home tonight with a good enough explanation for ping-pong balls.'

'Well, not unless you happen to find yourself playing ping pong during the next couple of hours,' Ben said, and laughed. 'And I have to say I think that's pretty unlikely.'

The other cab was ahead of us in the traffic and had already pulled up outside the club when we arrived. Mister Park was standing on the pavement with his hands on his hips, looking up at the neon lights, which featured a stacked cartoonish Annie Oakley type blowing smoke from a discharged revolver, and winking. He pointed something out to Mister Kim, who was following him out of the cab.

The last of Warrant's Cherry Pie could be heard playing inside the club as Ben, Max and I caught up with the others at the entrance. There was shouting, and applause which faded quickly.

'So this'd be four, five and six then?' the woman at the box office said through a microphone as she passed drink vouchers and raffle tickets to Vincent on a turntable.

Vincent was putting his wallet away. 'Group discount for six,' he said to us. 'Max, try not to look as if we're taking you out the back to shoot you.'

The huge Pacific Islander on the door eyed us impassively and lifted a curtain aside for us to enter the club. He wore all black and had an old-fashioned crew cut and an ID tag with the number forty-three on it. He had the kind of look that might take third prize as the Rock's character in a Get Smart movie look-alike competition.

The club was decked out like a Wild-West saloon, with barmaids in bustier tops and high hair. The lights were low and the ceiling lost in darkness, the walls near the stage draped with heavy burgundy curtains. Above the bar, I thought I could make out the outlines of wagon wheels, arranged like disjointed Olympic rings. At the far end of the room, two unoccupied pool tables glowed green under hooded lights, their balls racked and waiting. They were the only patches of brightness in the room. There were entrances off to other rooms, though the signs above them were too dark to read. I thought I could just make out the distinctive hook of Van Halen's Hot for Teacher coming from one of them and assumed that, behind the closed door, a stripper in a cruelly short skirt, a bun and librarian glasses was in the process of misbehaving, or dispensing discipline.

The stage in the saloon room was golden and keyhole-shaped, with a pole in the centre of the circle. Even there the lights were down for now, as two staff members on their knees squeegeed away the last of the faux-cream from the Cherry Pie act. On three sides of them, men clustered around upturned barrels or stood by themselves holding their drinks and gazing at the curtains, as if waiting for a bus. A few were in business suits, but most were at the shabby end of casual, in jeans and short-sleeved shirts with checks or raucous patterns.

We found an unoccupied barrel and formed a loose semicircle around it, facing the stage. Mister Park was talking animatedly, and pointing to the trashy themeing.

'Mister Park says this is very like Anchorage,' Mister Kim said. 'Very happy. And will there be horses? In Anchorage there was a lady with a horse.'

A woman, snugly laced into her bustier and with her blonde hair piled high on her head, arrived with a platter of dark brown spring rolls and dim sims.

'I'm Bianca. I'll be your hostess. Would you like to order any drinks, gentlemen?' she said, in a tone more brisk than friendly, as Mister Park gawked at her straightforward cleavage as if it was better than real. She had stripped at one time herself, perhaps, but those days looked to be in the past. 'Your vouchers will cover any non-premium domestic beer, house wine or single shot of spirits with mixer, but I can also take orders for other drinks. I can also organise any special shows or personal dances that you may require.'

Vincent leaned across to Mister Kim and said, 'Please don't translate non-premium,' as if the subtleties might suddenly matter. 'We should just order whatever we like.'

'I am sure Scotch will be fine for Mister Park,' Mister Kim said, without checking. 'On the rocks. And water will be fine for me.'

Bianca took our drink vouchers and left us with a pile of lap-dance raffle tickets on our barrel top. Mister Kim clarified their purpose to Mister Park who swept them all up with his large hand and pocketed them. Mister Kim adjusted his glasses, and looked at the floor.

The muzak fired up, and heart-shaped lights fell upon the catwalk and started swirling.

An announcer's voice cut in over the fading murmur of conversation. 'And now, gentlemen, start your engines and please make welcome . . . Jett.'

A jet-engine sound effect swooped in and, just as it lifted away, Wings' song Jet opened up and a spotlight swept to a back corner of the stage, catching the next performer striking a pose in black leather − a jacket, thigh-high boots, tiny spray-on shorts. She pulled off her leather cap, and long straight black hair fell down past her shoulders. She had dark eyes and even in the shifting stagy light I could see they were made up like Cleopatra's. She bit her lip and unzipped her jacket, as if a very sexual thought had just crossed her mind and she was powerless to fight it.

She made her way down the catwalk in time to the music and, in the spill of the light, I could see the pale faces of men opposite gazing up at her. She slid the jacket from her shoulders, grabbed the pole and the song hit the word 'suffragette'. Half a world away, around the grave of Mrs Pankhurst, visitors paying their respects swore to each other that the noise they had just heard couldn't be a body turning over, no matter how much it sounded like it.

Jett moved from the Wings song into Fever. The boots came off, and the tight, tight shorts. She swung up onto the pole, and spun slowly around. She unrolled her fishnets.

Ben nudged me, and I nearly spilled my beer. 'You're going to catch flies with that mouth,' he said.

'It's for the blog,' I told him without turning his way. 'I've got nothing if I don't pick up the details.'

Jett started rubbing her body, the music turned into Mazzy Star's Fade Into You. The lights dipped to blue and her moves became more trance-like. She had her hands under her top, stroking herself, exposing more skin as her hands moved to her breasts. She lifted the top off over her head and undid her bra, holding it in place at the front with one arm before letting it fall away. She hooked her fingers into the sides of her black G-string and started to draw it lower, her head tipped back, her eyes closed, her mouth open.

And then it was over. The song was over and the stage went to black and, when the house lights lifted, Jett was gone. A few dozen men stood looking awkwardly at the empty space in front of them, as if they had just been caught out farting in a meeting. Blood was pounding in my head and my mouth was dry. She had suckered me, just like the rest of them. Sold it as if she'd gone from something raunchy to some kind of intimacy. I wanted to shake it out of my head, loosen the hold it had.

I turned to my right and saw Max Visser, gripping his beer with both hands and looking like a hostage about to plead for his life in a video.

'I really thought this'd be karaoke,' he said when he noticed me. 'This stuff creeps me out. My oldest daughter's not much younger than that girl, and it was only a few years ago that she was wearing my horsehair wig for dress-ups and calling it the sheep hat.' He took a deep breath and then let it out. He looked around the room.

75

'God, you can tell you're old when the first thing you want to say to them is, "Do your parents know you're doing this?"'

It was the most unsexual thought imaginable, and it had me right back in the world of the un-suckered, turned off. I took a mouthful of lukewarm non-premium domestic beer. Mister Park was talking animatedly. Mister Kim was not translating.

The next act began a few minutes later. She was introduced as Elektra, and she strode out to Motley Crue's Girls, Girls, Girls, looking very eighties with her big blonde hair, bad eye make-up and temporary lace. She worked the pole hard, but like a construction worker or someone on an oil rig. The song switched to the J Geils Band's Centrefold, which brought on some strutting and posing. A garter was flicked into the crowd. The eighties motif carried through to the bitter end, with bursts of strobe lighting and Duran Duran's Girls on Film as Elektra let loose her large solid breasts and Mister Park punched the air in delight. Mister Kim picked up a spring roll, inspected it closely in the flickering light and put it back down on the platter. He wiped his hand on a serviette.

There was a final twitch of the strobe as the G-string came away, then darkness.

As the house lights came up, with Elektra's act done and the stage empty, I saw a patron being led off towards the private rooms, stuffing his credit card receipt into his pocket. As he passed through a gap in the curtains, a cowgirl near the bar caught me looking. She had a low-cut denim top, denim miniskirt, boots and a cowboy hat, and she wore a toy gun loosely on one hip.

As she started to walk our way, I realised it was Jett.

Ben, all set to pay out on me again for staring, turned to watch her too. She stopped in front of us. She smiled, as if she had it all worked out.

'I'm guessing you two aren't the personal dance kind of crowd,' she said. 'You're here for work, right?' She was looking at me, still smiling. She had gone from leather chick to near naked to cowgirl, and the costume changes had put me off balance. Her voice sounded completely and pleasantly normal. I had imagined her talking like someone in a movie.

'Good guess,' I said, when the words eventually came. 'Some of us were promised karaoke, but . . . What's a personal dance?'

She laughed, then stopped herself. 'Sorry, you're serious. Okay. A personal is just you and the dancer. And a comfy seat. Starting at a bargain fifty-five dollars for ten minutes, but you don't get a whole lot for that. And neither does the dancer, obviously. It's what we do after the show. You might know it as a lap dance, though legislation came in a while back that means we can't actually sit on you. So, sorry if you wanted me to sit on you.'

'So the lap's out of play now?'

She was flirting, professionally. She had dangled her flirting in front of me like bait on a hook, and all I could do was bite at it.

'It is, plenty isn't.' She rolled her eyes. Perhaps we were just two people having a conversation after all. And perhaps I was even more taken with the prospect of that. 'Hey, is that Max Visser?' She was looking past me. 'He's one of my lecturers at uni . . . Poor guy. This is so not his kind of place.'

'You're doing law, then?' Ben said.

And Jett the cowgirl said, 'Yeah, fourth year. Nearly finished.' She pulled her pistol from its holster and gave it a spin on her finger. She pointed it at me, lined me up in her sights and said, 'Bang. I totally don't feel like working the room tonight. If you think I'm using you, you could be right. Just pretend you're interested.' She tilted the brim of her hat up with the end of her gun barrel, and whatever light there was fell on her face. All my energy was going into pretending *not* to be interested. 'You've never been to one of these places before, have you? What do you think?'

'Well, it's probably less sleazy than I was expecting . . .' I said, in lieu of the brilliant answer I'd been looking for.

'Seriously? I'd hate to think what you were expecting. Don't you think the themeing's hilarious? We're themed to within an inch of our lives. These spurs can take chunks out of the carpet.' I wasn't sure it was true, but it was a good line. I couldn't even see the spurs, down there in the dark. 'The girls who are stacked up top mostly go for the bordello look for the personals, those of us who aren't default to cowgirl.'

'Yeah, but . . .' There was no good response, but my mouth had got started anyway. She had been talking about her breasts, which we both knew I had seen. And which were neat and compact and . . . 'You know, if they've had work done the seams show from here, where they . . .'

My index fingers were drawing semicircles on my chest, two smiley faces under my nipples, quite without my consent, swinging like windscreen-wipers and marking out the arcs of cosmetic surgery. I meant Elektra. Elektra had had work done, had had gourds attached to the front of her chest, and not subtly. Ben was laughing, and hardly trying to suppress it at all. There was a burst of music from the PA system, and an announcement.

'But that's not you, of course,' I said, struck by an insanity that I was hoping was temporary.

'Dig, Josh, dig. Take it deeper,' Ben said, and slapped me on the shoulder.

Jett laughed. 'How nice of you to . . .' She stopped. She was looking past me again. She holstered her pistol. 'I'd better keep moving. Looks like your friend might have the lucky ticket.'

Behind us, Mister Park was excitedly waving one of his tickets in the air, and Bianca was closing in to do the business. The unflappable Mister Kim was bracing for negotiations and Max looked close to throwing up. I glanced back over my shoulder, but Jett was already gone somewhere in the dark, finding new ways to avoid the paying customers, some other safe conversation that might look enough like work from a distance.

'You are so fucking suave,' Ben said to me. 'I'm glad you haven't lost that. She was totally eating out of your hand.'

She had been killing time, hiding with us in the middle of the crowd. She was cool and I had taken about a minute to draw breasts on myself, and then correct it by talking about hers.

'Well, congratulations, sir,' Bianca was saying to Mister Park as we stepped closer. 'Now, here's the deal. You've won five free minutes topless, one-on-one, no touching between the legs, no mouth contact, and you can upgrade if you want to fifteen minutes fully nude and including open leg work, for half price.'

'Bring her over and rub her with butter,' Mister Park said proudly and about no one in particular. He took Bianca's hand and shook it firmly.

Bianca hardly blinked. 'We've probably got some margarine out the back. We could work with margarine. But the girl would have to do herself. Nothing funny.'

Mister Kim stepped in. 'It's just a phrase he picked up in his travels. It means he is very happy. I will now translate your earlier offer. The margarine is not necessary. Probably not necessary.'

He recounted the deal to Mister Park, who listened and nodded. And then said something, just a few words, that made Mister Kim flinch. Mister Kim pushed his glasses back to the bridge of his nose, and tried to find the exact right words.

'Mister Park wants to enquire about a particular entertainment he has heard of from some Australian businessmen friends in Manila,' he said, with all the care of someone negotiating a missile stand-off. 'He was told it was very famous. He was told he should ask for it whenever he was in Australia. That it was a special Australian treat. He would like to know how much it would cost to watch a lady move her bowel. He would like to appreciate this spectacle. He would prefer large volume, and a table with a glass top.'

Was it real? Had it ever happened? Max stared at Vincent. Vincent stared at Max. Neither of them moved. As special Australian treats went, it certainly put Vegemite in its place. Max, a long long way from karaoke, cracked first.

He pulled his mobile from his pocket. 'Oh fuck, oh fuck, I think my phone's ringing.' The words rattled out of him, as quickly as he could manage them. 'One of my children has a fever.' He lurched away, his lie hot on his tail. 'Yes, yes, I'm coming,' he said to the phone, a finger in his other ear.

'I'm sorry, sir,' Bianca said, matching every bit of Mister Kim's sense of calm. 'When I checked before, all our girls had just moved their bowels. But if Mister Park's interested we have plenty of other options. We can do a nude shower show, duo show, dildo show, toy show or fruit and veg. Dildoes, toys and fruit and veg can go Greek for an extra fifty. Dildoes and toys stay here, fruit and veg vary seasonally, are fresh every night and Mister Park's to keep as a souvenir if he wishes. He could also go for a massage – Mister Park does the lady, she does Mister Park or both. And after the massage there's a shower where Mister Park can wash the oil off, and he can feel free to give himself relief in there if he wishes.'

Mister Kim smiled, for perhaps the first time. He took a platinum credit card from his wallet. 'I am sure there is something there that will make Mister Park very happy.'

★ ★ ★

WHEN BEN AND I left the club, a new stripper was grinding out some moves to Alannah Myles's Black Velvet and Mister Park was down the back, playing pool with Elektra, each of them wearing only a cowboy hat, boots and spurs. Mister Park had requested fully nude, but had been told that safety regs required footwear, as drink spillage was liable to make the floor hazardous.

Ben began to explain his exit to Vincent, saying something about making an early start on some documents for him, and Vincent said, 'Go. Save yourself while you still can.' He was still on his first Crownie, still in his suit, with his tie rolled up in his pocket. 'Just make sure I make a lot of money out of this.'

We were almost at the door when something poked me in the ribs. It was a revolver, and on the other end of it was Jett.

'Okay,' she said, 'there's this rumour going out the back that the big guy asked for the poo-on-the-table routine. Please, please tell me it's true.'

The security guard had opened the curtain for us, and a triangle of foyer light fell in and mostly on Jett. Her lipstick looked redder, her skin paler, her eyes a darker brown. I could see fine freckles on her cheeks, not quite obliterated by make-up, by the cowgirl cartoon that had overtaken her. For one clear moment, I knew I had nothing to lose.

'I think "prefer large volume" was the expression,' I said. 'I don't know how big it needs to be to have the desired effect. I mean, does he need it to beep as it backs out?'

'You're welcome to stay, gentlemen,' the security guard said, still holding the curtain, 'but I might need you to make your minds up.'

Jett laughed and kept her eyes on me as she stepped back into the darkness. She lifted her non-gun hand to wave, and the curtain fell.

The crowds on Ann Street pushed past as Ben and I paused briefly in the small foyer, repressurising for the normal world.

'You so lifted your game with that line,' he said. 'I can't believe you made a girl like you with a line about a turd.'

'It's a gift,' I told him. 'That kind of stuff went down a treat in London.'

Traffic banked up at the Brunswick Street lights and drunks ambled onto the road among the cars, shouting harmlessly into windows or up at the sky as their friends tried to pull them back. On the other side of the road, a huge and unruly cab queue blocked half the pavement, without a cab in sight. I was thinking of home, of the girl who had just vanished into the dark, of my unlikely winning line, now spent and gone. I couldn't go back in there, I knew that. I needed to be in a cab and on my way.

'You'll wait forever here,' Ben said. He could see me sizing up the cab queue. 'Come back to my place and call one from there. They're much better if you call from a landline. Otherwise you're just another pisshead in the Valley. It's a couple of blocks.'

He led the way through the crowd, keeping his head down and looking like someone with somewhere to go, his dark suit incongruous among people who had come out dressed for drinking or for clubbing, who presumably had nowhere to be in the morning and all night to celebrate that. There were hard men with gym bodies and sleeve tattoos, a girl with her shoes in her hand, crying and shouting at friends who were trying to settle her, emos in clumps in their op-shop flannos or shirts with ironic slogans.

Ben turned into a side street and we passed two new apartment blocks and stopped at an old industrial building that had had a recent makeover. He keyed in an entry code and the heavy steel-and-glass door unlocked with a clunk. When it shut behind us, the building seemed almost silent.

Ben's apartment was on the third floor, with only the rooftop garden above it. He called me a cab and then opened the doors to a balcony overlooking the street, so that we could hear when it arrived.

I wondered if we would talk about Eloise, and what I would say if we did.

The noise of the Valley came in through the open doors. It was an indistinct mess of traffic and people, like the sound of a TV in a nearby room. His flat was no bigger than mine, but it was a loft with a mezzanine, and the dark brick walls were scored with graffiti. The appliances in the kitchenette were European and fire-engine red, and the furniture was made in uncomfortable designer-ish shapes in pale curved wood. The longest wall had a row of three huge porthole windows just below ceiling height, through which blue light fell from a recently disturbed rooftop lap pool.

'It'll be a while,' Ben said. 'Even calling from here. This time of night it'd be a while anywhere.' His fridge had an ice dispenser, and he put ice into two glasses before opening the door and taking out a bottle of Perrier. 'Do you want anything to eat? I have some olives.'

'No. Thanks.'

I took my mineral water over to the open doors, but the balcony was too small to fit the two of us. I leaned against a nearby wall so that I would still hear the cab in the street below, and then the graffiti caught my eye. I stepped back and checked my sleeve before I could stop myself.

'It's all right,' he said. 'The walls are treated. The graffiti's authentic. Most of it's just tags, though. Junkies, probably.'

A car passed below, slowly, but it was just a car. Not a taxi.

'How's your mother?' I couldn't talk about graffiti as some hip urban design aesthetic. I couldn't talk about why all his appliances needed to be red, or the story behind the olives. I knew there would be one. 'I've been meaning to ask.'

'She's fine,' he said. 'She's good.'

'How was she about your father?'

'Fine. That history was way too ancient.' He looked out into the night.

'And how are *you* feeling about your father?'

'That sounds like a therapy question.' He made himself smile as if he'd meant it as a joke. He hadn't. 'I said no to counselling already. After the incident. I'm sure it would have been a great chance for an absent-father grilling if I'd taken it up.'

'It was just a question.' I had hit a weak spot. 'A "one human being to another" question. And maybe if you'd said yes to the counselling, you'd have a better term for it than "incident". I don't imagine it was quite that abstract at the time.'

He was about to have a go at me. Here I was, drinking his mineral water and taking his hospitality and trying, not for the first time, to back him into the corner in which he would tell me about the siege.

'I haven't missed him yet,' he said eventually. 'If you want to know where things stand with my father. I've missed him hardly at all. I couldn't do business and be his son. I'm not his son. I'm a guy with the bad luck to have his name. Absence is the way I've known him best. He worked long hours, he left us, he died.'

So there, in the eyes of his only known child, was Kerry Benson Harkin's epitaph, ungracious and probably richly deserved. Above us, a swimmer pushed off in the lap pool, sending bubbles down into the water and against Ben's portholes.

'Number six,' he said, of the gleaming white body in black Speedos. 'Never sleeps, as far as I'm aware. Or does an IT job in a different time zone. Something like that. They can't see us down here, not with the water lights on. The windows just look black.'

'Could have been you. The IT . . .'

He made a dismissive noise. 'Not with my rudimentary web skills. I don't think they even call it IT any more. I'd be doing websites for community groups at a thousand bucks a time, tops. I wouldn't have this place if I was doing that.'

He looked around his apartment, mood lit for a mood we were nowhere near. It had the appearance of an apartment in a magazine, with barely a sign of life but for the unnamed swimmer, tumble-turning and making his way back along the windows.

'You were really into the animation, though.' I wasn't going to let him pretend that he had never had the dream. 'The Japanese-style thing. Maybe you could have done something there.'

'Looks like I didn't. With that or the web stuff.' The

topic was over for him. 'It's only the porn magnates in this town who make real money from websites. Not that there's anything wrong with that. But what about you? All the blogging and the articles? All this . . . whimsy.' It was probably the most dismissive word he could find. 'Was that the London plan? I thought of you when that guy came out as Deep Throat not long after you left.'

'Mark Felt. W Mark Felt.' I had assumed we would never know the real Deep Throat. His anonymity was a fixed truth I had been born into, and I had watched the movie too many times to imagine that that might change. And the London plan was only partly about All the President's Men and journalistic ambition. It was as much to do with escape from Ben and from Eloise, from the fallout. He knew that. 'I don't mind the articles,' I said, though just at that second I hated them. I could choke on whimsy, gag on it. 'They make a lot of stupid things tax deductible. And people are starting to pay properly. And they're starting to come to me. I got a call a few days ago from a magazine pitching me a story. A national magazine.'

'Really? What about?'

'Well, actually . . .' The point had been that it was a national magazine, and they had come to me. I wanted to lie. I wanted it to be some important truth-breaking feature. I wanted to be better than him, to have a better life, a more successful life. Eloise had loved me, I thought, until he got involved. 'They wanted to send me out speed-dating.'

He laughed. He laughed until mineral water sloshed up the side of his glass and ran down onto his hand. 'Which you said no to in case you got a crush on someone. Right? You could get a crush on that Jett chick in five seconds. You probably already did. I saw how you were looking at her. Even when she was fully dressed and your jaw wasn't on the carpet.'

'She was an interesting phenomenon. I was looking at her as a law student who happened to be . . .'

'Dressed like a cowgirl, or a biker chick, or kind of close to naked?' He shook his head, and laughed again.

He was right, of course. I had already fantasised about cooking her Gergovian meatballs, which I would call 'a very old French recipe', on my Bunsen burner or, better still, at her place, which would be quite stylish, et cetera et cetera (fade out during excellent sex, wake the following morning to find her searching for synonyms for ecstasy – it was a movie already, this fantasy). Other than that, I had no kind of crush on her at all.

'You're very superficial,' I said to him, once I had rolled the closing credits. 'Our connection was all about personality.'

'Have you ever told a lie that anyone believed?'

'Not so far.' I didn't think I had. I wasn't good at it, when it was about me. 'It's amazing I'm in this job. Maybe I can send other people out to lie about themselves. Maybe I'm good at that. But I'm all about the truth, remember. Just finding the best, most survivable version of the truth. I spin the truth – I'll admit to that – but I don't dismember it.'

'Really?' He was giving it thought. 'Is that a genuine distinction, or is it what you tell yourself?'

'Don't get all meta on me. I'm not sure this bears analysis. It's what I do, for now. For the next week or so. That's all.'

He took a mouthful of his drink, stepped out onto the balcony and looked up and down the street. 'No cab,' he said. 'They're not quick tonight.'

In the distance, glass smashed. Someone had dropped a bottle. Ben didn't seem to hear it.

As he came back in, his elbow touched a lamp that stood on a table next to the door. He stopped to steady it, to check that it was okay. Its base was a graceful bronze woman's body that held up a canopy or a pair of curved wings made out of tiles of green glass.

He noticed me looking at it and said, 'Paul Behrens, from the twenties. The glass is Tiffany. He made it for his own house. He made every fitting and every piece of furniture from scratch. It's often copied, this lamp, but this one was his.'

'It's from your father's apartment at Surfers, isn't it?' I could remember it. Ben had thrown lavish parties when he had the chance. When he had access to better real estate than he tended to live in, usually a place in the temporary hold of his father, but at times when Kerry was conveniently out of town. The theme of that party had been the twenties, The Great Gatsby. He had studied the novel, I thought.

'It's the one thing of his I still have,' he said. He reached beneath the lampshade, pulled a cord, and broken green light refracted onto the walls. 'I took it years ago. The receivers had been called. It was one of those times. I was there on the right day, before they came and made their list.'

'But it smashed at that party, didn't it?' It seemed a stupid thing to say with the lamp intact in front of us, but I remembered it distinctly.

'Well,' he said, touching the glass, 'here it is.'

I had been the one to find the dustpan and brush. I had swept up the broken glass.

'Anyway, how about that Jett chick?' he said. He stepped away from the table. 'Aside from the crush. Look at her. We could get the band back together. She'd be just right for it.'

'There was no band. Or does that not matter to you?' It must have been another lamp back then. But I was sure he had told me the Behrens story before the party started – the Tiffany glass, everything made from scratch. And then the Gold Coast social crowd turned up. There were models and iron men and some local TV people, and a guy who'd made it through a couple of seasons in Formula One. Not friends of his, but Ben always knew who to call.

'Cloud-Sized Cloud could have been a hit.' He was still on about the band, as if he had a genuine point to make.

'It wasn't even a song.'

'It *sounded* like it could have been.' He was smiling, making some kind of game of it. 'She'd be great. Just for a photo. Everyone believes a photo. We know that. We only need her top half, and we know it's up to the job. A cowgirl drummer. Think about it.'

'You'll have me writing articles next if I think about it.' I was thinking about it. Thinking about the cowgirl drummer, who would be extremely cool. I was dreaming about Jett in a useless way. She had used us to kill time. That was all. She had chosen me as the room's most innocuous person. 'I'm not going to think about it.' He knew I already had. 'So, tell me about this Rob Mueller guy.'

He kept the smile up, but it was less real now. 'Rob Mueller . . . I don't know. In the end, I don't know. He seemed crazy. I don't know what does that. I don't know what makes you get a gun, or how you get a gun and what makes you . . .' I could almost watch the ideas falling apart. 'I don't know.'

'Sorry, I . . .' I had pushed him there, dragged him back to the trauma, just because I'd had enough of the game, enough of him picking away at my work, my stupid gawking at a stripper.

'No. No, it's fine. We've got to talk. *I've* got to talk. I signed the thing saying yes to the medal.'

Maybe it was better starting it here, on his turf, his sterile designer turf, away from the glass walls and co-owners of the story at Randall Hood Beckett.

'So what was it like for you afterwards? It doesn't seem to have been easy.'

'What was it like? I've got no idea how to describe what it was like. One day, actually one night, I went up and down the street and took free Toilet Duck samples out of all the mailboxes. Why? Why? I've got no idea. So I wouldn't have to go to a shop to buy it? I don't know. I wasn't even aware I was doing it, and then suddenly I was in the foyer with my pockets full of samples. I came in here and locked the door for two days after that. Until I could account for everything I was doing again, every minute.' He was looking around the room, picturing himself there on those two days. 'I thought about having another life. Maybe delivering stuff. Going round in a van screwing in new light globes – there's a guy who does that. It's an actual job. How about that?'

'It's pretty extreme outsourcing.' He had said no to therapy. I was guarding against sounding therapeutic, and I had defaulted to glib. Default. Jett said she had *defaulted* to cowgirl. I could play our conversation through, entirely. Every word of it was still there.

'There's a whole lot of stuff like that going on,' Ben said, in the world outside my head, my selfish head. 'Coffee carts, Gutter Vac. I could be the Gutter Vac guy. There are all these jobs where it's just you and the van and the mobile phone. But it's all practical stuff, and it turns out I don't have a clue about anything practical. You can get lost in these suburbs, you know. And do all kinds of things. There's a story – or maybe an allegation – that the fourth-largest music piracy site in the world is run out of an unassuming brick house in Bellbowrie. Fortunately I kept the city job. Things still feel different, I guess. But I'm okay. And Rob Mueller, since that was your question . . . Maybe it was his one clear way out. Maybe there's a point where every other way forward gets sabotaged. Or you just run out of possibilities . . .' He left it there, as if the idea couldn't be finished. 'Hey, you're looking for an oven, aren't you? Come and take a look at this.'

He led me across the living area to the kitchenette.

'I thought he was crazy,' I said.

'Yeah, well. That too. I already said he was crazy, didn't I?' Ben was down on his knees, one hand on the handle of the oven door. 'You should get one of these. Miele. It's triple glass so it's never hot to touch. Matt finish too. Nice. He stroked the glass. 'Not that I'm much of a cook.'

I didn't know if the oven had been used at all. I

couldn't even be certain that it was an oven, rather than an oven-look design feature, red enamelled steel with its square of matt glass and a long anodised rod for a handle. I wanted to open the door, just to prove there was an oven behind it.

A car horn sounded outside. My cab had arrived.

'We'll talk more about the siege, okay?' I said to him as he stood up. 'We've got a few days.'

'Sure. Here, let me take your glass.' He set both our glasses down on the empty granite counter, and then said, 'Oh, hang on a second.' He reached into his back pocket and took out his wallet. He pulled out a cabcharge ticket. 'You should have one of these. To get home. Let Randall Hood Beckett pick up the tab.'

He handed it over, and I took it. Perhaps it was a considerate act on his part but it felt like largesse, as if he had just handed me money, tipped me for some unknown and probably menial service before dismissing me from his designer life and sending me off into the night.

'I bumped into Eloise's mother a few weeks ago,' I told him, though I knew it was a cheap shot. Eloise was not a fair exit line. 'Complete coincidence. She said Eloise is in Sydney now and doing well in HR, "but she's not the Eloise you'd remember". That's how she put it.'

Ben nodded, and kept his face close to blank. 'That cab's not going to stay forever,' he said.

★ ★ ★

THE CAB TURNED LEFT and then left again, merging with the traffic and the world given over to drunks and clubbers, bottle smashers and shoeless girls who had lost the plot.

I met Eloise through Ben, when he first lifted his habitual veil of secrecy and invited me to a party at their flat. I hadn't known him long and I went to see who his friends were, as much as anything, and how his life worked. Most of the guests were Eloise's, though, and Ben's seemed to have been picked almost at random, as if he had a share of numbers to make up. There was no one from TV, or Formula One, though I didn't know to look for them then. It was Eloise's party, I realised some time later. It wasn't a Ben party at all.

They had a two-bedroom place near uni, in an old block from the sixties or seventies. The pavers of the path that led in from the front gate had long ago been lifted by poinciana roots, and the railings on the steps had a coat of new green paint over blooming rust. Ben had not been there long. Eloise had stated a preference for a female flatmate in her notice on the campus accommodation board, but Ben projected fastidiousness and never looked like someone with a posse of boozy mates. She told me later that she had thought he might be gay. I never knew why Ben had moved in, why he happened to be looking at the board at that time and had torn off a tab with Eloise's number on it.

I met her late in the evening, just as I was about to cut my losses and head to the bus stop. I had drunk most of the bottle of cheap red that I had brought, spilled a little while dancing and pulverised my share of Jatz into the carpet. I was the standard unremarkable partygoer in the world of student parties, but she noticed me anyway and introduced herself. She had fought with her boyfriend and he had left with someone else. I kissed her when I had the chance. I missed the second-last bus and then the last one. I slept on the floor of her room, on an ancient brown shag-pile rug at the foot of her bed, because she had worked out she was drunk by then and said she'd prefer to make her next mistake sober.

I fell for Eloise in a big way. She seemed to be into me too. We loved and hated the same things, and usually to the same degree. Red wine over white, indie bands over stadium acts, the book over the movie. In our first conversation, she said she thought palimpsest was a fair description of the relationship between the book and movie of The Name of the Rose. We had both seen the word in the opening titles, and looked it up afterwards.

It worked for more than a year, or I thought it did. I started telling her I didn't want it to end. Maybe I rushed it, or rushed her somewhere she wasn't sure about going. Or maybe the future just didn't look the same to her. I had turned the dial to 'crush' and perhaps she saw me as nothing special.

'You could get a crush on that Jett chick in five seconds. You probably already did.' Ben had talked as if he knew me completely, and as though we would both be amused by his snide remarks. I wanted him to be wrong, but he read me well enough and it felt as if I had laid a weakness bare to someone who could choose to be an enemy.

When I got home I knew I wouldn't sleep, so I got online and checked responses to my recent blogs. I had the intention of interacting, as I was supposed to, but it turned out I couldn't care enough. It felt even more pointless than it usually did, and I was happy for it to go on without me. I fell asleep on the sofa with late-night TV doing its worst and cookie fortunes on my lap. 'You will enjoy good health and be surrounded by luxury . . . A pleasant surprise is in store for you.'

I made a slow start to Thursday. I missed breakfast TV and moved straight to mornings, through which infomercials had long ago spread with a metastatic force. Among the toning devices and multi-function peelers and diet schemes, I found myself paying far too much attention to a classic package of low-res eighties video games, eighty-four in one, with free second console and light gun for credit card orders. 'That's under three dollars a game,' the spruiker said, his eyes bulging at the prospect of the hours that might be blissfully wiled away.

I dragged my laptop over, typed 'Eloise MacLean' into Google and then deleted it. I turned the TV off and added the two new fortunes to the pile, though I was sure I had had them both before, so far without either change in my luck.

I opened the siege file from Randall Hood Beckett.

By day three, the media focus had moved from Rob Mueller to Ben. The headline was a quote from one of the law-firm staff: 'He Saved All Our Lives'. There was a photo of Ben taken outside the building. He was in fresh clothes and his arms were folded. The wind had swept some hair across his eyes. 'This is a very brave young man,' a police sergeant was quoted as saying.

I had never seen that in him. I was still making room for bravery in the picture I had of Ben from years before.

I was bringing grudges to bear, and a mean spirit, as I sat in my shabby flat among unpacked boxes and a life without a plan.

* * *

'HOW ABOUT THAT?' Selina said from behind me. I had just written 'CONFIRMED' on the whiteboard next to Who Weekly. 'You do realise we put you in the junk room, and that old whiteboard was the only piece of junk that was too big to put somewhere else?' She scanned the names on the board. 'That'll keep him on his toes. You've got him on *all* the TV newses?'

'Well, they're all sending crews, and they know Ben's the story. I've talked it through with them. They're as confirmed as they can be. You can't totally confirm TV news.' Who Weekly was a feature, locked in, probably three pages. I had just sent them hi-res news pics.

'He's out of his meeting and back in his office.' She leaned against the doorframe and the chains around her neck rearranged themselves. They made a sound like a pocketful of change. 'If you want to grab him, now would be a good time.'

Ben was at his laptop working on a document when I got to his door. He held up one hand, then went back to typing at high speed. He hit a full stop theatrically and pushed his chair away from the desk, looking up at me properly for the first time.

'Sorry,' he said. 'I was on a roll. So, have you blogged about last night yet?'

'I've already got a panicky email from Max practically begging me not to and telling me how sincere he was about it being karaoke. Then there's the issue of how to write the piece without looking like a racist.'

'Racist? It wasn't the Koreans who came up with it. Didn't they get the idea from those Aussies in Manila?' He reached out and straightened up his pen. 'Lucky there was nude pool to come to the rescue. Who'd have thought?'

'Did you get my email?'

'No, I've been out. When did you . . .' He looked back at the screen, checked for it and found it. He read it quickly. 'News. TV news. Is that really . . .' I had sent him my pitch to the TV news reporters. It was headed 'He Saved All Our Lives'. 'Anything could happen with TV news, like . . .' He seemed to get stuck there. He looked at the screen again, and frowned.

'Like what? Like you could be on it?'

He shut the document. 'There were TV crews on the day, when it happened. That was the last thing I saw before the ambulance doors shut. TV cameras. I didn't . . . I'm really not sure about this medal, the more I think about it.' He looked at me, as if I could somehow let him off the hook.

'Look, this is going to work.' Tough love, part of the job. I was used to doubt surfacing. 'You deserve a way through it, and we'll find it. That's why I'm here. And I've got a major appliance riding on it. It has to work.'

'Well, if you put it like that . . . We can't have you living on toast. But how far does it have to go? Honestly. Between you and me. How much of the whole thing will I have to get into? How much of the father thing?'

'It'll be okay.'

It wasn't just the job, I realised. I wasn't sitting there working my way through a script because there was an appliance at the end of it. I had taken the job for money, but his fears were real, and mine to fix. Ben needed me. More than tailor-made suits and three-hundred-dollar haircuts and designer appliances. At uni, when his father's most recent disgrace had finally lost the eye of the media, he gave me a bottle of Hill of Grace that he said had ended up in his car. 'It's not a fair swap for what you did when the shit was at its deepest,' he said. 'Not a lot of other people stuck by me. You kept calling. A lot of semi-famous people didn't.'

The bottle was dusty when he gave it to me. It was from his father's cellar, I was sure. At first I thought it was too good to open, and then I hated him and couldn't. It had ended up in a box somewhere at my parents' house, with junk.

Ben was waiting for more, for the next line in my script and some details that would show I had found him a way through the week ahead.

'It really will be okay. I gave Who an exclusive, so that takes other magazines out. They'll do a good, warm story. We'll keep it to one serious TV piece, and I think we've scored there with Australian Story. And there'll be news coverage on the day and around it. Some print, some TV, some radio interviews. But they're short. We'll work on some messages you can stick to for them, some straightforward things to say. It's all fine. There's only two big stories.'

He nodded. 'Okay. Good.'

'And don't be too concerned about them. Australian Story will be one longish interview, probably. They'll talk to Max and Frank as well, and I'll be putting some time in with the two of them to get them ready for it. And you and I can do a walk-through on the weekend, room-to-room on the thirty-eighth floor, with you taking me through what happened. As far as Who Weekly goes, they want to mix it up a bit, get a look at the real you. "Hero at leisure" photoshoot stuff.'

He looked amused. 'Really? And what do I do for leisure?'

'It turns out mini-golf.'

He laughed, and leaned back in his chair, putting his hands behind his head. 'Okay, this is much better now.'

'My plan is for us to go to the Gold Coast, if you're okay with that. Or maybe even if you're not, since I had the place booked weeks ago. Mini-golf tour. Feature article. And you can crap on that all you like, but Who totally loves it for the photoshoot, and it's locked in. Max and Frank have okayed it too. They've decided you'll need a break between Monday and the lunch on Friday. Australian Story'll do their taping around the lunch.'

'They want that lunch, don't they? Frank wants that lunch.' He clunked his seat forward, reached out to his laptop and hit a key. Something on the screen had distracted him. 'I think it's part of a plan some org psych person came up with. They don't get it. It changes your life in a place like this – one nutter with a gun. It's never the same again. And a panini platter isn't going to change it back, isn't going to finish it.' It felt like we had struck the bedrock of truth at least a glancing blow. 'Who you are changes if you get stuck in the middle of something like that. You're far better off being one of the crowd running down the fire escape. You've got a good deal, you know. You'll be free of all this next week. Or soon anyway.'

'Sure. I'm poor but happy.' It was glib again, glib at the wrong time, and it sounded defensive. 'It's okay for it not to be over for you. It's okay to even talk about that in the interviews if you want. The media will go with you. They'll be good about it. They're not looking to cut you down. This is not your father's story.'

'Yeah. They're going to want to talk about him, though. For the two big stories anyway. I know we can't avoid it . . . He doesn't seem dead yet. I know that's strange. Even though I went to the funeral. It's his kind of story. It's too much like a stunt − reported dead in a lagoon on Bora Bora, making the papers and nobody taking a look at his body back here. I never trusted his stories. I have to keep telling myself this one's true. That he's not out there somewhere, working on some new scam. He left nothing, of course. Other than a web of arrangements that adds up to debt. Wife Number Three's back at work as a personal trainer. I think she rents somewhere not far from me.'

He stood up and pulled his phone out of his pocket. He flipped it open and checked something before closing it again. I was trying to find something to say about the loss of his father, wondering what could hit the right mark.

'You're coming on Monday, aren't you?' he said. 'To the medal thing? Is that part of what you do? I've got to give names. You can be my plus one.'

'I'll be there. We'll have it all mapped out by then, and I'll make it work. I think you get more than one. Max and Frank are planning to be there. Are you going to invite your mother?'

Australian Story had called back asking about family and I had half-promised them Ben's mother. I had told myself that meant I would only be half-breaking the promise when she failed to materialise. She would fall through at the last minute, by which time half-a-dozen interviews would be in the can and they would be committed.

'My mother won't get me through the media,' he said. I wondered if she even knew about the medal. I wondered if he had any other plus-one prospects in his life. 'I guess I can't stop Max and Frank. They're part of the story. And it's all about the story.' He looked me up and down, and half-smiled. 'You might need a suit, though. For the Governor. Is that a possibility?'

★ ★ ★

'UM, YEAH, SURE,' Brett said when I called him later in the afternoon. He was my last and only resort. 'I've got quite a few suits. I can't say they'll fit, exactly. I've got a bit more width than you. Is it safe to assume you've got a belt?'

Because he was my brother, he was entitled to a shot at me any time the chance arose. 'A belt? Is that what you rich people do instead of rope? Yeah, I've got a belt. I can cover the shoes too.'

'You're doing well for yourself then. Maybe I'm paying

you too much.' He laughed at his own joke. 'Francesca thought we'd have a barbecue on Saturday. You should come. The kids'd love to see you. You can fill me in on how the job's going. You could pick the suit up then.'

'Sounds good.' Some bits did anyway. 'I'm up for some Uncle Josh time.'

'So how is the job going?' Brett couldn't resist.

'Good, I think. Interviews are locked in. I emailed the itinerary to Frank and he's happy. There's a bit of talent tuning to be done yet, but that's okay.'

'Talent tuning? Is that Frank? I'm assuming he's on the list for any of the bigger things.'

'Yeah. He'll be fine, though. He's already Mister Quotable Quote on the subject. I've got to get Max to focus and Ben to cough up the story. But that'll happen. Don't worry.' I was better at sounding confident over the phone.

Ben walked past my office just as I was finishing the call. He signalled through the glass that he wanted to speak to me, and I nodded and waved for him to come in.

'You were wanting to talk to Max, weren't you?' he said when he got to the door.

'Yeah. I think he's gone, though.' I shut my phone and put it in my pocket. 'It's not urgent. It can wait till tomorrow.'

'I've got some documents to get to him.' He held up his briefcase, though I had seen it through the glass already. 'They've got to be sorted out and on their way to Mister Park's legal people in Korea while they're all still at work. Before they drop their pants, chalk their pool cues and head out for the night. So let's go.'

'Go?'

'Yeah. To Max. Selina's called us a cab.'

'What's the urgency all of a sudden?' My mind was already on home, fortune cookies, channel surfing.

'A more relevant question would be what else were you planning to do right now? Answer: nothing. It'll put you closer to home anyway. And you can bill us for every minute, I'm sure. Think of the quality appliances you'll be buying when this is done. Miele, my friend, Miele. Maybe even Gaggenau.'

It felt, for a moment, like the best of old times, not that we'd talked about appliances then. I had missed a part of him, I realised.

Max lived somewhere near me in West End. I could picture his house. It would be a nineteenth-century place with wide verandahs and a renovation that hadn't demolished its character. As we pushed through the CBD traffic, I assumed that was where we were going. Ben sorted through some sheets of paper, and fixed them together with a clip.

'I like the coast idea,' he said. 'Even if I have to have my photo taken playing mini-golf. I can't believe you talked someone into a feature on a Gold Coast mini-golf tour.' He put the documents away. 'And yet I can. Nice work. You'll never be envying the Gutter Vac guy.' He looked out the window, to the figs hanging over the railings of the Botanic Gardens and the litter of seeds and debris they had cast onto the pavement. 'I've got Cairns again tomorrow. A Japanese business deal to unravel, but this trip'll be the end of it, hopefully.'

He said it to the figs or to himself, as much as to me. It sounded like conversation, but it wasn't. Maybe he was still thinking of the Gutter Vac guy, working the suburbs, leading a different life. Or me, openly scheming towards indolence, as he saw it, and without a career to speak of. Or perhaps he was off somewhere else entirely.

The cab changed lanes. We rose on a loop of freeway and swung down into the westbound lanes of cars, with West End over to our left across the river.

'Where is he?' We weren't going to Max's house. 'Where's Max?'

'Don't worry about that,' Ben said, like a magician with a trick starting to come together.

'Is this some mystery tour?' I realised I hadn't heard him tell the driver our destination. I'd been walking around the cab to the other door at the time.

'If I tell you where we're going you're at risk of exiting the vehicle while it's still in motion. You'll thank me. Eventually. Or if you don't, it won't be my fault.' He had decided to be cryptic.

'So this is the Mister Park thing you're taking to Max?'

He waited for more, for me to crack and push him about our destination. I wasn't going to.

'Yeah. He's on his way back to Korea. We want this to be at his office before he arrives.' He stopped there, but still I didn't push him. 'Are you really interested in Mister Park?'

'No.'

As we passed through Toowong, the cabbie half-turned and said, 'Which bit of the campus did you want?'

Ben leaned forward and said, 'Forgan Smith Building.' He tried to hide it, but he looked pleased with himself.

Forgan Smith Building, University of Queensland. Max Visser was lecturing in law. He was giving his weekly guest lecture. And we both knew who else would be there.

'Come on,' Ben said, as if he was challenging me. 'You've only ever thought of her as a law student. That's how I heard it. So this should be fine. And I want to see it. Her worlds colliding, you wrestling with one of your awkward silences.'

'Fuck you. I don't have awkward silences.'

'Sure you don't. That was years ago. It'll be no problem at all as long as you're able to get those perky non-surgically-enhanced breasts out of your –'

'It's not about the breasts,' I said too loudly. 'You are making something out of nothing.'

'Sure I am. That's why you're so . . . tetchy.'

I was going to go with him, despite my protests, and despite my interest in talking to Max Visser temporarily falling close to zero.

'I'm only coming so that I can talk to Max,' I said.

'Yep. Keep telling yourself that.'

It was close to six pm as we drove onto the campus. Through the cab window, the students were just darkening shapes in the twilight. I felt like a kid at a school dance, hoping to see the girl he had bumped into once on the bus but not even knowing whether she would be there.

Ben signed the cabcharge printout and led the way up the granite steps into the building. The terrazzo floors and turned wooden stair railings were the same as ever, the same as the last time I had been in there, years before. And the smell was still the sweet musty old-book smell that the building had had when we had studied there, even though I had been given the impression they had moved way beyond books by now.

'Takes you back,' Ben said, just as it was taking me back.

He turned right down the bright central corridor and we walked past noticeboards and lecturers' offices. We had almost reached the double doors to the lecture theatre when they swung open and started disgorging students. The noise from inside sounded like an evacuation, an impossible number of feet making an impossible noise as they rushed to the exit. Ben stood us against the wall directly opposite, so that we couldn't be missed.

Jett came out quite early, behind a clump of students but by herself, a folder held to her chest, her hair much shorter than the night before. She was turning away when she saw us. She stopped, and the student behind her tried to swerve but caught her shoulder on the way past. Jett stepped clear of them, and towards us. She was trying to look less surprised. She had no make-up on at all. I wanted to tell her she didn't need it. It had been part of the job, like the toy pistol, the spurs.

'So what are you guys doing here?' she said. She was smiling, as if the night before had given the three of us a secret to share.

Ben gave me half a chance to answer her. I didn't take it.

'Work,' he said. 'I've got to get Max to sign off on something.' He looked at me. It was the second half of my chance to speak.

Inside the lecture theatre, students clustered around Max, asking him questions. My head was overcrowded with things I wanted to say.

'So I should push in,' Ben said. 'It's got to be in Korea pretty much right away. Josh? Did you want to see him or . . .'

'Could you tell him I'll catch him in the morning?'

'Sure. No problem.' He lifted his hand, and I thought he was about to pat me on the shoulder. He turned it into a wave to Jett and started to move towards the door, where the student traffic was now thinning out.

'So what are you?' she said. 'The minder?'

'That's closer than you might think. I've got a media role with the firm for a few weeks.' I was unstuck. She had unstuck me, partially at least. 'The rest of the time I blog for a newspaper and I write magazine articles. Freelance. About whatever bizarre things I come across.'

'You should hear about some of the stuff that goes on at work.'

'Actually, could I?' It was an opening, a chance for the conversation not to end.

'Probably not. Maybe some things. But I'd have to give it to you W Mark Felt-style.' She misread the look I must have had on my face. 'Sorry, that's a bit obscure.'

'No.' It was the most important movie of my life. I had fallen in love with people based on less. I wanted to impress her with a quote, something from Woodward to Deep Throat, but the only one I could think of mentioned chicken shit. 'So do I call you Deep, or would you prefer Ms Throat?' I felt myself crumpling inside like an empty piñata.

'Ha. Not so obscure then,' she said. She rearranged her folder, tucking it under one arm. 'I was just going to get a coffee before putting in some library time.'

Ms Throat . . . Ms Throat . . . The worst line of the millennium was playing over and over in my head.

'Let me buy you the coffee,' I said, in case I still had any chance. 'You can tell me a thing or two about work. It's fine if you give it to me . . .' I couldn't say Deep Throat-style. 'Anonymously.'

'That's it,' she said. 'Where was that word when I needed it?'

She led me out the other side of the building and along the sandstone colonnade at the edge of the Great Court to the nearest source of real coffee.

'You should call me Hayley,' she said. 'That's the name I go by in the world outside the Spur. Hayley Throat.'

'Could we just . . .' No, we couldn't pretend I hadn't said it. She was amusing herself too much for that.

There was a stand selling coffee in takeaway cups, and we sat near it, at a round table closest to the grass and the dark courtyard. All but one of the other tables were empty. People were buying their coffees and moving on.

I mentioned that her hair looked different and she said, 'That'd be Desley you'd be thinking of. Desley's my hair extension.'

'Not a complete wig, though.' I was thinking of Elektra, though her hair might have been real. 'You could have worn a platinum-blonde wig.'

'I could, I guess. I could have bought some big tits too. Would that be better? If I had a platinum-blonde wig and big tits?'

'I wouldn't change a thing,' I said and went bright flaming red. I could feel it. I went to drink my coffee, and slurped it.

'Good. Well, Desley's enough then. It's about . . . shifting from this world to that world. Creating a character. And my character is the antidote to platinum-blonde wigs and big tits. She clips on. Plus, long hair and that kind of act . . . it's a thing. There's more that you can do with it, but a lot of guys seem to look for it too. I actually cut my hair myself. My real hair. I read this thing in a magazine that said if you bunch it forward . . .' She tossed her hair in front of her face and then gathered it with one hand, using the other to demonstrate scissor-work. 'And cut into it kind of randomly, you can get this rock-chick look.' She let it fall, and shook it back into the look. She held her hands up, as if displaying it.

'I think I've got that piece at home,' I said, wanting not to go red again. 'Sitting in my research file of things people would never do. There's always a blog in that.'

'You arsehole.' She laughed, leaned forward and punched me in the arm.

'The hair's great, though. Really.'

'Way too late, my friend. Way too late. And don't try passing yourself off as normal. Things people would never do, number one: keep some crazy-arse file of things people would never do.'

'It's my job. Bizarre magazine advice is a gift for blogs.' The more I thought about it, the more I thought I actually did have the hair article. 'Though obviously the hair article wouldn't make the cut, since it's really sensible. Just don't tell me you've covered your kitchen walls with foreign newspapers and lacquered them for a bistro feel, or decoupaged hat boxes as gifts or covered your car in Astroturf.'

She gave it the appearance of serious consideration. 'Hey, I think I might be tempted by the wall thing. Is that a problem? Who doesn't want a bistro feel?' I wondered where she lived, what kind of life she had. 'Someone really covered their car in Astroturf?'

'Apparently. It was a green car – environmentally, I mean – with the ironic exception of the Astroturf. Which is green in colour but actually polypropylene, I think. It ran on bio fuel. They were proving a point. I think the point was that, if you covered your car in Astroturf, no one would pay attention to anything else. The bio fuel bit of the story got kind of lost.'

She straightened her watch so that it sat better on her wrist. She looked across the Great Court, at the dark lawn and the glowing row of columns around it.

'Did you know that close to forty percent of people in my line of work are doing it to pay their way through uni?' she said. 'It's not what you'd think.'

'I don't think I was thinking anything.'

'You said the Spur was less sleazy than you were expecting.'

'Yeah, but . . .' There was no denying it. 'Yeah, but I'd never had a law-student cowgirl walk up to me like that before. I probably said a lot of stupid things.'

She looked into her coffee cup, which was almost empty. 'Dammit. Study time. That'll teach me to go for espressos.' She drank the last of it, and scrunched the cup in her hand. 'And I haven't even told you any trade secrets yet. The only thing I've given up is Desley, and there can't be more than six words in her.'

'You should give me another chance then. I'm sure my expenses can stretch to another coffee some time. Or something else.' Nothing to lose, I told myself, nothing to lose.

'I think I might take you up on that,' she said. 'Why don't you give me your number?'

She put it into her phone, and then refused to give me hers.

'You'll have it when I call you. That's my best offer.' And then she stood and said, 'Well, thanks for the coffee,' and she was gone.

I watched her walk along the colonnade, caught by the light of each archway until she turned into Forgan Smith without a backward glance. I sat with my coffee for a minute or two but she didn't reappear.

'You want another one of those?' the guy at the coffee cart said. All the other tables were empty now, and I was his only potential customer.

I told him I had to be somewhere, and I left the Great Court imagining Hayley among the shelves of the law library, deleting my number. Or calling me at any second, telling me she couldn't possibly concentrate on study and had to see me now. My head was full of her, because that's what I did. I got crushes, I got big ideas, I got ten steps ahead of myself. I placed any small prospect in a vice-like grip, and I applied the crushing force that broke it. Francesca, Eloise, Emily in London and not just them.

Heart on my sleeve, my mother had said, and I didn't know what was wrong with having a heart and not keeping it hidden like some state secret.

I imagined introducing Hayley to my mother. My mother, who saw me with a patchwork job that she didn't understand, and no oven, currently being bailed out by her more successful son. Add dating a stripper to that list, and my fall would be seen as complete. Add being turned down by a stripper, brushed off by a stripper . . .

But she took my number. There was rapport.

She refused to give me hers. There was nothing.

Athletes were training as I walked along the top of the grassy slope that led down to the running track. They were practising their starts under the lights, launching themselves forward and then turning the engines off and coasting to a stop. They were too far away for me to hear a thing. They were focused, purposeful. I couldn't tell how good they were. A coach was talking to one of them, explaining something, while the athlete stood with his hands on his hips and looked down at the ground.

I felt unusually solitary watching them, down there in the light, even though they were mostly in their own heads as well.

I had just passed the rowing sheds and left the campus when a text message came through to my phone. It was the loudest noise in the street. It was from Ben, and it said, 'yr business with max was clrly important . . . b'.

I caught the next CityCat that was going downstream and I sat behind some college girls who were showing each other pictures on their phones. They were heading into town and talking about boys.

The ride lasted about a minute and I wasn't yet ready to be boxed in for the night, so I took a long way home and walked around West End. I followed the river, and eventually turned in near Vulture Street. There was a new signal box at the traffic lights near the school. It had been painted to resemble a CBD skyline and already graffitied with 'greed sux'. I had written something for a magazine on the city's signal-box art, so I knew that most of the artists were neither rich nor greedy, and they spent seventy dollars a time on materials.

On one of the power poles outside the cafés, there was a soup recipe. Someone had taped it there, and written 'So good I had to share it with you all' at the top. The soup was mostly sweet potato, with smoked almonds and basil and garlic to flavour it. I borrowed a pen and paper from Café Checocho and I copied it out.

As I walked down the side street towards my flat with the recipe folded in my pocket, I imagined making it for Hayley. But coffee was just coffee, and it was done, and it was better to believe that she would never call.

I re-heated a serve of Gergovian meatballs and I told myself not to crack a fortune cookie, because I would read far too much into it, either way.

★ ★ ★

THE NEXT MORNING, after emailing Max Visser to book a meeting in his diary, I played the DVD footage of the siege for the first time. It was a compilation of news pieces from that week. I took the days in order, matching the print coverage with TV and watching the story evolve.

The siege had occurred in late September almost nineteen months before. Summer came early that year and a hot dry spring brought the jacarandas madly into bloom by the time Ben was led from the building, his head down, his shirt soaked with blood. The cameras followed him, as he had told me, all the way to the ambulance. It looked like a re-creation, with the trees out of season, as if they had got no good pictures at the time and staged it again a month later to do better.

It was something Frank said two days afterwards at a press conference that caught my attention. 'Ben showed conspicuous courage in circumstances of great personal danger.' He was sitting at a table with a bandage around his head and two police behind him. He was speaking without notes. He had a work shirt on, but no tie, and his blue eyes looked straight ahead into the cameras.

I had seen that line before, or something very like it.

I searched through Frank's written statements and newspaper articles, and the dry and circumspect reports of the police, and finally found it in the Australian Bravery Decorations pamphlet. The Star of Courage was 'awarded only for acts of conspicuous courage in circumstances of great peril'. It wasn't identical, but it was close.

So Ben's bravery was either an almost exact natural fit for the Star of Courage or, by day two post-siege, Frank was tailor-making quotes with the medal in mind.

I went back a day, to Frank's hospital bed interview.

'We're very grateful for Ben's . . . intervention,' he said. He was sitting up in bed in new pyjamas. 'I'm very grateful. I could have been killed in there. That was the gunman's intention. And it's unlikely I would have been the only victim.'

Even then there was a formality to the way he spoke, a composure, but it was nothing like the fit with the

Star of Courage wording. I went forward again to the next day.

He talked about the siege itself, recalling the details, and then he stopped himself and seemed to refocus, and that was when he said, 'There's one point I want to make clear. Ben showed conspicuous courage in circumstances of great personal danger. I could have understood if he had escaped alone and left me there, but he chose not to. He chose to remain.'

It wasn't all out of the manual. I could find nothing in the pamphlet to match Frank's observation about Ben's choice to remain. Perhaps Frank, to use Hayley's word, had simply defaulted to formality. When he had most wanted to make his point, he had talked like the lawyer he was.

I looked for Ben's version of the story, but he went unquoted on the first two days. One newspaper article said he had been sedated. He surfaced on day three, but didn't have much to say. He called it a blur, and said he couldn't put it all together yet. But Frank had done all the telling by then already. Perhaps the story was what it was, Ben was a shell-shocked hero and Frank was focusing on gratitude. Maybe it was as simple as it looked, and Ben had been precisely as brave as a person needed to be to win a Star of Courage.

★ ★ ★

THAT AFTERNOON, WITH five minutes to kill before my meeting with Max Visser, I put 'Randall Hood Beckett' into Google, just to see what would come of it. There were hundreds of hits – newspaper reports about the siege, all of which I recognised from their dates and key words, and among them other sites that suggested a firm simply going about its business. There were several hits from their own website, a Lawyers Weekly web announcement about a new commercial property partner, an appeal to the Planning and Environment Court, and appearances in Chinese and Japanese business directories. There seemed to be nothing on the siege that I didn't already have.

The first few hits on the second page looked as unremarkable as the first, but one stood out halfway down. It was a newspaper report from months before the siege, and I brought the article up on screen. It was headed, 'Law partner "foul-mouthed and aggressive"' and the article read, 'Complaints have been made to the Law Society from three former administrative staff at the Brisbane firm of solicitors Randall Hood Beckett. The most serious alleges that managing partner, Frank Ainsworth, called one staff member a "stupid slut" when she questioned his billing practices. The complaints called Mister Ainsworth intimidating and aggressive, and claimed he commonly used language that was offensive and demeaning.'

I wasn't shocked, though I hadn't expected to see it put so plainly. I wondered where the story had gone from there, where it had come from. But it was time to find Max.

Selina walked out of his office as I stepped into the corridor. She saw me ahead of her and said, 'He's all yours, hon.' She was holding her security pass by its lanyard and swinging it. 'Oh, and I got your email about

Rob Mueller's legal file. I put the request in, but I don't think I've seen it. I'm just going to chase it up for you.' She caught the pass in her other hand.

'Thanks.'

I wanted to ask her about Frank, about the Courier-Mail story and the allegations, but Max was standing in his doorway.

'Josh. Come in,' he said. 'Come in.'

He waited in the doorway for me, and then pointed me towards a seat.

'Oh my God, I still can't believe Wednesday night,' he said, as he went back around to the other side of the desk. He made it sound as if it had happened about a minute before. 'Vince said they were there for hours more. The things you do to nail down a deal . . . I had to go home and tell my wife everything. She's not a big fan of strip clubs. She quite likes the karaoke, since she says it gets the singing out of my system. Oh my God. "Watch a lady move her bowel." I really think the toilet should be private.' He shook his head, as if it would shake the bad image away. He was moving his mouse around and clicking. He found my email on the screen. 'Okay, what's first? It's background as well as the incident, right?'

I waited while he read through it again. I could picture Frank with the bandage, his composed recounting of events.

'I know this is jumping to the end,' I said, 'but what about afterwards? Were you part of the nominating process? Part of writing the nomination?'

'Oh that was all Frank,' he said. 'I wasn't even aware of the system. We were all right behind him, of course.'

'So, all Frank, despite his head injury?'

'Yeah. He can be pretty determined.'

'Did he talk about which award he was putting Ben up for?'

'Yeah, a bravery award. I don't think you get to specify which one. You just put down the details and I guess they rate it against some criteria. I don't know. Frank came in the day after the siege, after he got out of hospital. He wasn't supposed to. He'd downloaded the forms.'

'How's Frank viewed within the firm? I'm just thinking of how he comes across, his manner. You said he's pretty determined. I'm wondering how he'll come up on TV. Obviously he's crucial for some parts of the story, but . . .' I needed the seam not to show. I hoped it looked like thoroughness, and not like trespass onto another subject.

'How's Frank viewed?' He stopped, to give it some thought. 'You could probably say he's seen as a tough negotiator. No nonsense. Old school. Some people go well with that. Not everyone. But no one's style is right for everyone. He'll be good on TV. He's got good coverage of the details. Better than Ben even. Sometimes it seems more like Ben's the one who got the whack on the head.'

'So, how long have you been at the firm, and what made you come here?' I hoped it sounded like nothing, background research.

'I've been here about two years. A couple of the partners left not long before that. One of them had been doing quite a bit of business involving China. The firm wanted to keep that going so they started looking everywhere for someone who was the right fit with the work and who could speak Chinese. I got a call from a recruitment firm. They made me a good offer. I was in Sydney at the time.'

'So what made the partners leave?'

'You're very thorough.' He looked uncertain about where I'd taken it. 'People leave. Do you really think Australian Story's going to want this much detail?' He said it affably enough, but then he waited to see if I'd let the topic slide. It made me more determined not to. 'Frank's style doesn't suit everyone,' he said eventually. 'I think that might have been part of it. Some people also want to go out on their own. Firms can be pretty fluid arrangements. But I'm South African. Frank wouldn't rate as a hard arse in South Africa. He tells it like it is. That's not a problem for me.'

'Okay, tell me about Ben.'

He looked happier about the prospect of that. 'I've got some notes,' he said, looking back at his screen and clicking to open another document. 'I put them together when I got your email earlier. I've got a story or two about Ben ready to go.'

★ ★ ★

WHEN I WAS BACK in my office, I googled the journalist who had written the article about the complaints. He had moved from the Courier-Mail to Sydney, where he was a senior feature writer for the Daily Telegraph. There was no sign of him following up the story.

I went to the Law Society website and searched using

Frank's name, but there were only mundane details. There was no mention of the complaint. I googled '"Randall Hood Beckett"+foul-mouthed'. A website called firmspy.com took the story a step forward: 'Word is that, over at Randalls, Foul-Mouthed Frankie Ainsworth has been talking tough but reaching for his wallet to hand out the FOM (that'd be go-away money, for you non-Randalls types).'

The original Courier-Mail article had more detail, so I read it again to see if I had missed anything. I knew Frank could be abrasive and I could see him being intimidating, but the world was full of people who could match him and it rarely provoked someone to run amok with a gun.

Rob Mueller was psychotic. The reports had said that. Perhaps there didn't need to be another reason.

I still had the article open on screen – 'Law partner "foul-mouthed and aggressive"' there in bold text – when Frank appeared at my door.

'Didn't mean to surprise you, Josh,' he said. Something must have shown on my face when I'd looked up. 'How's it going?'

I couldn't touch my computer, couldn't minimise the article. It glowed brightly in front of me.

'Good. It's going well.' His picture was on screen, an out-of-date head shot with Frank scowling as he looked into the sun. He was a step away from being able to see it. 'I've just got to get some information to Australian Story –' I took a look at my watch – 'in the next couple of minutes, and then I think everything's sorted out. I'll email you the final interview schedule as soon as it's done.'

'Good,' he said. He looked at his watch too. It was a nothing time, not two minutes to any normal deadline. 'That's good. Well, I should leave you to it then. Oh, and . . .' He changed his tone to sound as if we were colleagues, and close. 'There's no need for you to be concerned about the Mueller file. Some of it's confidential, as you'd probably expect, and I'm sure you've got enough to do already.' It was nonchalance that he was attempting, but there was nothing nonchalant about it.

'Just being thorough,' I said.

'Yeah, good. Good for you. There's nothing useful in it, though.'

'No problem.' Still the story glowed on the screen – 'foul-mouthed', 'aggressive', 'stupid slut'. 'I'd better get back to Australian Story.'

'Good. Next Thursday, then,' he said, as if we had made a plan about golf, and he was looking forward to it.

With that, he was gone. I shut the article down. I wondered what Thursday was, and then I remembered I had booked some time in his diary to talk through his Australian Story interview, which would happen on the day of the lunch.

I stood up and checked the corridor. He had almost reached his office.

I went back to my computer and I tracked down the number of the journalist at the Telegraph in Sydney. I called him and pitched Ben's story, in the same way as I had every other time, and I kept the firm's name out of it, and Frank's.

'Yeah, look,' he said, taking it exactly at face value,

'we'd probably be more interested if he was New South Wales. Or is this like a big deal? Do they hardly ever give these out?'

'It's the second-highest level,' I told him. 'They don't give out many of them.'

'Yeah . . .' He was giving it more consideration than I'd expected. 'It doesn't exactly sound like a VC, does it? I think you'd be better off trying closer to home.'

'Yeah, they mainly operate here,' I said. 'The firm. Randall Hood Beckett.'

I waited. There was a noise as something bumped against his phone.

'Randall Hood Beckett,' he said. 'I used to be up in Brisbane, you know. Did a story on them, on one of the partners. Nasty piece of work. Can't remember his name. He called me up and abused me afterwards. He sounded like the "I know where you live" type. There was some issue with the staff.'

'Really? What happened with that? I've only been here this week so I'm not sure who I should avoid yet.' Someone walked past my window, an admin person I didn't know. 'I just got back from a few years in London. And needless to say, that story's not one of the big topics around the office.'

'Ainsworth,' he said. 'Or Hainsworth. Frank. That was it. Something like that. Ainscough. It seemed to go quiet. I think some money changed hands. That's usually what happens. They probably withdrew the complaint for some nice quiet cash. But if you can find out more, do let me know.' He laughed. 'In the meantime, good luck with your hero. I'd better get back to the villains of New South Wales.'

I NEEDED TO BE at least two blogs ahead before the medal presentation and the trip to the coast, and I had one more to bank over the weekend. Late on Friday night, it was ranking third in my priorities behind staring at my phone in the hope that Hayley would call and scrutinising every appearance of Frank's on the siege DVDs.

I had a cookie fortune somewhere telling me that a feather in the hand was better than a bird in the air. Hayley would or wouldn't call. Ben might truly be a hero and Frank just an irascible man, caught on the spike of someone's psychosis, then trying to do good by seeing courage recognised. Whatever the truth, whatever would happen, I needed five hundred words on the business of toothbrushes, a half-smart idea I had once had that was now under pressure to amount to something.

With an output of three blogs a week, not every one could be driven by a great idea or by genuine enthusiasm. The job was about crafting the veneer of enthusiasm, but a wholly convincing veneer on top of a big, broad, solid plank of toil, thumping one clause in after another, building it like a gang building a rail track, all the way from word one to word five hundred.

Toothbrushes, I told myself. Go. Toothbrushes and marketing. Toothbrushes and the research that said chewing on a stick was slightly better, despite the swivel-headed chubby-grip tongue-scraping gadgetry now on offer.

I was halfway there, 273 words, and I hadn't even mentioned toothpaste – multi-function plaque-busting, enamel-whitening, anti-bacterial toothpaste, or the perennial riddle of how they got the stripes into stripy toothpaste. Okay, perhaps it wasn't such a perennial. It might have fascinated generations of eight-year-olds – or just me – but did stripy toothpaste still exist? Who knew? I wasn't going to let my blogging be contaminated by any real-world research. If I had to get out of my seat, I was trying too hard for the money. That was now the benchmark.

She hadn't called. It was late and Hayley would be in the Silver Spur, stripping again for a crowd who had no appreciation of how smart she was, or her true charm. And Frank was a prick and I didn't trust him, and Ben was holding something back too.

Two hundred and seventy-three words, and the toothbrushes had gone. Was there five hundred words in stupid crushes? No, there were novels in that, for too many of us.

* * *

BEN HAD AGREED TO come over to my side of town for breakfast on Saturday morning. He had ducked and he had weaved and he had gone away for work, and the time had come to talk properly. The investiture was two days away and so far I had prepared him only to play the role of a deer in headlights.

'Have you checked out the table art?' he said, as we sat in Café Checocho with our second coffees in front of us.

I had walked him through the interview itinerary once we had put our orders in, but he had called a halt when our food arrived. The café was styled with a mixture of found furniture and a few matching pieces, and our particular tabletop had been ruthlessly decoupaged with pictures of chessboards and Aztecs and lutes.

'It's all chess, I think,' he said, moving his plate to reveal more of the surface. 'Chess games and pieces throughout the centuries.' He looked around the café, at the people dressed like poets who were working on wireless laptops and at the shelves behind me selling second-hand books. I knew from previous visits that they were grouped into categories, and the categories included 'faeries', 'occult/magical/shamanism' and 'esoteric'. 'So this is your life every day?'

'Grand, isn't it?' I didn't want the place deconstructed, and I could see that coming. 'No, it's not my life every day.'

'This and daytime TV.'

'Since when did this get to be about my life?' He had me with the TV. 'I do happen to have breakfast here from time to time once the rush has gone, and maybe the TV does get turned on occasionally at odd hours. I'm sure you're more than adequately compensated for being at the office instead, with your lawyer's eye view of the eastern suburbs. And I do write, you know. That takes up some time.' Wikipedia had given up the secret of stripy toothpaste in a second, but that had never been the point and the blog was still just as stuck. 'I've cleared for us to do the walk-through tomorrow morning. So could you have a think today about what we should take a look at?' He didn't give me any kind of answer. 'I'll

126

need you to take me through it step-by-step, from when he arrived on the floor, to the others going down the fire exit . . . all the way to the bathroom. And I'll need you to think through what was on your mind and how you felt at each stage of it.'

'Sure.'

'I want us to get it all clear now. It's a chance for us to work out how we tell it. How you'll tell it on Friday.' He was nodding. 'It's the one time we'll have a TV crew there. And they'll want to walk through it too, and that'll be it. Okay? TV's all about the pictures, and tomorrow is when we get to work out what pictures we give them. So how about nine o'clock?'

'Nine? AM? How about ten? Some of us have a life and might do something on a Saturday night.' He had shown no signs of a life. His entire apartment looked as if it had just been unwrapped from plastic. 'Of course, maybe you've got a life now . . .' He made his hands into two imaginary six-shooters and fired them at me, then straightened the stetson that went with them.

'You would make one ugly cowgirl stripper,' I told him. 'Or maybe you're just androgynous enough to pull it off. I really hope you're going to give some straight answers in these interviews.'

'Of course. What other kind is there? But in the meantime . . .' He pulled out the six-shooters again and put a pantomime-style quizzical look on his face. 'Got a life now?'

'I can't say that I exactly have a life, but we did have coffee. And she did take my number afterwards.' And didn't call.

'And you took hers as well, presumably.'

'That's not how she played it.'

He laughed. I would probably have done the same. 'She's smarter than you, then?'

'She probably is. So, how about the interview messages? Radio interviews. Can you give me a sub-thirty-second version of the crucial moment in the siege?'

Between us on the table was a bamboo plant growing out of a cup, and he reached for it with both hands. I thought it was about to become another random talking point when he said, 'Okay. It's still a blur. Is it all right to say that?' He rotated the cup ninety degrees and looked at the bamboo from the new angle.

'Completely. As long as it's only part of the answer. It's four words. We need another fifty. And you might need to make eye contact. Even on radio. Because that's what normal people do. When did you decide to make the move?'

'Okay.' He gave me a look that was close to a glare. 'It's still a blur, but there was this moment when Frank was on the ground. And I just knew . . . Rob Mueller was focused on him, not on me, and that was my chance.' Ben was still leaning forward, which made his look more intense.

'Okay, not crazy-man eye contact, but thanks for trying it out.' I was going to keep pushing him and he needed to know it. 'Had you met him before? Rob Mueller? You mention his name as if you knew him. Usually people say "the gunman", or something like that.'

One of the staff discreetly set our bill on the table, folded on a saucer.

'I didn't know him. It's a matter of public record. Do I have to forget his name now?' He let go of the bamboo plant and sat back in his seat. 'This is hard, okay? It happened quickly. I can't see it all, sitting here. It doesn't work, sitting here.' He was closing it down again, making the first move towards the end of the conversation. He picked the bill up and started reading it.

'You can tell me tomorrow, when we do the walk-through. But you have to tell me then. I'm going to make you tell me then. Once you tell me, I will make you ready. We'll put it together step-by-step. So, I want you to think about it today, and make notes. Notes will help you turn this into something that's easier to tell. How did it feel, when all the others got to leave and you realised you didn't? How did it feel to work out your life was genuinely in danger? How did the gunman treat you? You need to think about those things, and about the moment when you went for him.'

'Yeah,' he said.

It was over for now. He took his credit card from his wallet. I pulled my wallet out too, but he waved it away.

'Work meeting.' He put the bill and his credit card on the plate. 'You've got to get used to how this goes.' He unfolded the bill where it lay, and took another look at it. 'Anyway, it's nothing.'

My wallet was still in my hand. I could have insisted, but I didn't. 'We haven't done much of the work yet.'

'We did enough for me to get homework,' he said. 'Notes.'

It was the homework for people who couldn't or wouldn't tell their stories, the homework for introverts and liars and people wedded to their secrets.

The credit card slip came back and he signed it. A woman sat down at the next table with an instrument case. She took out a flute and started to clean it. Ben smirked, and didn't try to hide it.

I turned right with him when we walked out the door.

'I think I can find my way back there,' he said. 'Don't I just reverse the directions you gave me to get here?'

'Sure. But I like to walk.'

I let him lead the way, past the two chess games being played at outside tables and the stacked crates of bok choy and choy sum at the front of the Asian grocery store.

'You so want them to like you in that boho coffee place, don't you?' he said. 'And they don't even know you exist.'

'Do you think you'll be a partner soon?' We were going with my plan, not his.

He lined up a bottle top that was on the pavement and he kicked it, sending it skidding across the concrete and into the gutter. 'Depends. I probably think about that less than you'd expect. How long have all these places been doing breakfast?' He had noticed more tables out in front of cafés on the other side of the street, ahead of us. There were cyclists drinking coffee, families with strollers. 'Don't you West Enders ever eat at home?'

We turned off Hardgrave Road and Ben picked up the pace on the downhill slope. An old manual mower whirred in a garden further down the block, pushed by a white-haired man in a singlet and boxer shorts. The wooden house next to his was now high up on metal poles, about to become two storeys. It must have happened the day before, without me noticing.

'I've got a question,' I said, as if it was nothing. 'A Randall Hood Beckett question. What happened with the issue a while back about some ex-staff members and Frank? Abusive language. Things like that.'

Ben kept looking at the uneven ground ahead. 'That was before my time.'

'No, it wasn't. It wasn't that long ago.'

'Before my time in that area. Frank's area.' He pulled his CityCat ticket from his pocket, as if he needed to check it. 'You realise this doesn't get me anywhere near my flat? I have to take a bus as well, from the ferry stop.' I had told him to give up the cabs for once, and take to the water. He waited for me to say something. 'I was on thirty-seven before,' he said, once the silence had dragged on a while. 'The thirty-seventh floor. So I don't know what happened. There were some complaints. They didn't go any further . . . I don't see what that's got to do with Monday.'

'Risk management. I've got to know these things. I've got to get you ready for any questions.'

We crossed the street and, through the shelter at the ferry stop, I could see a few people clustered at the far end of the jetty. In the park nearby, a two-year-old girl ran after a ball, waving her arms in the air.

'Why didn't you tell me about it the other night? At Terroir?' I wasn't letting it go yet. 'I asked you about Frank and his abrasiveness. And consequences. That's a pretty big consequence.'

'It didn't occur to me that way. I didn't think of it. And it got sorted out. It was before my time in that area.'

'Okay.' People who are telling the truth have one explanation, and they go straight to it. They don't stick pieces together in front of you and hope for the best. 'It probably won't come up. The journo moved on long ago. No one'll make the link. They haven't so far.'

'Good.' He was annoyed with me, annoyed that I had trapped him here on this street in my neighbourhood without a cab in sight. 'I don't know who picked the colours of the carpets either, in case you're wondering. Or the middle names of any of Randall, Hood or Beckett.'

'What about billing practices? Do you know about any issues with billing practices?'

He stopped. We were metres from the ferry shelter.

He looked at me and said, very clearly, 'I keep a timesheet. We bill every six minutes, same as everyone else. That's what I know.'

'There was an allegation that Frank called someone a stupid slut when she questioned his billing practices.'

He turned away from me, as if he had a need to watch the two-year-old catch up with the ball, and then trip over it. She landed on it, and rolled off the side as the ball skidded away. She scrambled to her feet and gave chase again.

'Are you insane?' he said. 'What are you doing pursuing this? It's just some accusation. From way back whenever. It's nothing. Allegations. Gone.' The two-year-old's mother looked over our way. Ben tried to let the tension go. His shoulders fell. 'Let it stay gone.

This is stressful enough without you introducing new stuff.' He said it as if we were just two friends again, and I would understand. 'My plane was late back from Cairns and I had to take the dawn flight there. Yesterday was a long day. I've got to get some sleep.'

'They won't go there,' I told him. 'In the interviews. They probably won't. But it's okay anyway, if it was before your time in that area. If there's anything else you need to tell me . . .'

A CityCat appeared from upstream. Water surged around it as it slowed down to pull in to the jetty.

'That's my ferry,' he said.

'Tomorrow then. Ten o'clock. Bring your pass to let us in.'

He was already going. 'Yeah, yeah,' he said over his shoulder. He jogged a few steps until he was on the jetty, and sure he was going to make it.

★ ★ ★

I WENT BACK TO the siege file and my notes, since they were all I had.

'Yeah, that sounds like Frank,' Ben should have said about the slut remark. 'Is it any surprise we've got trouble keeping staff?'

Something like that. But he got all twisted up instead.

There was another shift of emphasis two days after the siege – one I hadn't picked up before. Early on the talk was all about Rob Mueller barricading the three of them in – Max Visser had even used the word 'trapped'

– but Frank, two days later, was talking differently. In the medal nomination form, he talked about Ben having 'opportunities to leave'. I went to the DVD and found the press conference at which Frank had talked about Ben's conspicuous courage.

He went on to say, 'He could have escaped, but he made the choice to stay. He could have got out. He could have got somewhere safe. He made a deliberate choice that increased the danger he was facing to a significant extent in order to save my life. True bravery is about that kind of choice.'

He looked like a dazed man stuck on a theme, with his pale blue eyes fixed in a stare and a bandage around his head. But when could Ben have escaped? When was his opportunity to leave? And why did it matter that he had had one, and not taken it?

I googled '"Star of Courage"+opportunity+leave+bravery', but got nothing. Then '"Star of Courage"+escape+choice+bravery', and got nothing again.

I tried '"Star of Courage"+deliberate+choice+bravery', and got a hit. One hit. It was a pdf with the unremarkable name of AR1997-98.pdf. It was the annual report of the office of the official secretary to the Governor-General for 1997–98.

A paragraph on page twenty-seven lit up with highlighted words: 'The Committee has recognised that *bravery* is subtly different from fortitude in a predicament in that it requires not only the presence of danger but an option of *choice* – the *choice* either to go from a safe place to a place of peril in order to help, or to remain at a hazardous post carrying out essential duties while others are moved, or after they had been moved, to a safer place.

Bravery is interpreted by the Committee as having been displayed through a *deliberate* act which would increase the danger to the person to a significant extent.'

Frank had almost quoted the last sentence directly. He hadn't just filled in the forms, he had made Ben's case for a bravery award uncontestable. Two days after the siege and with a head injury, he had found the words he needed to *guarantee* that Ben would receive a bravery award he had never once seemed to want.

★ ★ ★

BRETT LOOKED AT THE BOTTLE of wine I had brought as if it wouldn't – couldn't – measure up. He turned it around to read the back label and held it at arm's length, squinting down at the small print.

'Great,' he said, without any conviction. I was still twenty to him, and liable to drink whatever I came across.

'So your close vision's going, then?' It was the second thing I thought of to say, after editing a question that might have gone: Did I just give you wine or did I shit in your hand?

'Your turn'll come,' he said, giving up on the label. 'We've got a few other people round. Just a couple of the more longstanding clients. I thought it'd do no harm if you met a few of them, in case you're interested in any future work.'

'Thanks,' I said. 'That's great.' Again second choice, this time to something like: I'd prefer it if you bundled me up in a sack with an anvil as my copilot and dropped me in the river.

He led me down the hall through the house, past their collection of Indigenous dot paintings that he knew by price tag but not by artist. I knew that each one amounted to a good oven plus change.

'Francesca's just put new curtains up in the family room,' he said as we walked. 'They're beige. It goes well if people notice.'

'Thanks. Thanks for trying.' He meant well. He wanted Francesca to dislike me less. I didn't know how often people noticed beige.

'I haven't seen this one before.' He was giving the wine bottle more attention as we walked. 'It'll be good to give it a go.'

I could hear music ahead. It sounded like James Blunt. It was probably one of those 'music for mellow people's parties' compilations. Francesca was tossing a salad as we walked into the large open-plan living area at the end of the hall.

'Oh, Josh, hi,' she said, without properly looking up. 'I'd come over but I'm up to my elbows in it.'

She tossed the salad another couple of times. Even now I could picture her in slinky yet outdated lingerie.

Brett went to put the bottle in the fridge but she stopped him and said, 'What have you got there?' She read the front label. 'Classic dry white. Ha.' She started to laugh. Brett smirked, but tried not to. 'Sorry, it's an old joke,' she said. 'A friend of ours, Ewen, he's a winemaker and he told us once that any old shit that you don't know what to do with, you just put it all together and call it classic dry white. I'm sure this'll be . . . good, though.'

'Lucky I got change from five bucks then.' It had cost me twenty.

'You should come downstairs and meet the others,' Brett said. 'I've told them a bit about you.'

Francesca stood there waiting for me to move on, her salad servers still in her hands like praying-mantis arm extensions. Below us, through the windows, I could see fat men standing nursing beers, and the blue-grey smoke of meat drifting up from the barbecue, even though it wasn't yet dark.

'The curtains look great,' I said. They were beige, though they didn't look particularly new.

'This isn't the family room,' Francesca said, sounding resigned to my unsalvageable crapness. 'The family room's downstairs.' She looked at Brett, and shook her head.

'I think the meat'll get overdone if someone doesn't pick up the tongs soon.' Brett was peering out the window, looking for any change of topic going. 'We're eating early. There's quite a kids' contingent. Let's get down there, Josh. Frannie, I'd say you've timed that salad perfectly.'

He led me down the stairs and, as we walked outside onto the pavers, he said, 'Sorry, my fault. Frannie's yet to find a beige she doesn't love. We're pretty big on beige curtains.'

'What kills me is how hard you tried. You primed me about the curtains, you managed not to shit on my classic dry white, and . . .'

A door crashed open behind us, at the foot of the steps. Darius and Aphrodite cannoned into me shouting, 'Uncle Josh, Uncle Josh.' They each grabbed a thigh and I tried unsuccessfully to wade forward. I reached down and picked up Aphrodite, her blonde hair spraying in a mess, ribbons detaching, purple texta on her face. I turned to prise Darius from my leg and he shouted, 'No, monster, no. You're going down.'

I tumbled in slow motion, and they climbed onto me, wrestling and throwing tiny-fisted punches. Big growly monster noises came out of me before I realised that I was lying on my back being pummelled while looking up at the stubbie-holding men who were the clients I was supposed to impress.

'Not monster time,' I growled in my monster voice, as quietly as possible. 'Must have meat.'

Aphrodite shrieked. 'Not me. Don't eat me, monster.'

'Monster has presents.'

They jumped off me. 'Yes,' Darius said, and punched the air.

When I stood up, I happened to be facing the house. I could see the room they had come from. There were other kids standing in the doorway, and beige curtains bunched at the end of the windows on the far side. It was the family room, and the curtains looked identical to the ones upstairs.

I reached into my pockets, and pulled out two plastic eggs. Darius and Aphrodite tore through the labels and opened them, pulling out the goopy, squishy fluoro-green men inside.

'Yuk,' they said in unison, loving the vile clammy cool feel and mucoid texture.

'Now throw them at the wall,' I said.

They threw and the men hit with a splat, spreading out across the wall. One slowly released his arms and flopped over backwards, re-sticking further down. They ran over, pulled the men off, threw them again, threw them at the pavers, threw them into the pebbles and picked them up with pebbles stuck all over them.

Francesca came out with the bowl of salad as Aphrodite was pulling garden debris from her sticky man.

'Is that toxic?' she said, holding the salad out for Brett to take. 'Aphrodite still puts a lot in her mouth.'

'Yes, I particularly search out toxic gifts for your children,' I told her. 'And they sell poisons over the counter now in toy stores. It's part of dealing with an overpopulated planet.' I showed her an egg, and its label guaranteeing that the contents were child-friendly. 'So safe it's practically a food group.'

She gave me her look that said: I don't get you and I never have, and it's quite likely that the main poison here is you.

'Aphrodite, Darius, come and wash your hands before dinner,' she said instead.

She led them away, Aphrodite demanding that her green man sit with her and have his own plate.

I watched Francesca for longer than I should have as she left. I had that back view locked away in my head. It was one of the finer moments of her Bras 'n' Things catalogue. She was kneeling on the bed, with her back to the camera, in a white G-string and white lace camisole. She had spray-tanned flawless buttocks and was looking over her shoulder in a way that told me she was open-minded and ready for adventure. She was holding a long pink feather in one hand, with nothing to explain it. There was no doubt, though, that the picture was full of illicit promise.

Sure, it was a lie – it was advertising – but I had plenty of imagination and it didn't call for much. And a picture that promised 'One day I will be the sister-in-law who hates you' wasn't going to sell a lot of lingerie.

It wasn't the treacherous promise that disappointed me now, though, even if it had crushed me once. And it was nothing to do with lingerie. I felt let down by her lack of scope, of imagination, of spirit. Vinyl billboard skins had more of those, and were more fun. There was no adventure in her.

Brett introduced me to the group, and one of the other guests said, 'Ah, the famous Uncle Josh. We've been waiting for you to arrive. There were high hopes for toys and it looks like you delivered.'

He shook my hand. His name was Ken and he told me he was in hotels. He asked about London. He'd been briefed, and not just about toys. Brett was refereeing me hard for a career I didn't want. Ken introduced me to his wife, Christine, and told me their daughter Alaska was with the rest of the kids in the family room.

'Probably drawing something,' he said. 'She's a big draw-er.' Purple pen on beige curtains, I hoped.

He mentioned London again, and I outlined what I'd done there, in a way that made it sound like a sensible linear success story.

'I hear things are pretty awful there at the moment in a lot of sectors,' he said. 'I wasn't sure if that'd make them call on you more, or less.'

'What we found was that a lot of people were trying to manage things in house, whether they had the expertise or not.' Behind Ken, I could see Brett at the barbecue, loading sausages onto a plate, not listening. 'It seemed like a good time to come home.'

Francesca arrived with a second salad and some freshly-baked bread, and told us we should take a seat wherever we liked. I ended up with Darius on one side of me and Aphrodite on the other, each of them competing for my attention and trying to stick their green goopy men to my legs under the table.

'Give Uncle Josh a chance to eat his dinner,' Brett said about five times, just managing to keep the more outrageous behaviour in check.

Once we'd finished eating I gave him a hand to take the dishes to the kitchen.

I was most of the way through stacking the plates in the dishwasher when he asked me how things were going at Randall Hood Beckett. I could hear people laughing outside. The CD was playing Chris Isaak.

'What makes you ask?' I took two more plates from him and fitted them in the rack. 'What have you been hearing?'

'Nothing to justify that paranoia.' He smiled, and picked up a handful of knives. 'Nothing at all actually. I expect it's going well.'

'Sorry. It's going well.' I reached up for the knives. 'Up or down with the blades?'

'Down. Down with steak knives, I think. Fran has a system.' He was sorting through the rest of the cutlery on the bench.

'You only took Randall Hood Beckett on as a client recently, yeah?'

'Yeah, maybe a couple of months ago. Why?'

'There's a story I found when I googled them.' I stood up. I'd been crouching long enough. 'It's from about two years ago, a newspaper story. About Frank Ainsworth using abusive language, and something about billing practices.'

'What are you doing, Nancy Drew?' He had separated the forks and the long barbecue tools, and bunched the forks in his hand. 'What are you saying?'

'I don't know what I'm saying. I just wondered how long you go back with them. What you know from the time before you took them on as a client, what you've picked up since.'

'Not a lot. Evidently. I can't say I've rushed to have Frank round for a barbecue.' Down below, Ken the hotelier picked up and started piggybacking the small girl who must have been his daughter. 'Nice work, though. One of us should have dug that up for you before now. What happened with it, in the end?'

'It seemed to go away. I think he handed over some money. It was just that one story, really.'

'So, not something that'll be an issue for you next week?'

'I don't think so. I'll deal with it if I have to. But I've done this enough times to know when something's not right. When there's a big ugly piece missing from the story. And that's how this job feels.'

He moved the forks to his other hand. 'I hope I haven't landed you in something.'

'I'm sure it'll be fine. I've been landed in things before. Just let me know if you come across anything.'

'And you let me know if there's anything you need.' He was about to bend down to load the forks, but he stopped. 'The suit. You wanted to borrow a suit, didn't you? For Monday? Make sure you don't leave without it.'

★ ★ ★

SO I WENT HOME with a suit that would do the job if I pulled the belt in and bunched the pants around the back. I'd had two suits in London, but gave them away as part of coming home, part of escaping a life in which suits had been obligatory.

When I left after dinner, Aphrodite was asleep in a beanbag, her sticky green man in her hand, and Darius was busy giving a new friend a pounding at Wii Tennis. 'Uncle Josh, no, you have to play next,' he said vainly, his eyes not leaving the screen as he swiped another clean winner down the line.

I hung the suit in my wardrobe, picked up my box of fortune cookies and slumped in front of the TV.

About a minute later, or in fact three hours, my phone rang cacophonously on my chest somewhere near the start of a dream about Britney Spears giving me a massage while I was lying face-up on a skateboard. The TV was playing a TeleCafe ad, offering the conversation of lingerie-clad women to lonely singles, and I was surrounded by fortune-cookie crumbs. There was a fortune tucked into my phone. It read: 'A bird does not sing because it has an answer. It sings because it has a song.'

I flipped the phone open and made a noise that was supposed to sound like hello. I didn't recognise the number.

'Well, hello,' a female voice said. My first thought was Britney Spears. I still wasn't awake. 'I know it's late in the regular world, but I figured all you freelance journos are up doing Quaaludes or coked to the eyeballs.'

143

It was Hayley. I needed consciousness, wit, charm. Maybe a Quaalude, though I didn't think I'd ever seen one outside the works of Hunter S Thompson. I still had Britney in my head, Britney as a cowgirl now, with very supple hands. Long thumbs. Tom Robbins.

'Yep, that'd be me,' I managed to say, brain still trundling along a track to nowhere. Hayley had not deleted my number. She had called it, and apparently deliberately. 'Living the gonzo life. Hang on a second while I wipe some honey off these hookers.'

She laughed. I muted the TV, but kept it on so that I had some light. There were now two women in lingerie on screen, writhing on a chintzy bed together and yet inexplicably needing my call to make their evening whole.

'Well, I'm done for the week,' Hayley said. 'This is five pm Friday for me. Five pm Friday and mid-semester break from uni. So do you want to . . . have a drink or something? Once the hookers are sorted?'

I stood up, flushed with the thought of a gonzo life involving a fabulous stripper girlfriend – hold the hookers, hold the honey – with non-ridiculous breasts and a sharp mind. Fortune-cookie crumbs cascaded to the carpet.

'Definitely,' I said. 'Yes.' I pressed my shirt flat, and it looked okay.

'Good,' she said. 'Well, maybe if you just come to the Spur? I'll get changed and we can go somewhere . . . regular.'

My shirt was terrible. Fine for a barbecue at Brett's, where the standard male wardrobe was an XXL Hawaiian shirt corseted around an XXXXL frame, but wrong now. I went to my wardrobe and threw my shirts onto the bed, one after another. In movies only girls did that. I needed a cool shirt, and all these were the shirts of someone who had partially given up on life, who didn't rate his prospects.

I settled on the least bad option and I cleaned my teeth. I told myself it would be presumptuous and wrong and would damn my night to hell if I stopped on the way to buy a condom for my wallet.

I drove into the Valley wishing I had a slightly better car, but not showy, not a pimp car. This was the gonzo life, driving late at night to the Valley to meet my fabulous stripper not-yet girlfriend, but stone-cold sober and in my mother's hand-me-down metallic blue Toyota Echo. She always bought two-door cars so that she could put her handbag behind the driver's seat with ease.

I fluked a park only two blocks and about two minutes fast walk from the Silver Spur. Number forty-three was on the door again, in a black shirt and black pants and with his rings glinting like knuckledusters. He nodded to let me know that he'd seen me.

'Uh, hi,' I said, making it sound tentative and wrong. 'I'm here to see . . .' Hayley? Jett? Hayley? 'Jett.'

'A lot of fellas pay money for that,' he said, electing not to crack a smile. 'And your name would be . . .?'

'Josh Lang.'

There was a burst of static. 'That's the one,' the woman in the ticket booth said to him over the intercom.

'I'm onto it, Colleen,' he said, in his calm bass voice. 'You said the magic word, bro. That'd be Josh. Didn't know the Lang. If you want to duck back out onto the street and take a left and head down the lane, I'll give her a call and she'll meet you at the back door.'

'Thanks.'

'Wayne,' he said, and thrust out his substantial hand, which wrapped around mine and gave it a firm squeeze.

'Thanks, Wayne.'

The lane was dark and litter-strewn and had all the ambience of a crime scene but, the moment I got to the end, the back door of the club opened and Hayley was standing there.

'Hi,' she said. The light from inside threw her into silhouette, catching the shape of her off-duty rock-chick hair. 'Glad I could drag you away from your big night.'

'Hey, once my four-year-old niece fell asleep in the beanbag, the party was pretty much over. The last four or five hours have been relatively low-key.'

'Do you want to have a look around?' she said. Her hand was still on the doorhandle. 'Behind the scenes? See if there's anything bloggable?'

I couldn't, wouldn't, say no. She led me inside, into a corridor with old movie posters framed on the walls, Paint Your Wagon, State Fair. She had wiped away her Cleopatra stripper eyes and swapped the tourniquet-tight short shorts for something longer and probably comfortable. She was wearing a sleeveless top, and I developed a crush on her shoulders right away.

There was a door to a storeroom on the right and, beyond it, the corridor widened into a small lounge area, with a coffee machine and bar fridge, and sofas on either side of a coffee table. A stripper sat in classic naughty-nurse costume working studiously at a laptop. Next to her, on the arm of the sofa, an espresso cup was balanced on top of a Penguin Classics edition of Proust.

As we passed through, Hayley was saying, 'You'll have to meet the owner, Ross. He's a bit of a classic.'

Like Proust. Or perhaps not. I had a lifetime of TV to teach me what the classic strip-club owner was like, and I had never set out to meet one. I had a picture of him in my head: a hard man, a short fuse, a heavy bat. Every year or two he'd snap a leg with it when someone crossed him, and that way he kept his turf.

We came to an open door, and Hayley reached in and knocked on it.

Ross sat at his desk, looking like he had had far too many fist fights in the eighties, or perhaps the seventies. His hair was a steely grey and slicked back, his nose was mostly flattened and he had a scar where the skin had been split under one eye. He had a plate of biscuits in front of him, and a cup of tea.

'Oh, g'day, love,' he said, sounding like anyone's shabby old favourite uncle. 'You're off then, are you?'

He was broad and solid, with a fine pair of man boobs and a big-man's Mambo shirt. There was mess spread all across his desk. On the walls there were old black-and-white photos of Ross with boxers, his hair black and slicked back, nose flat even in those days.

'Yep, done for the night,' Hayley told him. 'Back late next week. I just thought I'd introduce you to a friend of mine. Josh. Josh, this is Ross.'

Ross came around the desk in a stiff-legged big-bellied way and he clenched my hand and shook it. It was a night for burly handshakes.

'Ross Sammut. Always good to meet a friend of our Jett's. She's an asset, she is.' Hayley told him I was a journalist and he said, 'Oh, yeah, we run a clean operation here. Nothing to hide.' He rubbed his nose with the back of his hand and sniffed. I was surprised any air could pass up there at all. 'It's a funny old game now. Not so many villains. Not since they disbanded Special Branch.' He gave a big throaty laugh. 'Well, what can I tell you? The licensing boys are through us all the time, but they're okay. They come in here with those fluoro jackets – cock softeners, I call 'em. Kills the mood for a while.' I wanted to reach past him, to his desk, for a pen and paper. I could see an article happening, and he was dictating it. 'You wouldn't believe it, but the steady money's in the merch. Well, maybe you would believe it. I mean, what bloke in this town hasn't scored one of our stubbie holders from the office Secret Santa?'

He went over to a nearby set of shelves and pulled a box open. He lifted out a black neoprene stubbie holder with their signature cartoon Annie Oakley on it and 'Silver Spur' scrawled beneath her in a neon font.

'Here you go,' he said, throwing it to me. 'On the house. We've got caps, calendars, the lot. The real trick . . . the real trick to this –' he said it as if he was about to deliver a closely held secret – 'is picking the right girls. You're nothing without the right girls. Too many of them who come in here are the wrong sort – messed up or drug-fucked or just plain soliciting. You can't be too careful. So, how do you know our Jett?'

It had been a monologue. I hadn't expected a question.

Hayley stepped in. 'He was here last week in an involuntary capacity. A work thing. With the Korean guy.'

(148)

'Not the turd guy?'

'Yeah, the turd guy. I was here with the turd guy.' I said it twice because I couldn't resist.

Ross laughed again. 'I bet you don't get to say that too often. Or maybe you do, and we can work with that too. Is it a Korean thing, do you know? Should we be expecting more interest in that kind of business?'

'That's a good question. Apparently he thought it was an Australian thing. Heard about it in Manila.'

'Before we get ahead of ourselves,' Hayley said, stepping in just as Ross's mind seemed set to turn to costings, 'I'm not sure that you'd get a lot of the girls to do it.'

'Not a problem, love. The wife's got me on a high-fibre diet.' He guffawed again at the ghastly prospect.

'I don't know how big the market is for that, Ross.'

'How big the market is for what, Hayles?' a voice said behind us. It came from a woman who looked late thirties, maybe forty. She was casually dressed and stood as if she had once been a dancer, all tone and muscle memory.

'Ross letting one go Korean-style on the coffee table.'

'Christ,' the woman said. 'Talk about a niche market. Now, if we could clean our acts up for a second, there's someone I'd like you to meet, Ross. This is Vixen.'

'Oh, good-oh,' Ross said, and took a step towards the door.

Vixen was in her early twenties and looked a particularly vampish kind of nervous. She had a long coat on and, beneath it, a complicated series of garments made of lace and leather. She was a stripper about to go to work for the first time. Ross appraised her like a proud father looking at a daughter dressed for her formal.

'Nice. Very nice. Very tasteful.' He said it without a trace of irony. 'You'll turn some heads, love.'

'Thanks, Ross,' she said, in a small self-conscious voice.

'Now, you're all set to go? Everything feels right?' This was Ross the boxing trainer at work, psyching her up for the crowd. 'You've got your ABN set up, and all that?' Ross was thorough. Had anyone − any of his numerous hangers-on − thought to ask Muhammad Ali about tax compliance as they fitted him with his mouth-guard and walked him in to the Rumble in the Jungle? 'Now, dance your tits off.'

'Righto,' Vixen said, sounding more perky. 'Here goes nothing.'

She turned, and sashayed out of the room stripper-style, with Ross saying, 'Beautiful, love, beautiful,' behind her.

There was a burst of mood music from inside the club as a door opened further down the corridor. It was like a cheap sound effect and gone in about two seconds when the door closed again, with Vixen on the business side of it.

'She'll do okay,' the woman I didn't know said. 'Once she gets through the nerves.'

Ross nodded. He'd seen it a thousand times before.

'Oh, sorry,' Hayley said. 'I don't think I've intro-duced you. Mel, this is my friend Josh. Josh, this is Melanie. She's our dance trainer − expert in stage and personal − wardrobe adviser extraordinaire . . .'

Melanie rolled her eyes. 'Solarium supervisor,

accommodation finder, ABN organiser, general dogs-body . . . Good to meet you.'

She shook my hand and, for less than a second, I thought I saw her give Hayley an is-this-your-new-boyfriend look. But it was gone too quickly and Hayley was moving on, ignoring it, if it had ever happened.

'I'm about ready for that drink,' she said to me. 'I'll see you two Thursday.'

'Be good,' Melanie said, making it sound as if it was all about the sub-text.

'I'll be great,' Hayley told her. Then she looked my way again, but at my chest, no eye contact. 'Let's wrap the tour up and get out of here.'

She led me into the corridor and pointed out the gym and the kitchen. I wasn't really listening. I was fantasising about a conversation between Hayley and Melanie the den mother, Hayley telling her about this great guy she'd met, and how she wanted him right now. Me. It was crush logic at work, and I was falling under its wheels again. Hayley was still pointing, wrapping up the tour.

'Beyond them you've got our change rooms,' she said. 'And on the right there are the ways in to different bits of the club. All pretty much invisible on the other side, since it's dark in there and they're hidden by curtains or the bar. And that's about it.' She turned her back to it all and shrugged, as if it hadn't had the climax that a good story should. 'Let's go.'

We left through the back door. It was darker out there than I remembered, and cooler. An umbrella tree hung over the bitumen courtyard and its battery of wheelie bins and crates of empty bottles.

'Okay,' Hayley said. 'How about Ric's?'

She led the way down the lane to Ann Street, and we crossed at the lights with the crowd. And perhaps I was on a date, for the first time in months. On a date and silenced by the thought of it, wanting too much for the next thing I said to be perfect.

There was a band playing inside Ric's, so Hayley grabbed an outside table and I pushed through to the bar. I held up two fingers and shouted, 'Hoegaarden,' and the bartender cupped his hand to his ear. I shouted again and he said something, twice, and then shrugged. He went to the fridge and came back with two bottles I didn't recognise. He pointed to the word 'Hoegaarden' and seemed to say it was all they had.

As I made my way out through the crowd, I had the idea that Hayley might be gone, that she'd changed her mind. I looked for her through the window and saw her, still sitting there, her arms resting on the steel arms of the chair, her hands in her lap.

There were bar stools lined up against the back wall, and I bumped my way past the knees of everyone on them to make it to the door. When I got to the table, Hayley took her beer from me and clinked it against the neck of mine in a toast.

'So, how was that?' she said. 'Back at the Spur. They're crazier than they know.'

'I think the word "character" may have been invented for guys like Ross. I had no idea there were people like that still around. And yet he's talking about ABNs and things. It was . . . very strange.'

'I know,' she said, emphatically, as if it was something she had needed to share for a while. 'And they don't have a clue. Out the front it's, like, sleazy to the point of cliché. Out the back it feels like a family business. They'll even line you up with an accountant and talk through your superannuation options. And you noticed that Ross wanted to get in the point about being okay with the Liquor Licensing crew? They're through us all the time, but Ross is pretty smart and they know he knows the rules at least as well as they do. I think there was a dicey moment in the early nineties when he nearly got done for body-slide massage, but it was all a question of interpretation.' She stopped, and took a mouthful of beer. 'I don't even know what it is – body-slide massage – I'm just aware of the case. He agreed to get the girls who did it to change technique slightly, so then it wasn't quite prostitution. I think that's why his wife has to be the licensee, though we never see her. He's still hilariously old school in some ways, though. He's got used to paying tax instead of paying bent cops, but he still keeps an old gun in his bottom drawer. I've seen it. An old handgun and a cardboard box with bullets in it.'

'Ross has a gun?'

'Police issue, from about 1980.' These were the stories she couldn't tell in the corridor of the Silver Spur. 'It's a hangover from back then.'

'And, what, he keeps it in case the accountant gives Vixen bad advice about her superannuation?'

She laughed, and put on a Ross voice and menaced me with a finger pistol. 'Didn't I tell you not to make her overweight in international equities? That's the last warning, Brian. Get ready to meet the fish.' She dropped her thumb, fired the gun. 'I don't know why he keeps it. He's a good guy, though. Flexible rosters, time off for exams. Plus the pay's not bad at all. Best job I've had in a while.' She turned her beer around, and took a close look at the label. 'So, this is Hoegaarden, but not the regular one?'

'Yeah. It was noisy in there.' The label featured Adam and Eve, falling to the temptation of beer. Above them, it read 'De Verboden Frucht'. 'I think this is the only Hoegaarden they've got. I was probably supposed to get it in a glass, but . . .'

'It's good. Never met a Belgian beer I didn't like. Hey, you wrote about Belgians, didn't you? Famous Belgians? I looked you up. I'm still not really sure how your job works.'

'That makes two of us. Or in fact several of us.'

She had gone looking for the blogs. She had looked me up.

She asked me how I came up with the ideas and I told her about the virtual life I tended to lead, search-engining my way to topics that might have some kind of spring to them, putting myself through tasks that might trigger stories. I told her about the photocopier repair guy, and my growing fascination with the evangelical promises of infomercials. There was a seed for a blog there, for certain. I talked about some of my best failed attempts to lead a blog-worthy life. For one entire week I had worn a red string on my wrist, feigning a kabbalah connection, and absolutely nothing happened. No one saw it, no one said a thing. But even in failure, there was room for speculation, and it all fitted into the 'Random' brief.

Would that week have been different if the string had been authentic, blessed by Rabbi Joseph Moor

Halevi from the Institute of Kabbalah and Mysticism in Jerusalem, thereby warding off the evil eye and denoting my commitment to the oneness of love for just $18.95 online? I put it out there and the replies came in, scorning me for my eternal cynicism and my blasphemy and my denigration of minority beliefs, and for wasting time, oxygen and red string.

'How weird,' she said, 'that you can hang out at home and talk to so many people. Make them laugh, shit them, whatever. Maybe you changed hundreds of people's minds about red string.'

'I expect so.' I was trying not to stare at her too much. Blogging, for once, felt like the game it was supposed to, and I felt liberated from the crud I waded through most weeks to make it happen. 'It's a lot of responsibility having all this power. I'm writing about toothbrushes at the moment.'

'So how do you end up doing this thing with the law firm?'

'Well, I'm as freelance as a lance can be,' I said, a line that kicked the legs out from under half-a-dozen winning blog stories. 'My job sort of makes itself up as it goes along. This month the extra bit's media wrangling for Ben – with whom I have a somewhat awkward past – over his act of heroism. If we manage to keep the part about him having sex with my girlfriend all those years ago out of it, we should be okay.'

Hayley's eyes opened wider, and her beer stopped on its way to her mouth. I had wanted to prove something by saying it, but I wasn't sure what.

'No, really, I'm not bitter.' I made a performance of it, and it drew the laugh I was hoping for. I wanted more of that. 'Actually, I'm not. Just this second I'm a lot less bitter than I have been for quite a while.'

'Good,' she said. 'That's good.' She drank her beer. 'It gets you nowhere.'

'We knew each other at uni. I actually took the job on without knowing it was him. My brother's company handles the firm's PR.'

I could imagine Ben, a few blocks away, working on his laptop in his pristine open-plan living area or lapping in his pool, his shadow dropping through the portholes to glide over his polished concrete floor. I couldn't picture him out somewhere, with people. 'Some of us have a life,' he had said.

'Ben seems to have done something genuinely heroic.' I wanted to give him his due. 'And pretty traumatising, so it's good that I can be there to get him through it. Get him through getting his medal on Monday, and the inevitable interviews. That's this month's one-off job. Mostly I seem to be getting a name for the blogs and quirky articles, and all that looks pretty trivial whenever I read Ben's medal nomination.'

The band had finished inside, and the audience was pushing to get out through the door and into the mall. Around us people drifted by, mostly in groups, high or tired or looking for a last drink. There were boys with chains hanging from their pants in loops, gentle ferals of the kind who sell dream catchers at markets, and two girls in Doc Martens who were carrying guitar cases and looking like they were heading home.

'What's not trivial, really, when you look at it?' Hayley said. 'There's only a handful of things that aren't. Any time my life feels fucked up or trivial, I just imagine it with a Morgan Freeman voiceover. Suddenly, dignity restored.' She cleared her throat, got ready to make the switch to her inner Morgan Freeman. 'Four days a week, come rain or shine, Hayley makes the long journey across the city in her second-hand Holden Barina to attend law lectures in the great sandstone buildings . . . Et cetera et cetera. He's the voice that made penguins feel good about themselves.'

I could imagine the penguins, huddled in snowdrifts in the Antarctic with their eggs balanced on their feet, the Morgan Freeman voice in their heads getting them through the long nights, the plummeting temperatures, saying to themselves 'this is noble after all'.

'I could really use that,' I told her. 'I could need it as soon as Monday. We're going to the Gold Coast after Ben gets his medal and finishes his hero interviews. It's for another article. I'm putting together a mini-golf tour. So, he puts his life on the line with a crazed gunman, I putt pink golf balls into the mouths of fibreglass dinosaurs.'

'Easy,' she said, and put on her Morgan Freeman voice again. 'Josh, armed with the wisdom earned during the long summer holidays of adolescence, drives the ball gracefully across Astroturf flattened by the feet of generations of putt-putters.' She paused, and tried not to look pleased with herself.

'Was that pathos?'

'I think it was.' She was back to her regular voice. 'Pull it up just short of ponderous and the smallest thing sounds like a triumph of the spirit. I get it, though, the mini-golf tour story. People fly from Japan to play golf at the Gold Coast, but who does the mini-golf tour? I think you're onto something.'

'Thank you. I've been waiting for someone to get it.'

'Hey,' she said, caught by a new idea. 'I know these people at the coast, they do doves for weddings. Japanese weddings. I used to do dove releases as a part-time job. You should do a story on that. I still do the occasional one midweek, when the owners have their weekend.'

'Why not?' It was an automatic response, just part of keeping the conversation going, but then I thought, really, why not? I saw us there, Hayley and me, on a manicured lawn at a Gold Coast reception venue, doves in our hands. I took a mouthful of beer and summed up all the nonchalance I could muster. 'You should come. Maybe you could line up a dove release. Ben and I could do it with you. We'll have suits, so we can look the part. But why not come even if you can't line it up? It's low season. I got this deal where I got the third night free and an upgrade to a three-bedroom place.' I was racing her to the end of the pitch, like a cold-caller pushing a holiday package, wanting to get every word out before the phone goes down. 'You should come.'

It was her turn to take a mouthful of beer. She picked up the plastic table number, as if it needed checking. The conversation had fallen into a hole. I had flung it into a hole, in a sack, with hammers.

'Maybe I will,' she said.

She turned the number ninety degrees and set it down again. Pizzas arrived at the table next to us, and we both stared at them as if they were really important.

'Hey, look at that,' she said. 'Pizzas. I didn't know they still served food this late.'

I needed to say something great about pizzas, late

service, but I was completely stuck. One beer, and I was pitching her three nights at the Gold Coast.

'You were in the UK, right?' she said, and I assumed we were forgetting my suggestion about the coast. 'Was that work, or backpacking or . . .'

'Mainly work.' Mainly work. Anything interesting? No. Learn anything about not rushing girls? No. 'Some backpacking, but I got sick of my clothes never drying.'

'Oh, I know what you mean. When I backpacked I used to wear my G-strings as scrunchies after I washed them just to get them dry.'

'I dare you to do it now.' I was out of my conversational death spiral and back in the game.

'It'd be wrong now. Scrunchies have been out for years. They weren't even in then.'

'It'd be wrong because it's putting underwear in your hair, so the fashion argument's pretty minor.'

'I can make it look quite convincing.' She wasn't backing down. 'The main issue is hiding the label.'

We talked about Europe and hostels and the antipodean ghettoes of London. Her worst accommodation was a barn that she shared with hens in the Czech Republic. Mine was a London sharehouse with skid-brown toilets everyone refused to clean and a South African who enforced his seniority by renting out any conceivable area under the roof at the rate of his choosing. For three weeks a New Zealander paid five pounds to live under our dining table at nights, rolling out his sleeping-bag after dinner and crawling into it when he had drunk or smoked himself stupid. We eventually overthrew Herschel when he made a move to rent out beds – all but his own – in shifts. He was last heard of running an escort agency from a houseboat at Camden Lock.

The pizza eaters ate and went, and an hour passed with us still talking. I was starting to wonder if I could do the crime-scene walk-through at Randall Hood Beckett on no sleep at all when Hayley checked the time on her phone and said she should be making a move.

I walked her to her car, which turned out to be in a side street in the opposite direction to mine. The mall noise didn't make it there. It was as if our last few lines to each other were to be delivered in some kind of close-up. It was a movie trick, cutting the background noise to heighten the intimacy, or the stakes.

Further down the street, a taxi pulled out from the kerb. I could just make out voices as two people moved through the shadows to their front door, then the sound of the door closing as they went inside.

'That's it. The red one,' Hayley said, pointing to a car ahead of us. We stopped next to it and she looked down into her bag, searching for her keys. 'So, the Gold Coast trip. What's the plan?' She looked up. 'Assuming you were serious.'

'I was serious. I was totally serious.' Light was falling on her face from a streetlight well behind me. 'We're going down Monday, for three nights. I can text you the address. It's at home. I don't have it with me now.'

'I can get there on Tuesday, some time during the day. I'm doing something on Monday. A family thing. So if Tuesday's okay . . .'

'Tuesday's perfect,' I said, because any day would have been. 'There's an interview Wednesday, but Tuesday's a day off. Nothing but putt putt. And whatever else we want to do. Not just putt putt.'

'Good.'

She looked at her keys, moved them from hand to hand. Then she set them on the roof of her car and stepped forward. She put her arms around my neck and kissed me on the mouth. I put my hands on her back, and then the bare skin of her shoulders and in her hair, and she pressed her body against me.

I could hear a car, coasting down the hill behind me. Its lights caught us, and we stepped apart to let it pass.

'Okay then,' Hayley said, as we watched its tail-lights move away from us, towards New Farm. 'I'll talk to the dove people.'

★ ★ ★

I COULD STILL TASTE her mouth all the way back to my car. I was replaying the conversation, the parts that said she was coming to the coast and that I would see her again in not much more than two days.

I got home and lay on the bed with my shoes still on, expecting my thoughts to keep racing, but the next thing I noticed it was light, and eight-thirty. Five hours had passed.

I found the address of the Gold Coast apartment, and I texted it to her. I made toast and willed my phone to beep with a reply, but it stayed quiet.

My notes about the siege were spread across the table, and I gathered them in a folder and read them through on the CityCat on the way into town. I waited ten minutes under one of the jacaranda trees before Ben arrived.

'Sorry,' he said. 'Lost track of time.'

He was wearing three-quarter pants and a snug-fitting Mighty Mouse T-shirt. He looked like a Japanese tourist. He swiped his card across the reader and the small side door unlocked with a clunk. Our footsteps echoed through the stone foyer as we walked to the lifts.

'Much less crazy here on weekends,' he said. 'I wish it was like this all the time.'

I wanted him to ask me about Hayley, to ask if I'd heard from her.

In the lift he used his card again, and pushed the button for the thirty-eighth floor.

'So, the grilling begins,' he said as the lift rose. He was looking down at my folder. 'I can't wait to see what you've got for me in there.'

'It's not about what I've got in here. It's just a few notes.' There was a pinging noise and the lift stopped, at thirty-seven. 'I wasn't there, so I can't keep it all in my head.'

The doors opened. A cleaner was standing there, with a trolley that would fill the lift. She had a blue uniform on, and the bright night cityscape painting covered most of the wall that was visible behind her.

'No problem,' she said. I thought her accent was South American. 'You go. I have thirty-nine next. I'll get the next elevator.'

'I like that painting,' I said to Ben once the doors were shut again. 'The one on the wall behind the reception desk.'

'Yeah?' He looked as if he couldn't recall it clearly,

even though it had been in front of him seconds before. 'They're all leased. They turn them over every couple of months. I think it's to stop us getting bored.'

The doors opened on thirty-eight, and we stepped out. The air was close and warm and lights started flickering on. Ben looked right and left down the corridor, as if someone might have just ducked from view.

'They're motion-activated,' he said. 'The lights. I think the lift doors opening activated them.' He put his security card into his pocket. 'So, grill. Let's get this over with.'

I asked him what had been going on before Rob Mueller arrived, and where he had been at the time. He walked us around to the open-plan area where Selina worked. A sunflower made out of yellow-and-red 'sign here' stickers had been left propped up against one of the computer screens.

'There was a table here,' he said, though there didn't seem to be room for a table of any size. 'We didn't have all these workstations then. There was an afternoon tea on. Someone was leaving to have a baby. This is where I was standing. Somewhere around here.'

He leaned on a divider and looked around at the desks, as if he might be about to show me the exact spot. A sheet of phone numbers, held to the divider by one pin, snagged on his shirt and fell off when he stood back. He picked it up, and set it down on a desk.

'So there were a lot of people around?' I was trying to imagine the scene.

'Yeah. But he got rid of them. Down the fire stairs. Two doors down the corridor.'

'But he didn't get rid of you?'

'No. He needed two of us to block the fire stairs door once the others were out. Frank and me. We used the table. Actually, we used a bookcase that isn't here any more. It was against that wall.' He pointed beyond the workstations. 'Then we used the table.' He nodded. 'Yeah. That was it. And Frank – God knows why – told him they'd break through it anyway.'

'How did Rob Mueller take that?'

'He said something like, "But I'll hear them and you'll be dead by then." Then he made us take a desk to the lifts. He'd already got one lift stuck on the floor by hitting the emergency stop and jamming the doors, and he got another one to come up and we jammed it with the desk. It seemed like we waited forever for the lift to come. We couldn't put the desk down. He wouldn't let us put it down. He pointed the gun at the doors. I don't know what would have happened if someone had been in there. No one was.'

'These are good details. This is exactly right. Exactly what you need to be able to say.' He wasn't listening. 'So, he was here for Frank, and you were just kept to move things?'

He sat on the edge of a desk and folded his arms. 'I guess.'

'You guess? But you'd know.'

'Would I? Frank's the managing partner. I suppose that made him a target.'

'I thought I'd been told Frank *was* the target. Rob Mueller was a client of his.' He had nothing to say to that. I opened my folder, and looked at my notes. 'So did you have any chance to get out?'

'We'd barricaded the fire door and disabled the lifts.' He said it as if I had just insulted his intelligence.

'So, no chance then?'

'I don't have wings.' He almost said more, but stopped himself. He smiled. 'That's a no. Tomorrow, or whenever this is official, I'll just say no.'

'That's good. Sarcasm, for some reason, seems unbecoming in a hero.' I took the copy of the nomination form out of the folder. 'Could you have got out before then? Before you barricaded the door?'

'I don't think so. No.'

Frank's report on the details of the incident was attached to the third page of the form. 'In Frank's nomination for your award, he says, "Ben could have left me there. He could have gone with the others."'

Ben stared at the form, though he couldn't see the part I had read. I wondered if he was going to take it from me. He stood up, and moved away from the desk. He looked towards the fire door, as if it might cue a memory.

'I don't really remember,' he said. 'Frank remembers better than I do.'

'Frank who got hit on the head?'

'Yeah.'

I waited for more, but there wasn't any. 'I'm just getting you ready, okay? Just getting you ready for the media. One of the criteria for bravery is that you have a choice. Which doesn't necessarily mean a choice to leave. It might be about other things.' I put the form back in the folder. 'So, everyone else has gone, you've blocked the fire door and jammed the lifts – where to next?'

'Frank's office.' He was already turning to go there.

'Have we covered everything we need to here?'

'Yes.' He didn't look around.

'You might want to think about why you don't remember some of the things Frank remembers.' I was behind him, still catching up. 'If it's because it was a traumatic experience, it's all right to say that. It's better to say that than not.' He made a hmmm noise. 'You won't look less heroic, or less worthy of a Star of Courage if your memory's patchy.'

We walked into the office, and Ben stopped just inside the door. Outside the window, the glass of the next building blazed brightly in the morning sun and the piece of sky beside it was a vivid blue.

'We were here for a while,' Ben said, this time without waiting for me to push him. 'This is where Frank got hit. With the butt of the gun. I think he fell . . .' He took a few steps into the room and indicated an area on the floor. 'About here. Round about here.'

He was staring down at the spot. There was sweat at his hairline, but I was starting to sweat too in the boxed-in air. I looked at the floor, as though it might have some sign of Frank's fall, but there was only the blue-and-green carpet, without a mark on it.

'And why was he hit? Do you know what provoked it?'

'No.' He thought about it. 'Not exactly. There was a lot of talk going on. But not involving me. I was . . .' He took several sideways steps, as if measuring a specific distance. 'I was here. Standing here. It was surreal. It was like I was watching it a lot of the time. Not part of it. It was like a TV with the sound down, or YouTube with a bad connection. Frank argued with him. I don't know what about, but I can see his face and I was thinking why the hell are you arguing with a guy who's got a gun?' He put his hand on the back of a nearby chair, perhaps to steady himself. 'And then he hit him. Rob Mueller hit him with the butt of the gun.'

'So, how did you feel when that happened? That's the kind of question they'll ask. You're doing really well, by the way.'

'Well, Frank was on the floor bleeding.' He was looking at the spot again, sizing it up from the position he had stood in at the time. 'There was a lot of blood. This carpet's totally new, the whole room. I thought he might be dead, for a second, but he was just unconscious. And I was shitting myself, obviously. Frank's head was split open where he'd been hit. There was nothing special about Rob Mueller physically, but he was wired and he'd hit him hard. He was really angry that Frank was knocked out, that he wasn't awake to . . .' He was back there, in the moment, putting it together. 'To suffer in the way he was supposed to. So he made me drag Frank by the feet to the bathroom. I had to pick him up and drag him. He was a dead weight. I had him by the ankles and I dragged. Blood ran into his eyes and his right ear and onto the floor.' He pointed to where the blood trail had gone, out the office door. 'Rob Mueller wanted to stick his head in the toilet to wake him up, so he would be awake when he killed him.'

For the first time, he had shocked me. It had been grotesque.

'So, the toilet then,' he said. 'That's next.'

It was close by, a few doors down the corridor on the way back to the lifts. Ben pushed the door open and reached for the light switch. The fluoro tubes in the ceiling flickered and blinked, and then came on fully. The room was tiled and a clinical grey-blue in colour. It smelt of cleaning fluid. There were basins near the door, a trough along one wall, and two cubicles. It didn't look like a place where anything significant might happen.

'So, this is it,' Ben said, looking around. 'This is where I had to . . . make my move.'

'So you tackled him, and that drove him against the far wall.' I was going by my notes.

'Yeah.'

'And Frank saw that?'

'No. He was still unconscious. He was . . .' He started to indicate an area of the floor, but then stopped. 'No, wait, maybe he was coming round then.'

'In his nomination, I think he even quotes what you said. What Rob Mueller said and what you said.'

'Well, then he was conscious. Obviously.' He shrugged the discrepancy off and walked over to the far wall. He stood close to it, facing it, and he put his hands up on the panel in front of him. 'I pushed him to here, and that's when the gun went off. It was between us.'

'Pressed between you and therefore pointing up.'

He took one hand from the wall and moved his arm into the position of the gun barrel. 'Pointing up. Yeah.'

He was wrong. I had led him to it, but he was wrong.

'Or actually pointing more like this.' I put my back to the wall panel next to him, and made an imaginary gun in front of me with one hand, moving it around until I had the angle about right. It needed to be about thirty degrees to the vertical. 'It's in the report, the inquest. There's a photo.'

I went to open the folder again, but he grabbed my hand.

'I actually don't need to see the photo,' he said. 'I don't know what you're doing.' He let my hand go.

'Just getting the details straight. We can't have you saying he shot the ceiling if he shot the wall. They'll get the photos too. Australian Story will.' I pulled the forensic report out, without the photo. 'Here, it says wall.' I went to show him, but he wouldn't look. '"Samples collected from the bathroom *wall* and floor revealed tissue consistent with cerebral cortex, bone and scalp. Blood and tissue dispersal, *wall* damage and the pattern of embedding of shotgun pellets in the *wall* . . ."' Et cetera. So, the wall, not the ceiling. It seems like there was no damage to the ceiling.'

'Your point being?'

'The gun wasn't pointing straight up. Which is worth remembering in itself, but here's another question. Somehow there was enough room between you for the gun not to be vertical. You'd tackled him, with the gun between you, and yet the gun was at an angle. A shotgun. They're quite long, aren't they? I'm just wondering how that all fits together. If you tackled him. The police asked you about all that, surely.'

He blinked, and stepped away. He took two steps towards the basins before turning back. He looked at the ceiling, and at the wall, again as if measuring something up. My phone beeped loudly with a text message, and the tones echoed around the hard surfaces of the room.

'Yeah, the wall,' he said. 'Not the ceiling. That's a new panel. And maybe the gun butt slipped out from between us. I don't know.'

'Okay.' I waited for more, but there wasn't any. 'Okay, let's go with that. And your clothes. They look pretty messed up in the news footage – the footage of you leaving the building – but there's no report on them.'

'What kind of report would there be? I threw them out.'

'Didn't the police want them for evidence?'

'No. I don't know. No one said they wanted them. Not to me. They got thrown out. That's the answer.' He was frowning. 'They had blood and urine all over them.'

'Urine?'

'Yes. Yes, fuck it, urine. That's what this was like. It's not about paragraphs of some report you can quote.' He started to pace up and down in the small space. 'It's about blood and piss and a guy's brains getting blown out.' He turned, and he pointed. His arm was shaking. 'Against that wall. We slipped. There was a struggle and we slipped. I fell on him as the gun went off. Or just after, or something. Neither of us stopped to make notes about the details. And his bladder emptied when I fell on him. And I didn't think I'd feel like wearing those clothes again. Does that surprise you?'

'I thought the police would have made sure they got your shirt for GSR.' I sounded like a bastard, I was certain of it, taking such a hard line and pushing him about the details in the face of his story of carnage.

'GSR?'

'Gunshot residue.'

'What the fuck . . .' He threw his arms up on 'fuck'. He turned away from me, and made it to the door in three or four steps. I wondered if he was going to leave, but he turned back to face me again. 'What are you doing?' I could smell his sweat now. It was in the air, with the caustic odour of the cleaning fluid. 'This isn't CSI. It was a hostage situation. There's no doubt about what happened. The police didn't need to ask how the gun fitted between us. They didn't need my shirt. The gun went off and it was fucking loud in here and there was smoke and all kinds of shit flying around. Blood and brain and bone and bits of wall panel. No one came in dabbing stuff for GSR, or doing any other smartarse thing.'

He pushed a cubicle door open and sat on the toilet, with the lid down. He put his elbows on his knees and his face in his hands, and he stayed quite still.

'Okay. Okay, I'm sorry.'

I had taken my doubts about his story and pistol-whipped him with them. I had wanted him to confess, though I didn't know to what. Something that meant that I was smarter than him. That there was a scam going, but it wasn't getting past me. It was old vengeance at work.

I opened my folder again. I had the relevant page of the report of the Governor-General's secretary in there. I had highlighted the wording that almost exactly matched Frank's nomination.

'No,' he said, down into his hands, before I could make him read it. 'No, *I'm* sorry.'

'What?'

He sat up. He looked calm, steady, as if his hands had been fitting a different face.

'I'm sorry about Eloise,' he said. 'You hate me because of Eloise. You think I'm some kind of liar because of what happened, and I'm sorry. I know you. You would have had such big ideas when she thought she was pregnant and you thought it was yours. I'm sorry for the way it turned out, for the whole thing.'

★ ★ ★

AND THAT WAS THE END of the interrogation. I didn't play my trump card.

Eloise had become pregnant. She sat me down, looking pale and in need of sleep, and she told me she was nauseated and had missed her period. And as I started to say that didn't necessarily mean just one thing, she told me about the positive pregnancy test. She said she didn't know what to do. I told her I would back her, whatever, but I said it because it was what you were supposed to say. I wanted to throw up. I wanted life to be less hard than it had become in that instant.

She cried into her hands and I felt like I'd hurt her in some way.

But the shock passed, or started to. And I worked out I wanted to be with her. That was what mattered. I had told her I had money – though I didn't, in fact, have much – and that I would drive her wherever she needed to go. I said we would get through it. She said, 'Do we tell people? How do we tell them? How do we not?'

But I started letting another possibility creep in, the

possibility of a different life. We would be together, this would be our child, the anguish would go. I let myself become amazed by the idea that we had made something that might one day be alive and breathing, and like us.

And then Eloise had to tell me no, not necessarily. That it would come half from her, but I was no sure thing. She told me she had been mad with me one night around the crucial time, or afraid of how quickly I was moving, and that she and Ben had had a stupid amount of wine to drink, and they had slept together.

She couldn't even remember it, but she had woken up in his bed and it was clear that it had happened.

A week after telling me that, she miscarried a blighted ovum. It was never a child in the making. She and Ben had planned not to tell me that they had slept together. They had lied to me for weeks already, and I had been clueless.

All of our relationships tore apart that same day. I didn't expect that I would ever trust Ben again, because he could betray me without a hint of it. I suspected – continued to suspect – that he had not been half as drunk as Eloise, but I couldn't face either of them over an argument about semantics.

I threw out everything she had given me, threw away shirts of mine that she had worn to bed.

I realised how little I had come to know Ben in the times we had spent together over close to two years. He had made himself a good listener, and a mirror, and that could seem like friendship sometimes. I knew almost nothing about him, and he knew everything about me. Including my feelings about Eloise, before he had opened the third bottle of wine and taken her to his bed.

I failed exams, but talked my way to conceded passes. I got through my degree, and I ran. To London, and the fantasy of a new start. I had lost a vision of a very different future, blighted just as I had seen it and wanted it. I still sometimes thought about how old that child would be, even though it could never have been a child at all.

So Randall Hood Beckett had picked the right media wrangler. I would not be soft on the talent in his vaguer moments. I would question everything.

I was home before I remembered the text message. I took my phone from my pocket and flipped it open.

It was from Hayley, and it read, 'Great. See you Tuesday morning. Save some putt putt for me.'

★ ★ ★

I CALLED BEN LATER that afternoon.

'We should make a fresh start,' I told him. 'As much as we can. We've got to focus to get through tomorrow.' I had made a mess of both of us. I had taken him to the scene of the crime, armed with pictures of shredded human tissue and something close to malice. 'We've got to be on the same team.' He said nothing. I could hear music in the background, though not a song I recognised. 'I believe that you're a hero.'

I said it because I owed him something. I said it because it was my job, and because even a liar might go through something horrible, something that might shear the clarity of his perspective and leave him a genuine hero in a jumbled story.

On Monday morning, we went through it again in my car, and I coached him. It was okay not to remember completely. It was okay to say that things had happened too quickly to grasp. There was only one moment he truly needed to own, and that was the moment when, faced with the impending death of Frank Ainsworth, he chose not to run or to cower or to stand numbly by, but instead he moved towards the loaded gun.

'All right,' he said, his eyes on the glove box. I thought he was picturing it then, Frank on the floor, Rob Mueller standing over him, all of them closing in on the moment. He reached forward and fiddled with the air conditioning, directing more of the air at his face. 'Let's talk about the mini-golf,' he said when he sat back in his seat. 'You've got the good life. You really have. Even though you don't appreciate it.'

So we talked about life, but not about any real details of either of our lives, until we drove up Fernberg Road, where cars were being parked, and families in suits and their best day dresses were making their way up the hill to Government House.

'Your parents – have they still got the news-agency?' Ben said, sounding as if he was already absent from his own question, but using it to stop me bringing up what was ahead. 'Have you told me that already? Are they still at the Sunshine Coast?' He was watching the people. A man with crutches was being helped out of a cab.

I talked about my parents for most of the walk from the car, and I knew he wasn't listening to any of it.

'Remember Paris Hilton's advice,' I told him at the Government House gates. He was looking up at the old stone building, and had stopped to let other guests pass us. 'Always act like you're wearing an invisible crown.'

'What?' A gust of wind blew down the hill and pushed his hair across his forehead. 'That's what you've got for me now? Paris Hilton?'

'You were expecting Henry the Fifth? I'm more widely read than that. Just remind yourself that you're entitled to be here. You got plunged into something ugly, and came out a hero. You have to let people acknowledge that today.'

An usher was standing nearby with a clipboard, and he marked our names off and said, 'Mister Harkin, congratulations. You'll need to be fitted with a decoration hook for the Governor to put your decoration on.'

'A hook . . .' Ben wasn't following. His eyes were on the vans from the TV networks, which were parked further up the hill.

'Yes, sir. It's much smoother than the Governor trying to pin it on you. It's a small black hook that's fitted before the ceremony. You won't even see it against your suit.'

He told Ben exactly where he needed to be and when, but he kept looking at me to see that I was taking it in too.

'Too late to run, then,' Ben said when it was just the two of us again.

We followed the crowd along the curved road, past the well-groomed bushes to the entrance steps. The function room had rows of chairs set out in front of a fireplace. There was a portrait of the Queen on the wall, and a display of Australian honours. I could see the bravery awards clustered together, with their two-tone ribbons the colours of venous and arterial blood.

Ben was taken away to have his hook fitted and I was left alone, wondering how the day would pan out. I tried to imagine Robert Redford at Government House, standing, in a useless moment between tasks, in a big borrowed suit that in daylight had turned out to be browner than he had realised. I checked my phone, but there were no new messages. The audience, yet to take their seats, stood around talking quietly, as if quiet was what the room demanded. Two young girls in bright dresses chased each other along the rows of chairs, almost tipping one over in their hurry.

From the other side of the room, Max Visser waved, and he and Frank came over, holding programs.

'All okay?' Frank said. His scar was a vivid pink and his scalp almost looked as if he had polished it.

'Well, he's here,' I told him. 'And he's as ready to play the hero as he's going to be.'

I threw it out like bait, *play* the hero.

I watched Frank for a reaction, but he just said, 'Good,' and looked past me, towards the front of the room. 'Been to one of these before?'

'No. I didn't make it onto the Queen's invite list in London.' Max laughed. Frank didn't. 'You're ready for this? Ready for afterwards?'

'It'll be brief today, won't it?' Frank said. 'Brief for me, if any of them want to talk to me.'

'That's it. That's the idea,' I said. 'Have one or two sound-bite-sized things ready to say and don't be afraid to use them more than once. Save the detail for Australian Story. Talk about the bravery, talk about the lives saved, talk about the danger, but try to keep it natural. Try not to sound too much like an award citation, or an official document.'

'Right,' he said. He glanced at me. He was trying to read me. The look was gone in no time, but I'd caught it while it lasted. 'Good advice. You're worth every cent.'

I had him. I had something. There had been a flicker of a response. If the wording overlap had been chance, I would have got nothing at all.

We were asked to take our seats for the ceremony. Frank moved first, which left Max sitting between us.

'Quite a few awards,' he said, looking at the program. 'Only Ben for the Star of Courage, though.'

I opened my program too, but I was still back at Frank's look. Nancy Drew would have had more to go on than that. And what did it mean − what could it mean − if Frank had searched out the wording and used it? It did nothing to alter the facts. The siege was real, and the gunshot, and the death of Rob Mueller. If Frank's search for the right wording amounted to anything, it was the act that gave the story a hero. And the simplest, most obvious motivation for it was that Ben was one.

The TV cameras set up on one side of the room. An attendant placed them where he wanted them, and appeared to mark out an imaginary line that they were not to cross. It would not be like the back of the ambulance, cameras careering around on the pavement and the steps nearby and closing in. That was good. I checked my list of reporters, and made certain I could see them all before putting the piece of paper back in my pocket.

Ben glanced at the cameras when he was led into the

room, then looked down at the floor. He was shown to a seat in the front row, next to other award recipients. His expression read like stoicism, but most of the others didn't seem too different.

The ceremony began. For twenty minutes or more, there was nothing I could do for him.

I wanted to be in the next phase of my life, my business with Randall Hood Beckett done. I let myself imagine Hayley in my future. I advanced myself several minutes of unrealistic expectations before pulling my hopes in and reminding myself of my mother's well-worn advice about taking one day at a time, not getting ahead of myself. I was ahead, always ahead. It was always better ahead.

And *she* had kissed *me*. In the recent past, in a dark street, the move had come from her. That was rocket fuel for high hopes. Back on earth, my mother's voice grew faint.

The Governor saved Ben until the end. By then I had pulled my head out of the clouds and back into the room. The warrant was read, briefly recounting the details of the siege, but more the when and where than the specifics of what had happened.

Ben got up from his chair and stood stiffly in front of the Governor. He seemed not to expect it when she spoke to him while placing the star on his chest, but he mumbled some kind of answer. She shook his hand, still talking to him, and then let him go back to his seat. Applause broke out. He was the picture of a self-deprecating hero. He sat facing forward as the clapping went on behind him, and the Governor smiled at him again to let him know he was okay.

I pushed through the crowd to get to him first on the way out. The TV crews would close in all too quickly. I told Frank and Max to stick with me, but I lost them. I got to Ben at the same time as Ten News.

'We spoke last week,' I said to the reporter, before she had a chance to talk to him. 'Josh Lang. I'm responsible for that piece of paper you're carrying.' She had my media release in her hand.

'Oh, great, Josh,' she said. 'Courtney Smith. Where can we go to get a few words from Ben? Preferably somewhere without a brass band.'

I found us a spot under a hoop pine some distance away, and that was the start of it. For the next half-hour, while a military band played in a striped marquee across the lawn and sandwiches of a polite size were served, I marshalled the reporters and the cameras around Ben and Frank. I had Ben's medal box and warrant in my hand as one camera after another framed him with the trees behind him and the star on his chest lit up by the late morning sun.

I listened to him, I listened to Frank, I listened for the messages we had talked about – the bite-sized pieces that TV needed or that would work on radio news.

'It was a split-second thing, I guess,' Ben said to one of them. 'Time was running out, and it was then or never.' He was on the money. There was tension in every muscle and it was clear to me that he was hating the interview, but they wouldn't see that.

'He's doing Afternoons with you,' I said to the radio reporter who was next in the queue. 'Do you still want him now for news?'

'It was a terrible risk he took,' Frank was saying, next

to me. 'He certainly saved my life, and maybe dozens more.'

Over in the marquee, the band was playing Click Go the Shears and the Governor was still shaking hands, still listening to the stories of the brave but not conspicuously courageous.

'And how do you feel about the death of Rob Mueller?' I heard the final TV reporter say to Ben, just as I thought my job at Government House was done.

Ben looked around until he saw me. The reporter had her microphone angled his way, waiting, just below the shot. I took a step closer. I could stop it if I had to.

'I feel very bad about that,' he said, unrehearsed. 'It wasn't what any of us wanted. I wish . . . we'd all come out of there alive.' He blinked, and put his hands up to shade his eyes from the sun. I believed him, this time completely.

'Thank you,' the reporter said. 'That'll do us.' She shook his hand. The cameraman stepped back, but the reporter stayed with Ben. 'You did an amazing thing,' she said, still holding his hand. 'I don't know how you did it.'

He looked uncomfortable, as if it was another question to answer just as he'd been told it was over. I stepped in and thanked the reporter, and said I might take Ben for something to eat.

I led the way towards the marquee and I told him to go for canapés, as many as he could get his hands on, since we had more interviews to do around town before he had any chance of a meal.

'Hey, that was really something,' Max said, his mouth half-full of white bread and cress. Some food had strayed beyond the marquee, and he hadn't missed it. 'Watching you bring all the media through, keeping them happy. A lot of them wanted to talk to him, didn't they?'

'That'd be all the phone calls Josh has been making, Max,' Ben said, as a platter of mini quiche came his way. He gave me his medal box and warrant certificate again so that he could take two. 'Mate, I couldn't have handled that without you, you know that.'

★ ★ ★

BEN TUCKED THE HEAVY STAR into his jacket pocket as we left Government House. It had been pinned just above the pocket by the Governor's ADC when she had come to take back the decoration hook after the ceremony.

'It was way out of line,' I said, about the reporter asking Ben how he felt about the death of Rob Mueller. 'It's not the question you ask someone in your position.'

'It's okay.' He sounded calm and, for the first time, looked it too. 'I thought I did okay with it. After the grilling you've been giving me the past few days, I was ready for just about anything.'

'I didn't get you ready for that. You did well.'

'Hey, go for the truth. That's what you said.' He kicked a stone off the path, and it left a mark on the toe of his shiny black shoe. 'I do feel bad that he died. It's a tragedy. He had a family.' Two taxis drove by, carrying guests away from Government House. 'I want them to run what I said. I hope they do. Do you think they will?'

'Yeah, I do. She knew she had something, that reporter. If Miriam Mueller sees it, or hears about it, I think it'll mean something to her.'

Our next interview was across town at 4BC. We listened to music all the way there. Ben didn't say much. We parked out the front, and I checked that he was ready and told him it was time to show the star again. He lifted it out and placed it on the outside of his pocket, running his hand over the ribbon as if it needed smoothing.

The producer met us at the door and said, 'So that's what it looks like.' She asked if she could touch it and she weighed the silver star in her hand and said, 'It's solid, isn't it?'

Two other staff members were walking in with their lunch and stopped to admire it as well. It was like an Olympian turning up with a medal, but the backstory here wasn't victory.

'What did you do?' one of them said. There was an eagerness about the way it came out. She was looking for good news.

'There was a siege,' Ben told her. 'A guy with a gun.' He wanted the story out of his life. He didn't want to be recounting it in doorways.

'Don't wear him out, girls,' the producer said. 'I want him on air with this.'

She led us inside and took Ben into the studio. I watched him through the glass, getting settled in the seat, picking the headphones up and then putting them back on the desk. The producer rearranged the microphone so that the height was right and showed him the cough button.

She came back out into the foyer as the weather report ended and the presenter said, 'We've now got a very special guest with us . . .'

It was live and I thought it would be close to seven minutes, not the sound bite Ben was used to giving. I hoped he was ready. He started well. The producer asked me if we were doing the rounds, and I told her we were being selective.

'I think it's a story people will want to hear,' I said, still watching Ben through the glass. 'But he's not a rock star with a new record doing thirty interviews a day. It's a tough story, and I only want to take him through it a few times.'

I could hear the interviewer saying, 'I don't know about that. I don't know that you can say anyone else would have done it if they'd been in your position. It took some courage. I think I would have been hiding under the desk.'

It was a hero interview, and it was going just the way I had wanted it to.

'Well, we were in the gents at the time,' Ben said, leaning back from the microphone, his voice falling away. 'So . . . No desk.' The interviewer signalled for him to get a little closer, and he nodded. 'That's just where we ended up. And then he was going to shoot Frank . . .'

'How did it feel? Tell us about that moment. That moment when you knew you had to act.'

'I don't know,' Ben said after a pause. 'I know that doesn't sound right, but it happened so quickly. I saw the gun come up. I saw that he was about to fire. I had to knock the gun away. But it didn't work out like that. I had some momentum and it carried us to the wall, and the gun went off. I think that was it, but it all took maybe a second.'

'And in that second, lives were saved. Would you have known you had it in you, to be the hero in a situation like that?'

'No,' Ben said. 'I'm still not sure I do. It's just what happened, I guess.'

He sounded like the perfect honest hero.

★ ★ ★

'YOU'RE AN HOUR from beach time.'

We were pulling away from the kerb outside 96five, another solid interview behind us.

'Yay.' Ben sounded weary, all talked out after four radio stations. 'Do we have any more when we get there, or is that it for the day?'

He pushed his seat back and adjusted his sunglasses. His jacket was now on the back seat, with his medal tucked into the pocket again. The box and warrant had ended up on the floor, near his feet.

'That's it. Nothing this evening. Next one's Wednesday, so you're on holiday until then. That'll be Who Weekly. Interview and photoshoot. You in the suit with the medal. You playing mini-golf with friends. Things like that.'

He lifted the sunglasses up, as if he needed to see me properly. 'Oh really?' he said. 'Who are the friends? I have friends? You've booked some friends for this?'

'Well, I'll be one of them.' Years before I would have been one of them as a matter of course. I had thought nothing of it when I'd planned it. I had seen the photoshoot as a straight role-play then, and not a mean joke at the expense of the past, or a hint at a fresh start. I didn't know which way he would take it, if he would see either of those in it. 'Maybe I should have asked if there were people you could call. I'm sure you've got plenty within range of the Gold Coast. But it's not a friend showcase, not really.' It was a photo, an image, a fake that I was setting out to craft. And I was doing that because it was easier than the real thing, because it gave me more control. I realised I didn't care about the truth of the photo, just that they ran the piece with the story the way I wanted it. 'They only need a couple of people. So, it's you, me and . . . we might be joined by someone.'

'*Might* be joined by someone?' He had picked up the scent.

'Okay, will be. And the someone is Hayley. Who you might know better as Jett. She'll be coming tomorrow. I happened to book a place with three rooms, so . . .'

He laughed. 'Because it's all about the three rooms, right? Don't want a room to go to waste, do we, so we'd better give it to the nearest hot law-student stripper? How long have you been keeping this to yourself? I thought you didn't have her number. When did you line her up?'

'I caught up with her on Saturday night.'

'And just invited her to the coast? We might have to give you one of these.'

He picked up his medal box, took out the miniature and tried to pin it on my shirt. I fought him off with one hand. The car swerved but stayed in the lane.

'Traffic, please. I have to focus. On driving.' The passenger in the car to our right stared at me as they passed, assessing me to see if I was some kind of hazard. 'It took practically no bravery at all. I met her when she finished work and we went to Ric's. You should see what it's like out the back of the club. It's really . . . normal. And then there's Ross, the boss, who's hilarious. He's this jolly fat guy who keeps a gun in his desk drawer.'

It felt like a mistake to mention Ross's gun to Ben, even as I said it. It was a secret I wasn't supposed to know. But it was as if we were friends again and I had stories to tell, and a girl to invite to the coast. I wasn't the loser who had left years ago, who had had his spirit broken by one bad act.

'You're serious? The boss keeps a gun in his drawer?' He was still working through it. 'That's crazy. Why would he do that? Has he been watching The Sopranos too much?'

'It's from the bad old days apparently. A handgun and a box of ammo. And they had this new stripper. Her name was Eugenia but her stripper name was Vixen.'

'Vixen. Is there some book of stripper names? You've been blogging your fingers raw since Saturday, haven't you?'

There had been a time, years before, when we had gone to the coast on weekends in my old car, and this trip felt remarkably like that, but with suits and a Star of Courage. I think we both wanted things not to have changed at all, no bust-up, no gap lasting years, no siege. We were talking as if history could be deleted rather than merely rewritten.

'Forty percent of them are students,' I said. 'The strippers. One of them was even reading Proust on a break.'

'I bet stripping pays better than flipping burgers,' he said. He had never flipped burgers. 'If it's forty percent now, there must have been at least a few in our day. Who would it have been?'

We made a list.

'You could have been a contender,' I said, figuring the list could do with some gender-balancing. 'They like the boys hairless, in the clubs that specialise in the boy thing.'

'I won't even ask how you know that. Maybe I'll add it to my options, if the law thing goes belly-up. I could probably walk to work.'

We passed Yatala, and the huge pie sign to the right of the highway.

'The canapés aren't holding me,' he said, one hand on his stomach. 'I think you got to eat more of them than I did. I could eat that sign.'

'Well, you were busier than me.' We were driving at a hundred and ten. In twenty minutes he could eat actual food.

'And I was more nauseated.'

'Less nauseated now?'

'Yes. It feels like it's nearly done. The big bit's done.' It was news time on the radio, and he muted it during the play-in. 'No news,' he said. 'I want to have a holiday from news. Hey, how about that time we stopped here for pies? We left uni one Friday in the middle of the day and made it this far before we had to eat. You ate a whole family-sized steak-and-kidney before you remembered you didn't eat organs, and I had to drive after that. We had to have the window down in case the thought of all that kidney got too much for you.'

'Yeah. I never did like kidney.'

That was true, and I was sure he was right about the pie, since he had been so specific. I couldn't place it, though. The more I thought about it, the less memory I had of it. But his recollection was precise and detailed, and it sounded like me, and like such a better, more uncomplicated time that I wanted it to be something we agreed on.

'I'm glad I kidnapped you and took you to Max's lecture,' he said. 'I really hoped that you'd do something with it, with that chance. I saw that she liked you in the club, you know. She came over to you twice. It was to you, not to us.'

'Yeah?' I didn't want to owe him Hayley. I didn't want to hear that he had noticed who she had been looking at, that he had been paying her any attention at all. 'Well, she called me when you didn't think she would. And she's coming.'

The conversation was about Eloise again, or turning that way. I would make it about mistrust if I said one more thing.

Ben looked straight ahead down the highway. The radio news went on in the background. There was a fizz of static as we passed under a bridge.

'How much longer, do you reckon?' he said. 'I may have to start eating my arm.'

★ ★ ★

BEN BOUGHT A BAG of apples from a convenience store while I was checking us in to our apartment at Focus. He ate two on the balcony, staring out to sea while the wind whipped his hair around. It was dark enough now that the ships had their lights on.

The apartment was bigger than I had expected, and curved since the building was circular. It had green sofas patterned with starfish and conch shells, and there were pastel Greek-island-style prints on its cream-coloured walls. There were probably a thousand places decked out just like it within walking distance. It would have seemed huge, stupidly huge, if I had been there alone. Alone and driving around the neighbourhood to tap balls across Astroturf in the name of work, and retiring to my laptop to massage it all into some kind of fun.

I drove us to Chang Mai Thai, where I had made a booking for dinner. Even on a Monday out of season, the outside tables were full. There were groups of ten and twelve, and milestones being toasted. Fairy lights beaded the roofline and twisted around the potted palms.

The manager ran her pen down the list of bookings, found my name and led us past the paintings of buffaloes and temples and the indoor greenery to a small square table tucked against the belly of a teak elephant that was close to life-size.

'You order,' Ben said, after a cursory look at the menu. 'I'm too tired. Let's go straight to mains. Those apples are only just holding me.' A platter of satay sticks passed us at high speed. 'Or maybe some of those would be good. They look good.'

'So is this you ordering now?'

'No, you're ordering. But include satays.'

'What kind?' The menu offered chicken, beef or lamb.

'Whatever you want. Not chicken. Beef. Make it beef. Unless you don't want beef. Whatever you want.'

'If this was a date, I'd be seriously thinking about dropping you.'

'Can't be a lot of second dates for you then, with those standards.'

For the first time, I wondered how we would go when the week was done, if there would be a reason to stay in contact. We could be adept at looking like friends.

I put our order in, and asked for the two serves of satay to come at the same time as the curry. That seemed to meet Ben's needs.

We ran out of conversation, or the conversation tapered off at least. We talked through the decor and I told him about my Cooking with Asterix blog, which was soon to surface.

He asked me how I was finding the rising mortgage interest rates, then told me he had to check something and got out his iPhone. He kept himself busy scrolling through emails until the food arrived.

It came on a brass tray, with the curry and rice in ornate brass bowls and the satay sticks in a row, in a slick of peanut sauce. Ben put his iPhone back into his pocket and started scooping rice onto his plate. He handed the spoon to me and took two satay sticks.

'Governors should serve this,' he said, as he set about unthreading the meat from a skewer with his fork.

'What? A Thai banquet? You think you should get a Thai banquet as well as a medal? I think I might have seen some satay sticks there this morning.' He had been doing interviews at the time. 'There's one thing I've been wondering about. And don't take this the wrong way. It's just a question.'

'Yes?' he said, putting on a suspicious tone as he mixed sauce into his rice and picked some up with his fork.

'How is it that Frank, two days after the siege, already knew exactly what to say to get you a Star of Courage?'

He lowered his fork and glared at me. He didn't speak.

'It's like he went home and looked it up. With a head injury. After having a gun in his face. It's like he googled it. Is that crazy?'

He ate the rice on his fork, and a chunk of meat, and he took his time over it.

'You should try this stuff,' he said. 'Instead of just looking at it. It's good.' He lifted two satay sticks onto my plate and spooned sauce onto them. 'This is the holiday part, isn't it?'

'Sure, but . . .'

'Or are you going to get that autopsy report out again and start reading about all the blood and brains and shit that got splattered on the wall? I think everyone here would like that. I think they'd find it really interesting.'

'It was just a question. And maybe it's complete

192

coincidence. Maybe he went home and had a stiff Scotch and wrote it then, and that's just how it turned out.'

'Maybe. And maybe I don't know.' He measured it out slowly, one word at a time. He wanted me to get the message.

'I'm sorry. This is the holiday.'

His mouth was full again, more beef satay and rice. This time he didn't wait to finish it before speaking. 'Bring on the mini-golf. Bring on the doves.'

★ ★ ★

THE MULTISTOREY apartment buildings were lined up along the beachfront for miles in either direction, all of them shaped to face out to sea, towers of lights and patches of dark with the city falling away immediately behind them.

Below us, the night life of Surfers Paradise went on. Several lanes of traffic crawled along and pedestrians ambled, mostly in groups, perhaps destined for the clubs a few blocks away that would stay open most of the night. From the height of our floor, the only sound was the wind skidding around the building and the distant beating of the sea on the sand.

Ben had decided we should finish our wine outside. We kept the balcony lights off and sat in semi-darkness on the weatherproof, and therefore mainly plastic, holiday furniture. He had been quiet since the restaurant, and he sat with his glass in his hand staring into the wind and out at the ocean. There was nothing to see out there but a few stars among the patches of cloud, and the slow lights of freighters working their way along the horizon.

I wondered what Hayley was doing, who she was with.

'I'm sorry,' I told him. 'For how I handled the situation with Eloise.'

'No, I . . .' He looked caught out. It had been one ambush after another from me, one pounding for ancient deceit or another for any recent minor inconsistency.

'No, let me,' I said. 'I was more attached than she wanted me to be. I know that can happen with me.' I waited, but he didn't speak. 'Thank you for not commenting on that. She chose to sleep with you. The *two* of you made that happen, not just you by yourself. I know she'd been drinking, but, still . . . I probably made it hard for her to talk, to bring up any problems. And that was the outlet she found. Or something like that.'

He stood up, still holding his wineglass. He turned and leaned against the railing, gripping it with his other hand. The light from inside fell across his white shirt, but not his face. I could see that he was looking at me, though, as if he was about to speak. But he said nothing.

'Or maybe you were more than an outlet.' I wondered if I had got it wrong, if I would have to rewrite my history yet again and come out of it a bigger fool. 'Maybe there was more to it.'

'No, no,' he said. 'No. That was it. An outlet.'

'So, I've been a shit to you the past few days, and I'm sorry. I've been picking at details because I couldn't stop myself. You went through a really horrendous experience . . .'

He breathed out, shook his head, came away from

the railing. 'Stop.' He held up his hand. 'Stop. I can't lie to you now. Any more.'

I waited, waited for the revelation to hit, for some key piece of our long-ago past to be exposed, to hit me like a hammer, if it had to.

'The story's not right,' he said. 'About the siege.'

'About the siege?' I was still back trying to be an adult about Eloise. 'What do you mean?'

'I don't know exactly . . . Rob Mueller was pacing around, trying to get up the guts to shoot Frank, I think. Frank was still out then. Still unconscious. And I was nothing to him, Rob Mueller. He made me drag Frank around the room. And then to the bathroom. That's all pretty much like I told you. I think he wanted to shoot Frank's head off in a toilet, or something. Something degrading.' He was frowning, picturing it, looking away from me. 'He lost it when we were in there. He started bawling. Frank woke up. And that's when Rob Mueller . . .' He turned my way again. He had stepped forward and his face was now in the light. 'That's when Rob Mueller shot himself. Backed himself up against the wall and shot himself. I was in the corner, the far corner. It was deafening and there was plaster and stuff everywhere. I moved towards him and I slipped on the mess on the floor – the blood and the urine, I guess – and I fell on him. So there I was, wrestling with this guy who had just blown his own head off. As brain came out the back of his skull and into my hands.' His grip on his wineglass shifted, and I wondered if he might drop it. 'Then we were on our way out. I couldn't believe how bright the daylight was when we got outside, I remember that. And I was the hero. Frank made me the hero, then and there, with his head still split open and bleeding. I couldn't speak. I couldn't hear properly and I had this shit all over me and people were shouting. Frank made me a hero, and that day I think I believed him. I had blanks and he filled in the details.'

'It was suicide.'

'Yeah. I was nowhere near him. And I wasn't brave. It's just how the story got told.'

I had picked at the story and picked at it, but it hadn't come undone and now, with my job days away from finished, it had fallen apart.

'You've got an interview on Wednesday with Who Weekly,' I said to him. 'I've been out there pitching this hero story pretty vigorously. You talked to sixteen media outlets today. You've got TV on Friday. How are you going to handle it?'

'I'm just going to handle it. I've *been* handling it. It's all over at the end of the week. That's what you said.'

So he was going to go through with it, and I had become part of the lie. There was no recanting now, not with it all over the radio that afternoon, the TV news that night and the papers in the morning. Two more stories and the lie could be put to bed.

'I could have fixed this if you'd told me yesterday. Or I could at least have done something.' I would have called him in sick. I would have worked the phones shutting interviews down. It would have been a start. 'Why didn't you tell me?'

'Because it's over at the end of the week. I've had a year and a half of this, and it's nearly done.' He was the runner stumbling in the home straight of the marathon, his eyes never on the medal but always on the end.

I had been fooled, but we had all been fooled. I'd had doubts, but not enough to back them up. These stories — siege stories, stories of disaster — called out for a hero, and worked best once a hero could be found. But this hero had been manufactured, not found, and by the one man who knew his story to be false.

'So, why did Frank do it?' I said. 'Why did he nominate you for a bravery award, and make damn sure you got one, if you weren't brave at all?'

'I don't know.' His voice was unsteady now. 'I don't know about that. I don't get it. He had a head injury. Maybe it was really how he saw it.'

'And you didn't think to set him straight?'

'It happened before I could stop it.'

'And why should I believe that, when you've just told me you've been lying to me for a week?'

There was no answer to that. He just shrugged.

'Two more interviews,' he said. 'Then you can forget about this.'

We were back to bare expediency, and the fragile thing between us that looked like a kind of trust was gone. I was back to doing my oven job, Ben to putting a long loud lie to bed. He had a fresh pair of letters after his name now, and a star in a box, and for them he had hidden in a corner and fallen on a dead man.

'I feel better, now that I've told you,' he said. He went to drink from his wineglass, but it was already empty.

I had to walk away then. I didn't want him feeling better, and I had run out of things to say.

MY WINE WAS STILL THERE in the morning, in its glass on the balcony table, warm in the sun.

It was the TV that woke me, a loud ad during a breakfast show. When I walked out of my room, Ben was sitting with his feet on the coffee table, eating a bowl of cereal. He was getting on as normal.

I turned my phone on and a text message came through from Hayley, sent late the night before. 'Doves booked in for 2pm. See you mid-morning.'

'I think I know who that might be . . .' Ben said.

But it was the opening line of a conversation from a different era and I couldn't do it. I couldn't let the two of us act like two uni students talking about a girl.

I took another look at the phone, as if I was checking something. 'Yeah? How did you know Frank was texting me? I didn't even tell you I'd tried to call him last night.'

For a second I had him. Then he said, 'Bullshit,' but he didn't sound confident. 'Frank never texted anybody.'

'Well, we've got to get this sorted out somehow.'

'We will.' On the TV behind him, the weather guy was being thrown around by acrobats. 'It'll be over by Friday. Just let it be over by Friday.'

'What does Frank get out of this? What does Frank get out of you ending up with a medal?'

'Nothing. It's how he saw it.' He was sounding clear about it now, clearer than the night before. 'And I was too traumatised to work it out. Give me a break. It was still a horrendous experience. We could both have been killed. And have you ever seen anyone blow their brains out? Everything afterwards happened before I could stop it.' He wanted me to believe him, but I had stopped doing that. 'Who was the text from, really?'

The TV weather guy was back on the ground, hamming it up and failing to walk a straight line.

I went out onto the balcony and called Hayley. I wanted to hear her voice. Her phone was off, though, and I went through to voicemail. I would ramble – I knew it – so I hung up and put some thought and far fewer words into a text message to let her know where we would be. I wanted to see her. I wanted Ben gone.

After breakfast Ben and I walked to King Tutt's Putt Putt. It was two short blocks away, since I had made sure we were staying at putt-putt central. King Tutt's promised, and it delivered. The front of its brochure featured a camel with a wide grin, dressed like a Florida retiree whose days revolved around golf. He wore sunglasses and a flowered shirt and was sitting in a giant cracked cerise-coloured golf ball, like a chick emerging from an egg. Above him was a curved line of jaunty text reading 'Mini-Golf at its Best'.

Ben was talking, but I wasn't listening. I should have forced his hand earlier, days earlier. He was walking beside me in three-quarter pants and slides, again looking more like a Japanese tourist than he would ever realise, looking like someone who might be scooped up by a minibus and taken away to pat koalas. I wanted his dirty secret out in public, and at the same time I wanted it buried deep for another few days, until I could outrun it. I wanted him to face the shame of handing his medal back in its box. I wanted that photo in the paper, instead of the one that would be there in newsagents across the state as we walked to King Tutt's. Neither of us had gone looking for the paper, or even talked about it. I expected he would be on page three. But this was the holiday. Bring on the mini-golf, bring on the doves.

King Tutt's was a warehouse, with indoor and outdoor courses set up to capture the three great eras of golf: Jurassic, ancient Egyptian and African jungle. The beauty of mini-golf – and the essence, surely, of any mini-golf tour article – was not so much to be found in the putting of a brightly-coloured ball across cunningly undulating fake grass. It was in the gratuitous themeing. The greatest moments in the sport would never be witnessed by the public, since they had already happened before the concrete pour, back in the planning stages when the theme dream kicked in. Mini-golf was a gift for the writer of quirk who had run out of steam, since it was quirk already, served up on Astroturf. No funny slant required, just two eyes and a pen.

The Egyptian course was on the left as we walked in. It featured small concrete pyramids as frequent obstacles, plus gold serpents coiled around holes, and a full-sized sarcophagus. The wall at the far end had columns set into it, along with the giant stunned face of a boy king, gazing across flattened fake grass and grit and a single group of holiday-makers leaning on their clubs, debating their scores.

Ben and I opted for the Jurassic course, with its volcanoes and palm trees and holes marked out by the sweep of dinosaur tails.

'I play some golf,' he said, weighing up the putter in his hand. 'But that's actual golf. You know, non-plastic grass, six other clubs. I don't imagine that'll do me much good here.'

By the end of the seventh hole he was six shots ahead, since I had maxed out at five shots on the first hill hole and almost come to grief on a second. He stood looking at the dinosaur murals as I klutzed it up, one hole after another, and each time he pencilled in my score without comment.

I teed off first at the eighth, putting up a slope towards two caves at the base of a volcano. Each cave had its own hidden tunnel leading to the plain that lay below and to our left. One tunnel opening put you right near the hole. The other left you in a far corner. There was no way of telling which was which. My first shot clarified nothing. The ball decelerated rapidly on its way up the slope, defied gravity for a millisecond and then rolled back down, gathering speed all the way to the back board. It ended up a few centimetres behind where it had started.

My second shot was crisp and firm, and drilled the wrong cave. I two-putted from there.

Ben picked the right cave and had a tap in for a birdie.

The ninth was surrounded by rock walls, but the path to the hole was easy enough and we both made twos.

I was lining up my first shot at the top of the steps at the tenth when Ben said, 'Come on, what's eight shots between friends? The brochure says this is the very best fun you can have on your feet.'

'That's why we're here.' My eye was still on the ball, and the track to the hole. I wanted him to talk on his own time, not on my putt. I didn't want him to talk.

The ball plunked down the steps, bounced well past the hole and ended up tucked in a corner.

'Experience the fantastic adventure of putting amongst the ruins of ancient Egypt and also the ferocious dinosaurs of Jurassic Park – both eighteen-hole courses,' he said, reading from the brochure. 'Light refreshments on site.'

There was a family playing back on five and there were two groups out on the Egyptian course. There was music in the background, and automated noise from the Bullseye Barn Shooting Gallery, which was unattended in the far corner. Ben was scanning the brochure for something else to read.

'How can you do this today after telling me what you did last night?' I should have been playing my second shot, edging my ball out of the corner that had trapped it and making some kind of attempt at the hole. 'How can you play mini-golf?'

He closed the brochure. He was irritated and didn't hide it. 'How can I do anything? For eighteen months now. I'm a hero, and I'm a guy who . . .' He looked around, checking to see how near the other mini-golfers were. He lowered his voice. 'I'm a guy who fell on a body and got a medal for it and I don't know what the hell I can do about it, okay? You should be taking more photos for your article. Here . . .'

He held his hand out for the camera, and clicked his fingers. He took it from me and placed his own blue ball in the worn tee-off zone, harder than he needed to, so that it hit the ground with a loud clunk. He stepped down to the hole and crouched, pointing the camera back up my way. 'Putt that and look happy.'

I putted, and the ball dropped down the steps and ended up in the same corner as my first shot.

'Well, it's a good photo anyway,' he said as he reached over and hooked the ball with his putter.

He came up the steps and gave me back the camera. He lined up his shot, tapped the ball gently and, as it fell step by step towards the hole with an unwelcome inevitability, I looked away and saw Hayley at the entrance to the building, standing in the bright sun. She waved, and started to walk the course in reverse to reach us. She was wearing a sundress with large hibiscus flowers on it, and sandals, but her hair still had a hint of the rock-chick look.

'If this doesn't stop you being shitty, there's no hope,' Ben said as she walked across seventeen, the triceratops-skull hole. He spun his putter in his hand.

Two more interviews, and we would be done. I nearly said it to him. And I nearly said that if he made one move on her, his secret would be out.

Hayley stopped on the tee-off circle at the eleventh and said, 'Well, this looks tense. Is it close?'

'No.' I got in first. 'I've had a few technical problems. Mostly to do with hitting the ball.'

She introduced herself to Ben, saying they hadn't met properly, not by name anyway. I didn't like the way he looked at her, as if she was still Jett in his head and not Hayley, as if he could recall almost every bit of her without the sundress.

She took a look at the scorecard and said, 'You'd better let me play a couple for you.'

I handed her my putter and she hit the ball wildly on eleven, but didn't seem to care. It pinged around like a bagatelle ball and no one could guess where each shot would finish. She even drove it fiercely at the hole when she was less than a metre away, sending it rattling around the boundary boards again and almost back to the start. With the addition of out-of-bounds penalties, I was fourteen shots behind when she gave the club back to me after the twelfth.

'There you go,' she said. 'You can finish him off.'

Ben outsmarted himself at the triceratops skull and wedged the ball behind the mandible, but that was as close as I came to having a chance to finish him. He was twelve strokes ahead when our balls dropped into the hole in the floor at the eighteenth.

Hayley had a black dress laid out on the back seat of her Barina, which she had parked on the gravel behind King Tutt's. Ben climbed in over the tilted passenger seat, and sat with one end of the dress on his lap for the two-minute drive. Hayley chatted like someone on a holiday. I wanted to match her. I wanted to impress her, to make her laugh. I kept looking for angles, as if I was blogging on the fly, while Ben talked like a normal person and made it seem easy.

'Nice,' she said when I opened the door to the apartment. 'It's big.' She stepped inside and put her bag down at her feet. 'So, where's the medal? Let me see the medal.'

Ben fetched it from his room and found himself in Olympic-champion mode again. He opened the box and took her through it item by item, explaining the different uses of the full-sized star, the miniature and the lapel badge. Like everyone else, Hayley took the star in her hand and talked about how solid it felt, how heavy.

'You realise it's part of the deal this afternoon?' she said to him. 'I pitched us as the deluxe wedding package. Suits, medals, little black dress for me. That's how I persuaded them to give us the job.'

'So, I wear this?' Ben said as she put the star back in his hand. He looked down at it. I couldn't tell what he was thinking.

'That's why they put the pin on it,' she said. 'I reckon they make these things for wearing. So don't be bashful. And don't go checking your pamphlet about it, since I'm sure Japanese weddings require the full big star.'

'Okay,' he said, closing his hand over it. He smiled at her. 'I'll wear it. And I won't be Bashful if Josh won't be Grumpy.'

His medal and its bits and pieces put an aura around him. It drew people in. I didn't want Hayley to be one of them.

'Some of us default to Grumpy,' I told him. 'Me, the Queen's face. Have you noticed how grumpy she looks when she's taking in yet another passing parade? The muscles relax and out comes Grumpy.'

'So, you've just got the Queen's face then,' he said. 'My mistake.'

'Was there a dwarf called Smartarse? Or did they get the shits with him and chuck him out before Snow White arrived?' My status as Grumpy was confirmed. 'We should hang this dress.' I was still holding the little black dress Hayley had brought for the wedding. 'Let me show you your room.'

I had kept the best one for her, but the unused room reminded us both that we were only acquaintances. I had already pictured us as much more. We had one-and-a-half good conversations behind us, and one rather fumbled kiss in the street. That was all. Separate rooms, no big assumptions.

I felt like a valet – like Anthony Hopkins in a stiff shirt with a wing collar, or an actor in an Edwardian play – as I walked in there with her dress and hung it in the wardrobe.

She set her bag down on the bed and said, 'Nice room. Thanks. I hope they're all this good.'

Over her shoulder, I could see Ben in the living room, watching us and smirking.

'Well, Ben and I don't have our own en suites,' I told her, 'but we should be able to share a bathroom as long as he's not in there for hours buffing and plucking before the photoshoot.'

'I already waxed,' he shouted out. He had picked up the TV remote, and was pretending to be interested in it while listening to every word.

'This is starting to sound just like work, like backstage at the Spur,' Hayley said, and he silently held a knuckle to his mouth and bit it.

* * *

WE WENT OUT FOR PIZZA, since it was the nearest option and the wedding was at two. It turned out I even liked the way she ate pizza.

When we got back to the apartment, Hayley changed into her dress and put on her hair extension. She wore it in a ponytail and said she was aiming for 'demure, but stylish demure'.

Ben came out of his room in his suit, looking like a suit model.

'Very nice,' she said, 'but where's the medal?' She took it from the box and pinned it on, smoothing it flat over the jacket pocket. 'We're not all brave, you know.'

She stood back to check that the star was sitting straight. He modelled the medal for her too, setting his chin at an angle that conveyed resilience in the face of an unspecified threat, or quiet nobility. He looked like the statue of an admiral who had lost men but won the day.

'That's better,' she said. 'That's deluxe. It's the free low-season upgrade I promised. Like this place. A dove wrangler, one of our nation's heroes and –' she turned to me – 'our driver.'

Ben laughed. 'I knew I'd been too wordy over the past week when anyone asked me what Josh's role was. He's our driver.'

'Well, your limo awaits,' I said. I picked up the keys from the counter, and told myself he would be gone from my life in three days.

In the basement, Ben squeezed into the back seat of the Echo, with his knees splayed around the passenger seat, and we drove to the hinterland to pick up the doves. Hayley took a sheet of paper from her bag and unfolded it. I thought the directions were on it, but she gave me those from memory. It was an email she had been sent, outlining the details of the job. The birds would be waiting in a cage on the owners' front verandah.

I had imagined something nice, somewhere well-maintained and lush, a restored old timber homestead with a tin roof, but the bird people lived in a two-storey brick house set back from the road and up a gravel driveway from which tufts of weeds had started to sprout. I parked in front of the double roll-a-doors of the garage, next to a planter box in which a shrub had recently died. Hayley walked up the front steps to a balcony, which had been enclosed and now had windows of patterned yellow glass. The cage was just inside the unlocked screen door, and she brought it down to the car. The birds cooed at each other and looked twitchily around, like two old ladies on a church excursion who might have just got on the wrong bus.

She pushed the passenger seat forward and passed the cage to Ben in the back. It was gilded, or at least sprayed with gold paint, and higher than it was wide, and the birds flapped their wings madly as it made its way through. A single small white underfeather was still in the air by the time Ben had them settled on the seat next to him.

He was inspecting them closely. 'They're not even doves, are they?'

'No, they're white pigeons,' Hayley said as she pushed the passenger seat back into his knees and got into the car. 'That way they always fly home.'

'But how can you call them doves then? They're just . . . albino vermin.'

I could see him in the rear-view mirror, a decorated man in a suit, suddenly aware that he was sharing the back seat of his non-limo with two rats with wings.

'Hey, enough of your lip, nation's hero,' Hayley told him. 'Don't diss the birds.'

The birds settled and cooed to each other as they took in their new surroundings in their twitchy-headed way. I turned the car around on the gravel.

'You'll have to keep giving me directions,' I said to Hayley when we reached the end of the driveway. 'Starting about now. Left or right?'

We drove right, down the hill and through acreage that had once been farms and would be suburbs soon enough. There were still a few lush green fields with well-fed black cattle in the dark shade of corrugated iron shelters, motionless but for their flicking tails. We passed a tavern and some shops, crossed the highway on an overpass and skirted the edge of a salmon-pink faux-Tuscan suburb from the early nineties.

We took Robina Parkway and the road dipped down to more low-lying land that was being reclaimed for golf courses and canal developments. In some parts it was swamp, with nothing but tall-legged birds stepping around behind the temporary fencing. In others the work was already done and three-storey show-off houses in navy and grey had risen out of the water shoulder-to-shoulder like some new Venice.

'So, give me an insider's view of the job,' I said to Hayley. I was thinking of the blog or article that I might write. 'What sort of skills do you need?'

'To wrangle homing pigeons?' She laughed. 'None. None that I'm aware of. You probably need skills to keep them, but for this you only need to be present-able and turn up on time. I do try to be nice to the birds. Other than that, you just have to remember that everyone else is taking it really seriously. The birds are a big moment.'

'So you're sure it'll be all right for me to take photos?'

'It's a Japanese wedding.' That was her whole answer. There would be photos in their thousands. 'We used to do lots more of them. I don't know where they go now. Maybe Hawaii. But maybe it's GFC'd out as well. I've had afternoons when I've had two cages on the back seat and one in the front. Six pigeons. If one gets stirred up, they all do. I tried playing music, but that only seemed to make it worse. Maybe it was the type of music.'

I wondered what music she liked. There was a lot I didn't know. Was there any music that would be a deal-breaker? I thought I would still want her even if she told me she had just bought us tickets to André Rieu.

We turned into Palm Meadows Drive, and golf spread out into the distance on both sides – verdant fairways, clumps of trees, more wader birds picking their way through patches of softer ground in the lower-lying areas. We passed a driving range where a few solid men were belting buckets of balls in the direction of the road. A tractor drove among the distance markers, raking up the spent shots. It was another for Ben's list of subur-ban-oddity jobs, perhaps – golf-ball retriever. Another chance to get lost, if you needed to.

We hit a speedbump and I took a look at him in the rear-view mirror. His hand was on his Star of Courage, keeping it still, covering it.

Hayley had her piece of paper out again as we drove up to the entrance of the Radisson.

'Nakajima-Toyama wedding,' she said to the guy who came over to the window. 'We've got the birds.'

He had a clipboard, and he turned over a couple of pages. 'Yeah, great.' He looked into the car, at the three of us, at Ben's Star of Courage. Ben pointed, helpfully, to the birds. 'It's at the gazebo, so park underneath and head out through the exit under Sandpiper. You've been here before, haven't you? It's the usual place, down by the lake. You've just got the one lot of birds?'

'Yeah.'

'No worries,' he said. 'Well, have a good one.'

He waved us on, and Hayley pointed to the car park entrance ahead.

'That question about the one lot of birds . . .' She said it like someone with a story to tell. 'Apparently there was one time, a few years ago, in the heyday of Japanese wedding dove releases, when someone had a bunch to do one day in the middle of summer and, at the second-last one, they parked in the sun. With the windows fully shut. And the wedding went longer than it should, or started later, and when they got back to their car? Two dead birds at the bottom of the cage. Apparently the doves had started to cook. It was sixty or seventy degrees in there. Or so the story goes. At the hotels now they always check if you're carrying extra birds and make sure you're parked in the shade, with the windows open a crack. Sometimes they even take the birds from you and look after them.'

'So do I get to use that in the article?' I was looking for parks, but there were none in the first row.

'You know you want to,' Ben said from the back. He put his hand on the top of my seat and leaned forward.

'All his life he's been looking for a genuine ex-po-zay –' he said it theatrically – 'and this could be it. Pigeongate. Welcome to the big time. The seedy side of the Gold Coast wedding dove-release scene. Bird substitution, death. And you can have that pun for free. Seedy side.'

'Well in that case it's a no,' Hayley said. 'And not just because of the pun, or because you thought you had to say it twice in case we missed it. It's an unsubstantiated rumour, and you didn't hear it from me.' She held both her hands up, disowning her slow-baked pigeon anecdote. 'No birds harmed in the writing of this article. I want to see that in there somewhere.'

'So ready to be a lawyer,' Ben said, as I got out of the car. He passed the cage to me. 'Over to you, driver.'

He climbed out over the seat and Hayley checked the alignment of his medal again and pretended to polish it. She made it seem like a piece of a costume, an accessory. I wanted him to look at me, but he wouldn't. I wanted to tell her not to fall for him, not to fall for anything he had to offer. I wanted her to know that he had pressed himself into a corner and waited for Frank to be shot.

I wondered what Frank was thinking, back in Brisbane, and I wondered if there was a thread I could pull to make the real story unravel.

A car drove past us, its tyres squeaking on the concrete as it turned at the end of the row.

Hayley led us through a doorway and outside. The air was warm and smelt of cut grass. We followed a path that seemed to be familiar to her. It led us around the next building to a lakeside lawn on which the gazebo stood under palm trees. It was white, with iron lacework and a grey domed roof, and in front of it were about forty chairs with white covers and sashes, arranged either side of a red carpet aisle. The guests were standing with their backs to us, looking out across the lake, pointing to bunkers in the distance, talking about the golf they would play or had played. Or the space, the clean air. I had no idea.

The celebrant, a gym-toned blonde, was wearing a pink jacket and skirt, a white top and a scarf. She waved to Hayley and started walking our way. She had a tan the colour of nutmeg and, as she got closer, I could see that her face at least had had some work done. It anchored her in the frightened part of early middle-age, her cheeks and forehead a little too taut. She might have been fifty, but she looked like a fake version of younger, or a younger version of fake.

'Leslie,' she said as she shook Hayley's hand. The scarf was Hermès, held in place by a brooch set with a green crystal the size of a baby's fist. She glanced at me and then looked properly at Ben and the Star of Courage. 'I like that. Nice and medally, but not too showy. You look like you might speak Japanese too.'

'Reckon I might,' he said. He waved his hand in front of his face, at a fly that I was certain wasn't there. 'If this is the Nakajima-Toyama wedding.' He made himself sound like Crocodile Dundee, and it made me realise how accentless his regular voice was, as if he came from no place at all.

'How thoughtful of them to send you,' Leslie said. 'We might get you and the birds set up at the table next to the gazebo.' She took a look at her watch. 'Akira and Yumi should be on their way.'

I placed the gold birdcage on the white tablecloth and the birds fussed around quietly, blinking in the brightness. 'Home soon,' I told them.

Leslie rounded up the guests and showed them to their places. They sat formally, expectantly, talking quietly if at all. Against the background noise of distant golf, I could hear an electric hum becoming louder. One of the guests pointed behind us and to our right. I looked around and saw two golf buggies coming towards us along a path, the groom in the first and the bride in the second, her hand on her veil.

It was a stunning, perfect afternoon for a wedding. The clouds had cleared, the sky was vividly blue and there was a gentle breeze over the lake, which rippled the fringes on the canopies of the two golf buggies. The groom stepped out and adjusted his charcoal-grey tailcoat and grinned at the guests. The bride was assisted from her buggy by her driver. She looked down at the grass in front of the rows of seats and smiled self-consciously. Her dress was a classic meringue, but I didn't have it in me to be cynical. There was a rush of fake shutter noises as twenty slimline digital cameras recorded the moment.

Leslie got the ceremony underway, delivering most of it in English, but interspersed with some sentences that sounded to me like cautious Japanese. Across the water, a pair of golfers stopped to watch before playing their next shots and driving on.

The formalities were brief, and soon Leslie declared Akira and Yumi to be husband and wife, first in English, in which it passed without response, and then presumably in Japanese, which set the cameras off again. She signalled for the bride and groom to kiss, and the shutter noises reached a crescendo.

'And now, to celebrate this union,' she said, with the tone of an announcement, 'and to let it take flight, Yumi and Akira will release a pair of doves.' Left alone in English, untranslated, the metaphor had to fend for itself.

Hayley reached into the cage, talking softly to the birds. She took one out, gave it to Ben and then took the other for herself. The guests left their chairs and stood in an arc, lining up their next shots, calling out to the bride and groom like paparazzi.

Hayley stepped forward and solemnly handed her dove to Yumi, who said, tentatively, 'Thank you.' Ben matched the solemnity, and gave a small bow as he passed his bird to Akira. He said something in Japanese, and both Akira and Yumi beamed. They started talking back to him, both at the same time, then stopped, looked at each other, and laughed.

Leslie steered them around so that they faced their guests. She said a few words, then backed them up by miming bird release. Akira and Yumi copied her and the birds lifted from their hands and, with just a few beats of their wings, they were above us, bright white against the perfect sky, then wheeling across the lake and away, setting a course for the hills, chased on by the shutter-beats of cameras and the ooh-ing and aah-ing of the crowd.

Hayley was in front of me, her eyes following the birds, though perhaps not with the fascination of the others. I noticed something in her hair, the white corner of a label or a tag sticking out from her black scrunchie.

I took a step closer, reached forward, and delicately tucked it in. She gave a small smile without turning around. Below the clip that held Desley in place, she was wearing not a scrunchie but a twisted black G-string.

★ ★ ★

AS SOON AS THEY had cleared our bowls at the Golden Fortune that night, one of the staff came through the servery doors with a plate of fortune cookies.

'Oh, excellent,' Hayley said. 'I love fortune cookies.'

'Me too,' I said. 'Sometimes I eat them as a meal.'

She looked at me as if I might retract it, but it just hovered there, a big glowing blimp above my head that read 'run away, run away'.

'Okay, I don't love them that much,' she said. 'I love them the *normal* amount.' She said 'normal' slowly and with great emphasis, as though I was very ab. She laughed and put her hand on my arm. 'Don't worry. It's endearing. While at the same time deeply dysfunctional.'

It was Ben's turn to laugh now. 'She's onto you,' he said. 'And she hasn't fled yet.'

We cracked our cookies, and Hayley pulled out her fortune. 'Never wrestle with a pig,' she read. 'You both get all dirty, and the pig likes it.'

'Hey, I get that one a bit,' I said, before I could stop myself. I was looking like a complete fortune-cookie gimp.

'I expect you get all of them a bit,' Ben said. He was holding his fortune in both hands, as if it was something that needed to be proclaimed rather than read. 'Every closed eye is not sleeping, and every open eye is not seeing.' Hayley went 'Oooh' and he said, 'I bet Josh gets that one all the time.'

He put the fortune down on the table. All around him there had been eyes that hadn't seen, people who hadn't worked out that his story wasn't right. I pulled the fortune out of my cookie and read it.

'A conclusion is simply the place where you got tired of thinking.' I'd had it a few days before. It was on the table at home, piled up with all the others like pick-up-sticks.

'Well, that's not you, is it?' he said to me. 'You'd never stop thinking.'

It was not exactly the in-joke that it must have sounded to Hayley. It was not about a long friendship marked by hapless rumination on my part.

'That's my job,' I said. 'Always thinking. You'd be surprised what turns up.'

Our bill arrived, folded on a white saucer. Ben picked it up and started to read it.

Hayley and I reached for our money and he held up his hand and said, 'Please, it's all work. I should have got that pizza earlier. You're my official friends for tomorrow's Who Weekly photoshoot, aren't you?' He looked over to Hayley. 'I hope Josh told you that. Anyway, Randalls still owes you from last week. Mister Park went home happy and Vince Duffy's deal's gone through smoothly.'

'Nothing to do with me,' she said. She still had her purse in her hand. 'I didn't play nudie pool with him.'

She pushed to try to pay her third, but he waved her attempt away and handed the bill back to the waiter with his credit card.

I pocketed my cookie fortune when we left, out of habit. Mini-Golf in Surfers was only a few blocks away, in the direction of Focus. We passed the mall and some restaurants that weren't busy, and shops piled high with a million toy koalas and racks of boomerangs.

'It's quiet,' Ben said, looking around. 'Even for out of season.'

I had forgotten how much time he must have spent at the Gold Coast when he was young, in his father's heyday. We were probably walking past buildings that his father had built, or financed in some precarious way. Kerry Harkin had made and lost fortunes on these streets. Ben's view of them could be like no one else's.

From a distance, it looked as though the Slingshot was firing right above the mini-golf, though it was in fact in the fun park behind it. A rider took off skyward in the seat, tethered by two elastic cables to towers at the sides. He flew up until the cables tightened and pulled him down again, and then he oscillated with ever decreasing amplitude until the ride was over and he was lowered to the ground. It was one of several carnival-style rides operating, though not with a big enough crowd to seem like a carnival.

Mini-Golf in Surfers had a small red-roofed 'club-house' that sold drinks and hired putters and balls. There were red plastic chairs and tables out the front, with the chairs arranged haphazardly as if they had just been vacated by people in a rush to putt. There was no sign of quirky themeing here, no gimmicks, but the course looked well-groomed, with its eighteen holes – blue fairways, green greens, burgundy trouble spots – laid out among wood chips, geometric topiary and water features.

'It's not as nutty,' Ben said, looking around. 'I think this is for your classy mini-golfer.'

Hayley took to it with less vigour this time, but still showed an admirable lack of purpose when it came to getting the ball in the hole.

'Hey, it's like a sock,' she said when we got to the third hole. 'It's laid out in the shape of a sock, with the hole down at the toe.'

Unfortunately there was a bonus slip of concrete in the middle of the foot part. My overambitious first shot hit it end-on and bounced back up the ankle.

'This is way better than last night,' Hayley said as I lined up my second. 'I went out with some girls from work on Sunday, so that started late and went later and they were buying rounds of cocktails. I don't usually drink cocktails. So I didn't feel like breakfast yesterday, or lunch, and then I had to take my nanna to bingo in the evening.' She watched the ball as it ran down the fairway, hitting the side first this time before glancing off the mid-foot concrete and finishing quite close to the hole. 'That was the family commitment I had and, trust me, it's a commitment. I do it every week. She waits at the front window with the blind open just a crack, and she calls me if I'm a minute late, in case I'm dead. Anyway, I must have been looking like crap – I was *feeling* like crap – because halfway through the bingo she snuck a bacon sandwich out of her handbag and passed it to me under the table.'

I walked over to the ball and tapped in. Ben played the hole in a neat two shots.

'Is that part of the deal every week? The emergency bacon sandwich?' I was two shots down to him already.

Hayley drove the ball to the heel of the sock, and it hit the concrete border at close to the perfect angle. It rattled around on its way into the foot and stopped a makeable distance from the hole.

'There's usually a sandwich,' she said. 'It's not always bacon.' She hit the putt too hard, but so straight that it dropped anyway. 'She grew up in the Depression. No way would she pay for a sandwich when you can make one at home from leftovers. The sandwich is normally for her. My crapness was the emergency. It was a one-off. In fact, I've got the job of taking her because I'm the only family member she could rely on to turn up every week. My mother went off on a bit of a tangent after she and my dad divorced. I think she decided she'd been missing out on something. I know I'm the one with the hair, but she wanted to be some kind of rock chick.'

'Which is a lot more interesting than some parents.' I was thinking of mine, and also realising that, if Hayley read from the back of a cereal box, I would probably pull up a seat.

'And I didn't mind it,' she said as Ben paced out the fourth, looking for tricks, 'but the awful bit to watch was the way she had to keep downgrading her expectations. She took friends along to hang out with bands. She wanted me to go, but there are limits. Plus I have

the thing that we refer to in my family as my "bar job",
so I don't get to go to a lot of bands, even without the
tempting offer of hanging out with the oldest groupies
in the room. She ended up for a while with a guy in his
fifties who filled in sometimes playing covers in a pub at
Stones Corner.'

Ben teed off, stroking the ball through a patch of
dark blue rough and setting up an easy second. He
continued to look good every time he played a shot. As
he sank the putt, Hayley put her ball down near the start
of the hole.

'One time she looked after his marijuana seedling,'
she said, as she lined up her shot in a perfunctory way.
'He thought the cops might be onto him. That's a quote.
She actually said "cops", and I'm sure she'd never said it
in her life before then. Always police.' Her ball clipped
a barrier and came off at a bad angle. 'She showed me
the seedling, as if it was wildly exciting.'

'My parents split up a while back,' Ben said. He was
leaning on a palm tree next to the green. 'My father
was such a shit. I used to stay there weekends and every
second Tuesday when I was still at school. He wasn't
there most of the time. And then Wife Number Two
wasn't there much of the time either.' He waited while
Hayley played her second shot. 'So it was just me,
feeding the tropical fish, drinking his gin and topping
the bottles up with water, pissing on his bonsai plants.
They've got these tiny leaves, but they're pretty bloody
hardy, I can tell you.'

Hayley laughed. Ben looked happy with himself,
pleased with his rebel pissing, and with eliciting the
laugh.

I had heard it before, of course, the boast about the bonsai plants, and I knew it was a fragment of the story. Ben had listened from another room to the exit conversations of his father's relationship with his mother. He had always avoided using the name of his father's second wife and, I realised, third, referring to them both only by number. I tried to recall the third wife's name from the newspaper article two months before, but I couldn't.

I could remember the house with the bonsai plants. It was a big place on acreage at Pullenvale, and it turned out to be leased by one of his companies. A few of us went there once when his father was away. 'Away' turned out to be Kerry Harkin trying to do a runner on his creditors. There was art on the wall, but there were no photographs of people or events and the decor seemed almost deliberately impersonal. There were plastic reeds set in jars of pale stones, an expensive but empty wooden magazine rack, a round white clock the size of a plate. It was as if the place had been hired, as if it was a function centre or a film set. I had seen Ben's own flat much more recently, though, and perhaps it was a look he preferred. It gave away nothing, betrayed none of the owner's tastes, or secrets.

'My mother got a new boyfriend not so long ago,' Hayley was saying. 'She asked me if I let men watch me on the toilet. I thought she was onto me about work, not that that happens there unless the Koreans are in town – I'm kidding – but she actually meant in relationships.' She was on the green now, and her fifth shot fell in the hole. 'There are some conversations you just don't want to have with your mother.' She lifted her ball out. 'Four or five?' she said to Ben, who had the scorecard.

'Four.'

He marked it down. I wasn't sure if the mistake was deliberate, or if he hadn't been counting.

I dropped my ball onto the ground and rolled it into place for my first shot.

'And *my* parents have a newsagency and a block of flats at the Sunshine Coast,' I said as I sized the shot up. 'Yep, that was as dull as I thought it'd sound.' There was one trick to the hole. Its middle third was diamond-shaped, with only a small opening at the far end where the sides of the diamond encroached on the fairway. 'Most Fridays they get to the surf club by six, and they don't mind claiming a senior's discount on the fish.'

Ben laughed. 'Well, they rock, obviously.'

'I'd kill for that kind of normality,' Hayley said, like someone who sensed it was a long way off. 'Well, not kill, but wound maliciously, maybe.'

I hit the ball and it passed perfectly through the narrow gap and came to a stop next to the hole.

'Nice one,' Ben said. He looked around, at the holes ahead of us, his putter swinging in his hand. 'I miss the dinosaurs. This is good, but it's not the same.'

★ ★ ★

IN THE SPILL OF LIGHT from the apartment blocks, the broken waves were dimly visible from the balcony as they spread themselves across the sand and then withdrew. I heard Ben's bedroom door shut. He was gone for the night. Hayley was fetching the wine from the fridge and my heart was clattering along like a train on a wooden bridge.

I tried to convince myself that the next ten minutes, or hour, or this night weren't the most important of my life. It was a feeling I'd had before – the feeling that a great and possibly critical moment was upon me – and it had usually not gone well. I looked out to sea and concentrated on the freighters making their slow progress up and down the coast. I pictured men with shovels hurling coal into furnaces. I think the image came from a movie, just before the U-boat's first torpedo hit them amidships. It was probably all done with one guy pushing a button now.

'You're looking very serious,' Hayley said as she stepped outside.

'Don't let me do that,' I told her. 'It all goes wrong when I get serious.'

'Is that an idea you got from Ben?'

Maybe it was. 'I don't know. I seemed to manage to get it wrong often enough without him in England for a few years.'

'Well, England's England,' she said. 'This is here. And this is my last glass of wine.' She looked down as she poured, measuring it out. 'I'm already having cold-bacon-sandwich flashbacks.'

She set the bottle on the table and took a sip from her glass. She looked out at the ocean, at the line of ships I'd been watching.

'Ben's charming, don't you think?' I couldn't quite get him out of my head, even though he'd gone to his room.

'I guess.' She sounded non-committal. 'I guess people could find him that way. It was the most charming pissing-on-bonsai story that I've heard. But, you know, bonsai – I was never really into it.'

'But he is our nation's hero . . .'

'Hmmm.' She took a bigger mouthful of wine. She turned away from the slow transit of the ships to face me again. 'I'm much more drawn to conflicted serious types. Heroism's so . . . unequivocal.'

For a line like that, I wanted her even more. I thought we would kiss then. I sensed we were about to, that we were both starting to move, but she stepped back. She dragged a plastic chair around, and sat in it.

'I think I scare men away sometimes,' she said. 'Sometimes it's my job, sometimes it's the speed I'm ready to move. If something's right, it's right. If it's all you think about . . .'

I moved over to the railing and leaned against it with my elbows hooked over it, facing her. My foot was next to the leg of her chair, my leg next to her leg.

'I went out with a guy once . . .' She made it sound as if it was a passing thought and perhaps not directed at me. 'This isn't so long ago. I think he didn't cope with my job and all of a sudden he stopped calling. That's a guy thing – and it's not a good one – to just stop calling. Weeks later I got an email – a group email to about fifty people – that said something like "Tomorrow I am starting the building of some retaining walls and need to borrow a couple of sawhorses. Anyone have them available for a loaner?"'

'That's intimate,' I said. I called too often and for too long. That had been my problem. With the exception of Eloise, I called until all hope had been wrung out of relationships and I was told not to call. I wanted to tell Hayley I didn't think I would ever ask people for sawhorses in my life.

'It's clear enough. A few weeks later I got one from him – another group email, and the last one I got – about sitting and lifting your right foot and moving it in clockwise circles, then drawing the number six in the air with your right hand. It makes your foot change direction and there's nothing you can do about it.' She laughed. 'Maybe if I'd had sawhorses, it would all have been different.'

I picked up another chair, and set it down beside her.

'Don't they have one for two people?' she said. 'What's that about?' She pulled the chair closer, so that its arm was lined up right next to hers.

'Well, who knows what might go on?'

'Exactly.'

I sat down. Her hand was still on the arm of my chair. Again, I was about to make the move. The signals were there, surely.

'I had a guy once at the club,' she said, lifting her hand and then wondering where to put it. 'I have no idea why I need to tell you this, but I had a guy once who gave me a thousand dollars to, well, kind of, fuck my feet.'

I couldn't be certain what was showing on my face. My head was nodding. 'Both feet or . . . or just the one?'

A man had fucked her feet. I didn't live in that world. I didn't even know what it meant.

'First he gave me fifty bucks to take off my shoes,'

she said. She sounded uneasy about going into the details. 'Which was no big deal. Then he wanted to massage my feet, and I'm not really into that, being paid for that, any touching, so we had to have a talk. Which was when he made the big offer. It was the start of the year. I had a lot of textbooks to buy. And I have to pay my own way through uni. I'm not some trustafarian with a river of family money coming in. That won't surprise you after what I've said about my parents. And it didn't even seem sexual, the foot thing. It was actually kind of . . . abstract. It was both feet. Between both feet.'

'So, it was your arches then.'

I had no idea why I was clarifying a point about the technicalities. I was trying to sound as if everything was normal. I was focusing on the sound of normal. Nothing was normal. A fetishist had fucked her feet. But I didn't think it mattered, not really. I had a smallish unremarkable life to compare it with and, it turned out, an abnormal relationship with fortune cookies. Other people's horizons were wider than mine. Some made money from their feet.

'Yeah, I think it was,' she said. She had great arches. She had one foot up on the lower railing and her legs were crossed at the ankles. I had flat feet. I had always been impressed by arches. And yet had never thought to have sex with them. 'It was. Fifty bucks for a look, a thousand for . . . more. I made him wear a condom and told him he'd pay double if I got any stuff on me. Legislatively I'm not sure where it stands. There's a real risk it's prostitution. It's not dancing, obviously.'

A gust of wind blew by, pulling the lounge-room curtains out through the open sliding door and onto the balcony, then dropping them again. We both turned and looked inside, but there was no other sign of movement.

'Tell me if that's too appalling,' she said.

'It's . . . very abstract.'

She waited for more. I had a crowd of things to say in my head, and they were blocking the exits.

'Here's where I stand,' she said when she had waited long enough. 'I don't have sex with people for money. I don't have any great moral objection to it, but it's about keeping some things so that they can happen when I actually want them to. I'll never want anyone to fuck my feet, so that seemed okay. At the time.' Her hand was on my arm. She didn't even seem to know. 'You're appalled, aren't you?'

'No. I . . .'

'There's worse than that out there.'

I was back with the kids who thought babies appeared under cabbages. There was a whole world of sexual practice in which feet were only the entrée and my education cut out early.

'I'm not even beginning to be appalled,' I told her. 'I can't match the foot story, but I want you so badly I am trying not to tell you in case you run away. That's all that's in my head.' It was a shock to hear it myself, a shock for it to be out, a dive from the ten-metre tower to blue water, hard as glass. I had met her in the doldrums, in a compromised life made up of bills and facile blogs and ambitions I had yet to come close to realising. 'You had me at "Mark Felt".'

(228)

She took a breath in. She took my face in her hands. She moved so that her face was inches in front of mine and she dropped her voice to a whisper and said, 'Okay, kiss me. Kiss me the way people kiss in a world where no money changes hands and they just have to do it.'

★ ★ ★

IT WAS LIKE CASABLANCA, that line. Like a line right out of a classic movie from the forties. But no one had to get on a plane and leave forever as the world fell into a long and terrible war. I kissed her, she kissed me, Ben kept his door closed.

'Let's go to your room,' she said after a while.

We ended up in hers, since I had to confess I'd taken the kids' room and had two single beds. We shut the sliding balcony door as quietly as possible and moved to her room like cat burglers. Moonlight came in through the glass doors on the far side and fell across the bed.

'I've got to tell you, I didn't bring anything for this.' My hands were on the warm skin of her back. She was pulling my shirt off and we were crab-walking towards the bed. Every spare second for six days had been spent dreaming up this moment, then telling myself it would never happen. 'I didn't want to make assumptions. Or look like I'd made assumptions.'

'So analytical,' she said. 'So excessively analytical.' She bent down, reached into her bag and rummaged around in the dark. She stood up with a strip of about ten condoms in her hand. 'So, now I look like I've made assumptions?'

'If the assumption is that we'll get through all those, well, I think I'm in love with your assumption. Or at least very serious like. And I'll definitely give it my best shot.'

She pushed me onto the bed and climbed on top of me. She whipped my chest with her string of condom packets, and laughed.

Then she said, 'Hang on a second.' She turned them over and looked at them closely in the moonlight. 'Just checking the expiry date. It's been a while.' She nodded and tore one from the end of the strip. 'I think we're good to go.'

★ ★ ★

THE LIGHT WOKE ME. Dawn was making its way into the sky ahead of the sun. Hayley was stretched out under the white sheet, her hair a mess on the pillow. Her shoulders were bare and one leg had kicked beyond the sheet. She had fine arches.

I willed her to wake. She didn't.

Around two hours later I was in a dream that started to smell like toast and sound like a kitchen. Ben was making breakfast. I listened to him, to how quiet he was trying to be.

Hayley had one eye open when I turned her way. She reached out and put her hand on my cheek.

'What kind of effort was that?' she said, her voice still full of sleep. 'I think I've still got at least seven of them left.'

'I made another assumption,' I told her. 'I assumed I didn't just have last night.'

'All right,' she said. Her eye sagged closed again. 'That works.' She rolled onto her back. 'Hungry now . . .'

I leaned over and kissed her on the mouth. Ben was stirring coffee. He was trying not to hit the sides of the cup with the spoon but failing every so often and sending out an arrhythmic tinging sound.

'Maybe he could just sit on the corner of the bed to drink it?' Hayley said. She pulled her right arm out from under the sheet and wrapped it around me. 'I'm sorry, he's your friend. Or some kind of friend, anyway.' She didn't wait for me to clarify. I didn't want to. 'I've got to go to the bathroom.'

She lifted her head off the pillow, kissed me again quickly, then slid out of bed.

The clothes from the night before were on the floor, and I picked them up and put them on. Ben was standing at the counter in the kitchen when I opened the bedroom door. He was holding a piece of toast, about to eat it.

'Lucky we got that upgrade to a three-bedroom place,' he said.

He had the TV on. He was watching a breakfast show, but he had it muted. Sports results were crawling across the bottom of the screen. The clock in the corner said it was eight fifty-five.

'So, you're on in an hour.' I was going to ignore his remark. Who Weekly was booked in for ten.

The interview had been right out of my head. I felt like I'd stumbled back in from another country, and meanwhile the lie had been festering away and I still had to answer to it.

I could hear Hayley in the en-suite shower. I walked

into the kitchen and poured myself a bowl of cereal. Ben leaned against the counter, eating toast.

'This is me and my friends playing mini-golf, yeah?' he said.

'Among other things. You and the suit and the medal, maybe a balcony shot, maybe the beach. And an interview. A sit-down interview, which they will probably record.' I could hear the work script starting to take shape. I was listening to the water fall in the shower, imagining Hayley in there, wanting to be with her, to have my hands on her wet body. 'Don't be freaked out by the recording. It's so they can quote you properly. It's about accuracy, not about catching you out.' I went to the fridge for the milk. 'That's the standard spiel, by the way. I tell it to everyone. People get paranoid sometimes when journalists record. So make sure you have a good story to tell, a good consistent story.' The fridge door swung shut. He was looking at me as if he somehow had the better of me, now that I was colluding. 'Or alternatively confess the whole thing, the whole big lie. What the hell. Clear your fucking conscience.'

I was surprised by how angry I had become, and so was he.

'This is the second-last one,' he said, steadily. 'Then it's all over.'

'Yeah.'

I picked up the TV remote from the counter and unmuted the sound. They were doing two minutes of news headlines at the close of the show.

We were both sitting eating breakfast when Hayley came out of the bedroom in a skirt and singlet top, her hair still wet, asking if we had any herbal tea. Ben was flicking through cable sports channels.

'Hey, stunning day outside,' she said, before either of us could give her an answer about the tea.

My phone rang. It was the Who reporter, calling from a cab at Coolangatta airport. Her flight had landed ahead of schedule and she was checking that it was okay to come early.

I followed Hayley into the kitchen. I thought I had seen some tea bags in the pantry.

'Let me make it for you,' I said to her. 'If I can find the bags.'

Ben settled on baseball, which I had never known him to like, and turned up the volume. There was no herbal tea, but Hayley said she'd make do with regular. I put the kettle on as she poured her cereal. I saw her look at Ben as he stared at the TV screen, and then past him and out at the tall buildings and the sky. I put my hand on her back and she took it and drew my arm around her.

'I'm going to have a shower,' Ben said without turning around.

I stepped away from Hayley as he got up. It was an instinctive move. Maybe I wanted her — whatever I had with her — to be his business as little as possible.

He fetched a towel from his bedroom, and some fresh clothes.

'So, your suit's ready?' I was trying to recall my notes, and the photoshoot plans I'd talked through with Who.

He looked at me, some smartarse remark about to come out. He kept it back. 'Yeah. It's on the bed. How's this shirt? Not to go with the suit obviously . . .'

He shook it out and held it up for me to see. It was a white T-shirt with rows of old cassettes on it, mock-up mix tapes from the eighties.

'Yeah, that's good. Start with that and we may well go back to it for the casual shots later. The mini-golf. Maybe just go with that and your three-quarter pants for now. That'll be good for the interview. Not too lawyerish. Everyman. Stylish everyman having some down time.'

'Cool,' he said, and took the shirt with him into the bathroom.

'You guys,' Hayley said when the door was shut. 'I'm not used to this. You dress him now?'

'Not physically. I want him ready. I have to get him ready. And he needs to be thinking only about the interview.' The story he would tell, the lie. 'It's my job to think about everything else, and I know more about what their photo plans are than he does. You drip-feed the talent. He gets it all on a need-to-know basis.' I heard the shower start. 'But I want to forget all about him and his wardrobe for the next few minutes.'

She was poised to pour milk on her cereal. She put the bottle down, put her arms around my neck and kissed me for as long as we could hear water running. The shower finished with a clunk. Hayley's cheeks and chin were blotchy. I didn't want to let her go.

'I'm next in the shower, I think,' I said to her. 'The journo'll be here soon.'

'You know your shirt's inside out, don't you?' she said.

She poured her milk and I went to the en suite.

I realised I needed to shave as well. I tried to recall the pieces of Aimee Duroux's that I had read. She would want some details and some backstory, but the lie would hold. Unless Ben blew it, in which case he would be on his own.

Once I was dressed, I rinsed some grapes, cut them into bunches and put them on a platter with some cherries. I went over Ben's wardrobe choices and told him not to do much with his hair, since there would probably be a make-up person with the photographer.

'So you're talking make-up now? Clothes, and now hair and make-up?' Hayley had come out of the bedroom wearing a bikini and a baggy T-shirt and holding a beach towel. 'If I come back from the pool and you guys are a couple, it's going to be a real kick in the guts for my self-esteem.'

'He's not my type,' Ben said, and I realised I had no clear idea what his type was. If it hadn't been for Eloise, I wouldn't be certain that he was sexual at all. He lived a neat finicky life, and I saw no room in it for anyone, no crack or gap anyone might fill.

'Well, in that case, have a good interview.' She came towards me, took my hand and kissed me in an uncomplicated way. There was an old intimacy to it that I liked. We had known each other for less than a week.

'Get a room,' Ben said, his hand up to his mouth, like a heckler. 'Better still, get three for the price of two, and then don't use one.'

Hayley took a step towards the door, and then stopped. 'Who says we haven't used them all? You weren't exactly quick in the shower this morning. Maybe we snuck into your room then.'

With that, she folded her towel over her arm and left for the pool.

'You didn't . . .' Ben said, still not certain.

'Allow me just a little mystery.'

The intercom buzzed. It was Aimee Duroux. I pressed the button to let her in and I waited for her by the door. Ben hovered nearby until I told him hovering was unbecoming. He walked out to the balcony and stared at the sea. I assumed he was rehearsing his story.

Aimee Duroux had long blonde hair and blue eyes and impractical shoes that might have been Jimmy Choos. They had high narrow teetering heels but she managed them well enough. She shook my hand and told me it had been years since she had been to the Gold Coast, this part of the Gold Coast anyway.

'I've been to a couple of premieres at Movie World,' she said. 'Which is . . . where? That way?' She pointed vaguely west. 'I flew into Brisbane for those, though.'

She was wearing tinted contact lenses. That was where the blue of her eyes came from, why it was so vivid. She looked past me, through the living area to the bright sky and the sea, and to Ben on the balcony. He happened to turn then, and he smiled and waved, almost as if he knew her. He walked inside and crossed the room to shake her hand.

'I thought I saw some whales out there,' he said. 'But I think it's the wrong time of year.'

He took her onto the balcony to look for them. I watched him point to the southeast as Aimee held her hand up to her eyes to block the sun. I took the platter of grapes and cherries out, and set it on the table. Ben was telling a story about swimming with dolphins. I had never heard it from him before. I wondered if it was someone else's, and he had seen it on TV or read it in a magazine.

'That would have been amazing,' she was saying.

I asked if they would like drinks and Ben said, 'A mineral water would be good.'

Aimee tucked some stray hair back into place. The breeze was strong on the balcony. 'Yeah, that'd be lovely, thanks, Josh.' Her eyes hardly left Ben.

I went back into the kitchen, put ice into two glasses and filled them with mineral water. I could hear Aimee laughing at something Ben had said. As I took the drinks out to the balcony she was reaching into her bag for her recorder and checking with him that it was okay to use it.

I set their glasses down on the table next to the fruit and told them I would leave them to it. As I turned to go back inside, I glanced down over the edge of the balcony to the swimming pool far below. Hayley had it all to herself, and she was swimming with a casual freestyle stroke along one of its two black lines.

I went inside and out another door, and I watched her from a different part of the balcony, her bright pale body in her yellow bikini, rocking from side to side with the stroke and with her breathing, the V of the waves moving out from her and lapping against the sides of the pool. She stopped at the end, turned and looked up. She saw me and waved.

I could hear voices from around the corner, but not the words. Aimee laughed again. Ben's charm had arrived like an invasion, with sensitive-guy whale-and-dolphin stories and me cast as his lumpen manservant. It was, I told myself, part of the job. It was the same as fetching cups of tea in Manchester or fruitcake in Nottingham, all of it breaking down the formality, making it more like a chat between two friends, less like a well-dressed interrogation. It was different only because it was Ben, different because his performance was so good.

Hayley pushed off on another lap, and I went back inside. I sat on a sofa within range of the interview, pretending to read a magazine.

Ben stumbled over something. They were talking about the siege. It sounded like a natural stumble, though, a tough part of a painful recollection. Rob Mueller had entered the building.

I went to the fridge for the bottle of mineral water, and took it out to the balcony. I wondered how crazy Rob Mueller had been, and who had heard his remarks about God.

'So tell me,' Aimee was saying. 'What made you move? What happened in that actual moment? Mueller was ready to kill Frank . . .'

I topped up her glass, then his.

'Well . . .' He looked at the bottle as I poured.

'I'm sorry. This can't be easy for you,' she said. She had a pen in her hand. She had been making notes as well as recording. She was leaning forward, trying to catch Ben's eye.

'Yeah . . . I don't know precisely what happened. I just knew that was the moment. I had to go for him then, or Frank would be dead.' He was frowning. He put both hands up to his forehead and massaged it.

'Are you having flashbacks right now?' It was honest

concern. She put her pen down. 'I've interviewed people who have been through trauma before.'

'Um, I don't know.' Ben picked up his glass of mineral water and took a mouthful. 'So, I went for him, and we hit the far wall and . . .' He stopped. He looked inside, and then looked at me. 'Is that my mobile? Could you go and check if that's my mobile?'

There was no sound, other than the breeze and the distant hum of life far below on the ground.

'Okay. No problem.'

Aimee was watching the interaction. Ben was traumatised and I was helping him through. I was sure that was what she saw — a storybook wounded hero who would rather swim with dolphins but who had risen at the moment of greatest danger and risked his life to save others. And here he was, his head still full of damage, still ringing with it, literally.

He wanted me gone, and he had managed it masterfully. I left to check his non-ringing phone. He would give her everything she needed about the moment on which his bravery pivoted, the instincts that drove him forward, the air-splitting crash of the gun, the shock of the blood, brain, bone, the tinnitus, the deafness. She would be completely convinced.

I went into his room, noted the silent phone on the bedside table and took my time going back out to the balcony. The story had reached the ambulance by then, and the crowding cameras of the TV news.

'I've seen photos of that,' Aimee said. I was ashamed for Ben that her empathy was so real. 'Josh sent me some and I've seen a few others as well.'

They both looked up as I got to the door.

'It was just Frank,' I told Ben. 'He wanted to check how you were going.'

If he was surprised, he didn't show it.

'I didn't even hear it,' Aimee said. She seemed relieved that there had been a call. 'Must be the wind out here. It blocks out a lot of noise. I hope we've been recording all right.' Her phone rang and she checked the number. 'Photographer,' she said, taking the call.

Down below, Hayley was standing by the pool with her towel around her shoulders. She was shaking water out of her ears.

Aimee stood up and walked to the far end of the balcony, talking into the phone. She looked over the edge. 'Yeah, I can see you from here. You're the white van, yeah?'

'Just about finished, I reckon,' Ben said to me. 'I could do with some more of that mineral water, though. Thirsty work out here.' He held up his empty glass.

'Yeah, well, we can't have you running to the toilet in the middle of the photoshoot.' I didn't take the glass. 'Got to watch that.'

Aimee closed her phone. 'Josh, would it be okay if you went down and met Richard? He's got an assistant but they've got a lot of stuff. It could really help if they had someone to hold open lift doors, and things. Just to make sure they make it here intact. They could start setting up while Ben and I finish off.'

Ben put the glass down, as though it had never mattered. He was smiling, waiting for me to move. As long as I was somebody's slave, my place in the universe was right.

The photographer had backed his van up to the foyer

door, and he and his assistant were unloading when I got there. I found two luggage trolleys and we piled them high with lights and screens, and boxes that looked like guitar amps.

The assistant and I took the first lift up with one trolley. Her name was Abi and she was studying photography. This was work experience. She told me she would get credit for it as part of her course.

'So, does Ben live here, or . . .?' she said as the lift passed the lower floors without stopping.

'No. He lives in Brisbane. This is a holiday. Just a few days.' The lift shook and one of the lights on the trolley rocked forward. I instinctively put my hand on it, though it was going nowhere.

'I saw him on the news on Monday. He's, what, Chinese? I wouldn't have brought the right make-up range if I hadn't seen the news. Ben Parkin, wasn't it? You're not thinking Chinese.'

'Japanese. His mother.' I didn't correct the surname.

The door to the apartment was wedged open, and Hayley was in the living area talking to Aimee.

'Josh has had us out testing the mini-golf options,' she was saying. She was still wrapped in her towel.

The living area was soon a mess of cables and boxes. Abi worked on Ben's make-up while Richard, Aimee and I talked through the plans. I showed them the medal pamphlet so there would be no doubt about how Ben's Star of Courage had to be treated. We could do medal shots and we could do mini-golf shots, but we wouldn't do medal-and-mini-golf shots.

Ben went to change into his suit, and Richard hooked a long roll of white paper onto a high stand and pulled the end of it to the floor. He got down on his knees, pulled out another metre or two and laid it out across the carpet. He asked me to stand on it while Abi arranged lights around me, and silver umbrellas, and he set up his camera.

'Instant studio,' he said. The paper met the floor in a curve and made the perfect blank backdrop. He took a picture and his flash popped. 'Yep,' he said as he checked the image. 'Looking good.'

Ben came out with his shoes in his hands and his Star of Courage on his jacket.

'Great,' Richard said when he saw him. 'This'll be great.'

Ben was looking at the stage that had been built for him while he had been out of the room. The white paper glowed under the lights. He stopped, as if he wasn't certain or needed to check something.

'Right in the middle,' Richard said. 'Abs?'

Abi moved him into position, tugged at his lapels, and made sure the star was sitting properly. She was arranging him like a shop-window dummy, and he didn't know how to take it. I wasn't sure how often people touched him, other than to shake his hand.

'Hang on a second,' she said, and she flicked at his hair. It wouldn't stay where she wanted it to, so she came back with a blast of spray.

'You look good, Ben,' Aimee said. 'Really good.' She was sitting with her legs crossed, clicking her pen in and out.

'Abs, if you could get the flekkie and put a bit more light on his left side . . .' Richard said as he looked through the camera.

Abi unzipped a bag, popped out a big silver disc and tried to catch the light with it.

Ben was stiff at first, but Richard loosened him up. He kept him talking, then got him laughing. He kept telling him how well he was doing, then asking for small changes. The flash popped and popped until Ben was more than used to it.

'That's it, that's it,' Richard said. 'That's beautiful. Okay, Ben, now smile. Give us that smile you were doing before. The . . . wistful one.'

'Like this?' Ben had no recollection of wistful, and did what he could.

'Yep, yep.' Richard's head was down over the camera, the flash was popping. 'A little bit more wistful . . . Beautiful.' He stood up, stepped back. 'Josh, is it okay if we lose the tie? Is that okay with the star protocol?'

'I think we could lose the tie. People do suits without ties.'

The tie came off, and Richard took a dozen more shots.

'Okay, those'll be great. Take a break. Step away from the lights. Cool down.' Richard was looking at his camera, scrolling through the images with his thumb. 'Next up I think we'll do some with you holding the medals in the presentation case. Aimee? That's right, isn't it? You want some like that?'

'Yeah.' Aimee watched Ben take his jacket off.

'But respectful of the medal again.' I was always the nag in these situations. 'Any time it's in shot we've got to think about that.'

'Of course, yeah,' she said, and laughed. 'I suppose we'd better keep the shirt on then. Damn the star protocol. Maybe with the jacket and tie off, and some kind of close-up?'

'If it was up to *me* the shirt'd be off,' Ben said. He fanned air across his face. 'You sweat a lot under those lights.'

'Maybe Josh could get you a drink?' she said, not even looking at me.

★ ★ ★

WHEN WE GOT TO King Tutt's, Richard decided he liked the light outside. It was overcast by then, but bright. He walked around taking readings with his meter, and chose a hole on the African jungle course. He crouched at the far end of the green, looking back up the slope to the tee, checking out the surroundings, framing the shot.

'Okay,' he said. 'Okay, this is good. If we could have Ben at the tee, with the friends in shot . . .' He had lost our names somewhere between Focus and King Tutt's. Hayley and I were the chorus. 'And, Aimee, if you could take two steps to the left and bend that branch down a bit so that it comes into shot, and Abs over to the right here with the flekkie . . .'

Two steps to the left put Aimee off the course. She looked at the spot where she was supposed to stand, as if looking might change it for the better. She took her Jimmy Choos off, lined them up on the edge of the Astroturf and stepped barefoot onto the wood chips.

Ben placed the ball and looked ahead towards the hole, lining up his shot. He was back in the T-shirt, three-quarter pants and slides.

'Just lean on your putters, guys,' Richard said to Hayley and me. 'Look casual, but also kind of impressed by Ben's shot. Fascinated by it.'

'Fascinated,' Hayley said, just to me. She gave me a look of mock fascination. She was wearing a polka-dot sundress. Back at the apartment, Richard had called it perfect.

Richard moved Ben a centimetre or two, redirected the light, asked Aimee to dip her palm frond a little further. He took a step back, to the edge of a water feature on a different hole, and he crouched again.

'All right, this is it, I reckon,' he said, looking down at the image on the back of his camera. 'Okay, Ben, what I want you to do is keep your body steady, and just putt the ball into the hole. I'll keep shooting all the way in. Sound okay? And if you could not drill it at the hole, that'd be good. I'd like to get about ten shots in. So, try to hit it so that it just drops in . . . Allowing for the slope of course.'

Aimee laughed. 'You didn't expect putting skills would be quite so important for this, did you?'

'You should have seen me on the Jurassic,' he said, like an old golfer recalling a mythical round from his youth. 'I tore it up.' He lined up the shot as she laughed again. 'Deepest darkest Africa? Somehow it's not so easy.'

'Ready when you are,' Richard said. 'And, Aimee, if you could hold the branch still . . .'

'Sorry,' she said, looking at Ben as though they had

both just been naughty. I couldn't see the look he gave her in return.

He putted, and he putted perfectly. He swung gracefully and the ball seemed to glide along the surface, picking up speed as it ran down the slope. It moved in an arc with the contour of the course, swung down from a bank and plopped into the hole.

Aimee let go of the branch and applauded.

Richard flicked through the images, checking them, and then showed the sequence to Ben and Aimee. She said they were exactly what she wanted. They were perfect. Richard, being a photographer, took twenty or thirty more photos of us just to be certain.

Aimee confirmed times for the next day for the brief phone interviews she needed with Frank and Max and then she said, 'You. I've got to get a quote or two from you as a friend.' She pulled out her notepad and clicked her pen. 'You've been friends since uni, yeah? Is this the kind of thing you would have imagined Ben doing?'

We had finished on the green, with Ben holing a short putt. It had been a tight shot, so I was close enough to touch him. He started bouncing an orange golf ball on the head of his putter, trying to keep it in the air. Friends since uni – had he told her that, or had I, when I was lining up the interview? Ben's eyes were on the bouncing golf ball. He started to move away, but the ball caught the edge of the putter and dropped into the wood chips.

'What he did was exactly the kind of thing I would have imagined him doing, in the circumstances,' I told Aimee. Lying, hiding something – exactly the kind of thing.

'Can you say any more about it? Anything particular about the siege?' She wanted a lie from me too, to put in print along with all the others.

'I was out of the country when it happened, but I've read the reports and it was obviously a harrowing experience. I think I'd just hide in a corner.' I wanted Ben to look at me, but he wouldn't.

'Good,' she said, writing it out longhand. 'That's good.'

She slipped her Jimmy Choos back on and instantly grew taller. She shook my hand and thanked me.

'This'll run the week after next,' she said, mainly to Ben. 'I think we'll get a great response.'

'We're off,' Richard said. He had a bag over his shoulder and his camera in his hand. Abi was taking a shortcut through the course with the lights. 'Nice one, that action sequence. Magic. Hope they use it.'

He followed Abi over a bridge and past a crocodile, in the direction of the car park. Aimee was already on the phone, calling for a cab.

'King Tutt's Putt Putt,' she said in the clear tone needed for voice-recognition software. *'King Tutt's Putt Putt.'* Her ankle buckled as her heel landed on the edge of a fairway ridge, but she corrected and kept walking.

'My vote is we play,' Ben said. He was putting his orange golf ball repetitively against a log that marked the edge of the Astroturf. 'We haven't done this one before.'

He led us back to the beginning of the course so that we could play the whole thing, and he decided that Hayley would go first.

'I reckon that went well,' he said to me as she played her tee shot. 'We should do all right with that piece. She seemed to like me.'

'I don't know if *like* is the word.' I couldn't let it go. I wanted to, but I couldn't. 'I'm not sure all that outrageous flirting of yours was such a good strategy.'

'I wasn't flirting.' He said it condescendingly, as if I wouldn't know enough to recognise it anyway. 'And she was the one who wanted me to get my shirt off.'

Hayley putted hard at the hole, and missed.

Ben tapped his putter against the side of his shoe. 'I thought the way I handled it would work well for the story. It was all about rapport. Remember rapport?'

'It wasn't rapport if she thought it was sleazy. Don't do it with Australian Story, okay?'

'All right, boys.' Hayley stepped towards us and waved her putter between us. 'Play nice. I didn't see the interview, but I've seen all those supermodel shows and no one oiled Ben's pecs, so I think it'll be okay. Now, you two can fight it out in some manly way to see who goes second. And whoever's scoring can put me down for a two.'

'How many did it take you?' I was sure it hadn't been two.

'Four, but you weren't paying attention, so I'll take a two. Except we don't have a scorecard, do we?' Abi had gone inside for balls and putters while Richard had checked the light. A scorecard hadn't been on the props list. 'I'll go get one, since I know you'll both want it to be a competition. And while I'm gone you can wrestle, or play the hole, whatever suits you.'

She handed me her club and ball, and Ben and I both

watched her walk past the stern mock-sandstone statues and plastic tables and into the building.

'Go ahead,' he said, pointing towards the tee-off circle with his putter. 'After you.'

I walked over, took a look in the direction of the hole and placed my ball. I worked out where I wanted to hit it, and brought the club head back. He *had* flirted with Aimee. I was in no doubt about that. And he had milked his story for all it was worth, choked on the moment of tragedy in a way that looked unquestionably real. Flashbacks, she had thought, as his eyes glazed over and he faced down his demons once again.

I stood up straight. 'Why did Frank nominate you for the medal?'

Ben looked over to the entrance, but Hayley was nowhere to be seen. 'This is nearly over.'

'Yeah, but why? When it wasn't true.'

'I don't know. I've told you that. He got hit on the head. Maybe it's exactly how he recalls it.' In its own way, it was now as practised as the flashbacks.

'That's all you've got? Still? And somehow by the next day he was recalling it in *exactly* the way that would make sure you'd end up with this country's second-highest decoration for courage. I've seen where the wording came from. I've found it. I know this story's rotten.'

He shrugged. I stepped away from the ball.

'I'm playing if you're not,' he said, moving past me.

He tapped my ball aside, placed his own on the circle and mis-hit it. It went off at an angle and rattled from one side to the other. It didn't make it halfway to the hole.

'Was it Frank who stopped them getting evidence, who stopped them getting your shirt? Who stopped them from taking it and showing it had no gunshot residue?'

'There was no . . .' He looked down at his grip on the putter, and adjusted it. 'I don't know. I honestly don't know about that. I got this kind of smock at the hospital and they put my stuff in a bag.'

I waited for more, for the bag to be explained. It was plausible that the hospital staff had done what he had said, but I wasn't inclined to believe any of it.

'I think I threw it away,' he said. 'I don't know. You can't expect me to remember that day as clearly as you'd like me to.' He walked down to where his ball lay, took a step off the course and into the wood chips and played an acceptable second shot.

'What the fuck is going on?'

As I said it, Hayley came out of the building, a score-card in one hand and a pencil stub in the other. She saw us watching her and she stopped to mime the writing of a two on the card.

'What's going on?' Ben spun the putter in his hand. 'I'm about to play my third. This hasn't been my hole.'

★ ★ ★

IT SEEMED THEN that I would get no more truth out of Ben. Predictably, he was a few shots up at the end. I was never going to beat him.

That evening was the warmest of the week as we set out from Focus looking for dinner. We had no plan, but Ben told us he felt like Italian. He found a Vintage Cellars that sold chianti and bought two bottles of it, carrying them along the street in brown paper bags, one in each hand.

Hayley put her arm around me. I didn't want her stripping again at the end of the week. It was the first time I'd had that thought, and I kept it to myself. I wasn't so concerned with the job itself, I just wanted her in my flat. My post-Ben life was scheduled to start on Friday evening and I wanted to spend it with her, not alone with bad TV and a box of fortune cookies, scrolling through blog responses and adding a line here and there.

'Perfect,' Ben said when we came upon a place where the waiters were arguing in Italian and the walls featured paint-by-numbers murals of the Tuscan countryside. There was a strong, enticing smell of frying garlic. 'Now, let's get pissed.'

I hadn't realised that had been on the agenda, but he said it was our last night at the coast and his big interview was done. He was over the hump now. He drank his first glass like cordial while we waited for bread, and then he drank a second. He announced that he was going to the bathroom and his toe clipped the leg of an empty chair on the way. He stumbled and almost pulled the chair over.

'You should challenge him to eighteen holes now,' Hayley said. 'I wouldn't have guessed today was so stressful for him.'

'Exactly. You weren't supposed to guess.' Down a corridor, the bathroom door slammed. 'He can be quite convincing.'

Ben refilled his glass as soon as he was back with us. He thanked me for everything I had done, he thanked Hayley and he raised his glass and toasted us both.

He asked Hayley about her Law degree, and if there were any particular areas that interested her. He said Randall Hood Beckett was expanding its commercial practice. He seemed to be implying that there might be something there for her, but he never specifically said it.

'Josh, Josh, Josh,' he said. 'One day you'll be like one of those Watergate reporters. You've got a nose for it. For other people's business.'

He put it as if he was being collegiate, but he wasn't. He raised his glass again. It was another toast, perhaps to me and my distant brilliant future, or my nose. I couldn't tell if he was genuinely as drunk as he seemed, or if it was an act that would give him permission to say things he otherwise might not.

The restaurant forgot our bread, but the mains were large serves when they came. Ben started talking about the Silver Spur and my behind-the-scenes tour. He said it sounded fascinating.

I told him that maybe Hayley didn't want to be grilled about work over dinner, but she said, 'It was okay to talk about law. Is it not okay to talk about this?'

'No, that's not . . .' I wanted to fix what I'd said. She didn't sound happy with me. 'It's not about the job itself.' It was about the gun. I was convinced he was about to mention it, to blurt that secret out with diners all around us. 'This is time off from work. I just thought it'd be like me having to go through the minute details of blogging.'

'But not much,' Ben said, before turning back to

Hayley, his half-full wineglass in his hand. 'So how does it work? How do you move between the backstage bit and the public area? You can't see anything connecting the two when you're in the club. It's as if you magically appear.'

'Well, from the stage is one way,' Hayley said. I tried to remember the other doors that she had shown me. 'But that's only if you're dancing. Or cleaning the stage, I guess. Like, if you're wiping up cream. Not that we use any actual dairy products, since it's a real hassle for the cleaning, even if it is great for your skin. There's also a door behind the bar and one next to the entrance to the fantasy room. It's behind a curtain. None of them are obvious inside the club. Unless the lights are all on and the curtains are back, which they never are when it's open.'

'I really wouldn't have thought you had a gym and a solarium and a sauna behind there.'

'It's not the operation people think.'

She picked up a couple of pieces of penne with her fork. Ben was looking around the restaurant. He was sitting with his back to one of the brown-brick archways that framed the murals, and he could see most of the room.

'Have either of you been here before?' he said. It was a new thought, though we had been in the restaurant close to an hour. 'I'm sure I've been here before.'

'I think it's been around for years.' I had driven past it on previous trips. That was all I could remember.

'Ah . . .' He reached for the bottle of chianti and topped up our glasses. 'It was a long time ago. It was the family holiday we had before my father left. Actually, no. That was a restaurant that looked just like this, but it was further down the coast. Da Carlo it was called, at Broadbeach. That was it. It was in a little strip of shops. Probably gone now.' It was another memory from his busted childhood. He was still holding the empty bottle in his hand. 'I kept the card. The guy gave me a card. No one had ever given me a business card before. I always wanted us to go back, just because of that. I wasn't used to that kind of respect. It had one of those black-and-white photos on it. A Roman street scene just after the war. Or Naples. A woman getting wolf-whistled, a guy on a Vespa. That kind of scene. Anyway, we didn't go back. My father had next-wife plans made that we didn't know about.'

'Were those the plans that led to you pissing on his bonsai plants?' Perhaps I should have been kinder.

'Ah, that's right . . . the bonsai plants.' He was smiling, but he didn't seem happy. He put the bottle down. 'I think he had them to make me feel at home. Which just goes to show how ignorant he is. Bonsai . . . why not a samurai sword? Most of the time I feel very un-Japanese. Like yesterday, those people at the wedding . . .' He stuck his fork into his pasta and started twisting it. 'I used to surprise myself when I looked in the mirror. When I was a kid. I'd look in the mirror and there was this Japanese guy. It was like the mirror was making it up.'

Neither of us knew what to say to that, but his attention was on his spaghetti so it didn't seem to matter.

When our mains were finished, we persuaded him we had no room for desserts and he made another fuss about paying the bill, taking it out of the waiter's hand and insisting loudly that it was his responsibility.

'Prick didn't even give me a card,' he said when we were out on the street. 'I tipped them too. Gave them a big tip.' He stood looking up at the tall buildings and the stars beyond as if he owned the lot of them.

He made us stop at Vintage Cellars again, where he bought two more bottles of the chianti, on the grounds that it was nice enough and the night was young.

'He's going nuts, isn't he?' Hayley said while we waited for him outside. 'I think he's losing it.'

We steered him back to the apartment and soon he was settled in on the balcony, unhappy and hardly saved at all from it by his nice chianti. We sat on the plastic chairs, and Ben cradled his glass in his lap and put his bare feet up on the railing. The breeze tossed the curtains around and he stared out to sea, his eyes half-closed.

'I read The Charterhouse of Parma – Stendhal's The Charterhouse of Parma – a few weeks ago,' he said, as though it was not long after the only other time he had mentioned it to me. That had been years before, but he knew I would remember. He turned to Hayley. 'You wouldn't know what I mean by that. On that last family holiday my father went out for two hours one morning. He came back with a book, and with this story about having been engrossed in it in a second-hand bookshop, and how he'd always wanted to read it. The Charterhouse of Parma. I found out later he'd seen his –' he thought for a while about the right term to use – 'new woman on that holiday. He'd been with her that morning, for about five minutes short of the two hours, and that's when he'd decided it was over with us. I think he ducked into the bookshop on the way back and picked up whatever shit he could for two bucks. So, anyway, I read it. Not long after he died. I was going through an airport and there was a new translation. It's this weird book from the 1830s. His name wasn't even Stendhal. And I don't get the history so . . .' He let the thought lapse. 'My father would never have read it. As if he would have read it. It was such a contemptuous choice really.'

He had told me about the book after the heat had abated from his father's failed attempt to escape to Spain. His father had insisted to the courts that it was a business trip, though he had no correspondence to back that up, no meetings in his diary. He told them that buying a return ticket was proof enough, but Ben put that down to him not being completely stupid and always having an instinct for covering his tracks. Stendhal, The Charterhouse of Parma. Close scrutiny might have found it wanting but, in the absence of suspicion, what is there that gets scrutinised so closely? He waved his plane tickets around in court, where suspicion was high and the scrutiny unrelenting, and they took his passport, kept him here and made sure he faced trial.

It hadn't played out that way with The Charterhouse of Parma and, if it had, the outcome would have been little different. The holiday ended acrimoniously, with Kerry Harkin stirring up discontent and smoothing the path to the exit. In his head, the deal was already done, his future was in another place and with another wife, and putting a wrecking ball through the holiday was a good first step towards getting there.

He married again a year later, since the divorce paper-work took time.

'It seemed to work, though. The Charterhouse of Parma.' I couldn't resist it. He had offered up his father as the villain of his story, his melodrama, because of one lie, and a less egregious lie than some. 'It held up as long as it needed to. Not every lie does that well.'

'You don't get it, do you?' he said. He was angry that I wasn't letting him set the tone. He wanted to be an innocent victim. 'You pick and pick and pick and you don't get it. You don't get that what's really killing me is how much of my family story, how much of everything told about us, ends up being about lies. About every-thing being built on lies. And I tried to change that, and it didn't work.' He shifted on his chair, brought his feet down from the railing. He leaned forward, and turned to Hayley. 'What you don't know – what I think you don't know – is where all of Josh's picking has got him. And I think you don't know about it because he's embarrassed to be doing what he's doing. Pitching this story, pitching me. And you know why?'

He waited, waited while she said, 'Why?' It had stopped making sense to her.

'Because Rob Mueller – that's the guy in the siege, the guy with the gun – his death was suicide and I did no more than fall on him.' He said it in a very measured way. Hayley's surprise was clear. He held up his hand to stop her speaking. 'But here's the whole story. The story no one knows, including your smartarse boy. Frank Ainsworth, the guy I "saved" –' the word, I was certain, had never been said more sarcastically – 'had been billing like a bandit. Fudging the figures. A bit here, a bit there. Maybe even siphoning money out. But in a smart way. I don't know the details and I never had any evidence. Some stuff may never have made it to the books.' Now that he was into the story, he almost looked pleased to be telling it. 'He had debts. He'd had margin calls when the stock market turned ugly. I know they were a problem. That's all I knew before the siege, actually. The margin calls. So it was greed. Just greed. Rob Mueller was a client. Ainsworth came up with bills he couldn't pay.'

He stopped to think, to bring it to the surface and put it into words. The base of his wineglass clunked against the arm of his chair. He jerked the glass away, as if wine might spill, though the glass was empty. He steadied himself again. 'With the right clients, you can probably make that work, that kind of deception. They don't know their rights, and they don't want to go up against their own lawyer. The best guess I can make is that Rob was suicidal. Miriam, his wife, got desperate. I think she agreed to sleep with Frank, or to have an affair. So Frank must have had money coming in in other ways that week, if he did that deal. She must have felt totally backed into a corner. Rob found out. That's the stuff he talked about when he was there with the gun.' Ben seemed less drunk, all of a sudden. 'There was not one second when I would have stood between him and Frank.'

It felt like the truth, finally. Ben put his glass down on the tiles.

'So what happened then?' I wanted to sound, this time, like someone asking, not picking. 'The hero part . . .'

'I was in shock. I couldn't process it. That's the truth. It was a horrible experience, regardless of the details. It was terrifying and then he blew his head practically off. Like, most of it came off. It burst like a melon. And before I could do a thing there were these stories about me out there. I saw my name in the papers before I'd got my head straight, and suddenly I wasn't a con man's son. For the first time in my life. There had never been a good word written about my family. I'd spent my whole life with us ducking for cover. And I thought, maybe we can change. Maybe this is when my name gets a fresh start. But the speed of it had overtaken me by then anyway.'

'I've seen the coverage. You only had a day or two before he'd dug you in too deep.'

'And once he made you a hero, he had you,' Hayley said. 'You'd have to stay quiet or the world would know you were . . . well, a fraud.'

'Yeah, that's it. A fraud,' he said, prepared to wear the word. 'Just like my father. Worse.'

So there it was, I thought. Harried forever by the stories of his father – the truth, the half-truths and the hyperbole – the second Kerry Benson Harkin had found himself trapped. By the hope of a better future and, soon after, by the realisation that he had little choice. He had been called a hero, with Frank Ainsworth pumping out detail, and he had appeared to acquiesce. Everyone within range had acquiesced, unwittingly – Max Visser and the staff, the police, the media, the committee who weighed up bravery and, in rare instances, handed out a star. The story came with a villain who was actually a victim and a victim who was a villain but, like many stories, it was better told with a hero. Shine the light on the hero, and all else falls into shadow.

Ben could imagine the destruction if the truth got out, because he had seen his father hounded, his reputation shredded, his face in the papers and on TV enough that passengers hurled abuse from passing buses.

'What would you have done?' he said to me. It didn't sound defensive. He simply seemed to be wondering where a person with a different past might have gone, where regular people went in such circumstances.

'I don't know.' I didn't. I couldn't know his state of mind at the time, or what capacity I might have had to stop the lie and tell the truth. To stand behind the clutch of microphones after Frank Ainsworth had had his turn, and praised me, and say to a crowded room and the wider world that the grateful man with the bandaged head was a thief who was fast-talking his way out of trouble. The choice was to call him a liar then, or become one.

I knew what I would do, and it was not the right thing. I had been Ben's liar already. I had not turned the medal story on its head when I knew it to be false. I had reconfirmed interviews instead of cancelling them. I had given quotes of my own. I had encoded them in a way that let Ben know they were not lies in themselves, but they were part of the lie just the same.

'And what would you do now?' he said. 'If you were me?'

'I don't know. I'm not brave. I'd do exactly what you're doing, I guess. I'd see the week out.' I had to accept that I probably would, and then I would bury the Star of Courage deep in a drawer and keep living with the shame of it. 'And I'd wonder about Miriam Mueller. I'd relive it a million times to find a moment when I might have handled things differently so that Rob Mueller lived and Frank Ainsworth got what was coming to him, whatever that is. But I probably wouldn't find one.'

'I've never met her,' he said, 'but I've thought about her. Miriam Mueller. She could see Rob was losing it, and she wanted to save him. She was desperate, and maybe what she did looked like the only way out. I don't know where she is now. I'm pretty sure Frank's got to her. Obviously he has. She's got nothing on him, no evidence. He's told me she's saying nothing. "Who's going to believe the wife of a crazed gunman out for a quick buck?" That's what he said. One word and he'll sue the house out from under her.'

I wondered if she would have been the motivation I might have needed, had I been in Ben's position. I wondered if I would have called Miriam Mueller and, with her, brought it out into the open. But Frank would have covered his tracks. There were still risks, beyond the pounding from the media for taking the medal.

I also wondered if I had spent years resenting Ben more deeply than I should have. I had put a lot down to our Tokyo Speed Ponies days. I had constructed a picture of my life then, with Eloise in it, as close to perfect, and I had refused to accept that it had been less than perfect for her. I had wanted to find that – find the thing I thought I had with her – in every relationship since, and that had been its own kind of sabotage. And I had given Ben the blame for every sunk relationship, for every year I spent fixing other people's stories and managing the telling of them.

I had left no space in my own story for the role I had played, or for the role Ben's father had played in shaping him. He had his own fears and weaknesses and ways of disguising them. And Frank Ainsworth had caught him in the fog of the siege and put a medal in his hand, or at least the prospect of it, before he could draw breath or work out right from wrong.

★ ★ ★

I THOUGHT I KNEW it all then. I thought the story was over. As I lay in bed that night with it kicking around in my head, I could find no good way of making the truth public, no way that would let me fix what had gone wrong. I was too far from the source, too far from evidence. I had nothing substantial.

I had two more days of it, and then it would be gone. I could picture Miriam Mueller. I had seen her talking to the media, tearful, bereft, an unfathomable space opened up in her life.

'What a terrible thing,' Hayley said, as she lay with her arm over me. 'Terrible for everyone.'

Except Frank Ainsworth, I thought. We had the window open and I could hear the sea, waves breaking and breaking far below on the beach that looked like it went forever.

It was hours later when she woke me. It was still dark. Ben was gone.

Hayley had been in the kitchen getting a glass of

water when she noticed that his door was wide open. Even in the dark, she could see his bed was empty. He wasn't in his bathroom or on the balcony. Then she noticed my car keys were missing.

'Maybe he just went out for something,' she said, though there was nothing to go out for, no reason for him to be driving around the Gold Coast at night.

I stood at the kitchen counter, still adjusting to the light, expecting my keys to be somewhere, Ben to be somewhere. I had pulled a T-shirt on, I realised, but no pants.

'I'll call him,' I said to her. 'He'll be somewhere.'

I found his number in my phone and called it. It rang three times, four. I thought he wasn't going to answer. I listened for his phone ringing, but it was nowhere in the apartment. Then there was a click, and a rush of sound.

'What's up?' he said. 'Couldn't sleep?' He was talking loudly. There was a roaring noise in the background, my car driving at speed.

'What are you doing?'

For a few seconds he said nothing. There was just the roaring noise. 'I have to fix this.'

'Fix what?' Dumb question. 'Fix it how?'

'You know what,' he said. 'And fix it definitively. I'll handle how. It's not your problem. You got me thinking. This isn't going to go away until I make it go away.'

'You can't be safe to drive. All that chianti.' I knew as I said it that it wouldn't stop him. 'Where are you?'

'In your car. But you knew that.' I was about to tell him to pull over, to say that we would come and get him and that there had to be a better way, when he said,

'Anyway, two hands for driving. That's the law. Going now.'

He hung up. I called back right away, but he didn't take it.

'What's he doing?' Hayley said. 'Where is he?'

We were both wide awake now. She was wearing a T-shirt of mine, I noticed, and probably nothing else. It came down to mid-thigh. Her hair was a mess. She pushed it out of her eyes.

'I think he's going to confront Frank.' It seemed like the worst idea in the middle of the night and in his present state of mind.

I called him again, and again he ignored it. I left a message on his voicemail telling him to stop, telling him that there was a better way, that he would be sober in a few hours, it would be daylight and we would fix it. I had no idea how. I sent him a text telling him to stop. I called again. No answer.

'We're going to have to go,' Hayley said. She reached out, took the phone from me and closed it. 'Where's Frank? Where does he live?'

I had no idea. I hardly knew these people. 'The award paperwork. The form Frank had to fill in for Ben to get the medal. It's on that.' He had to put his home address.

I went to my room, my original single-bed room. All my junk was there, all my siege notes and the file from Randall Hood Beckett. In England I had got into the habit of carrying everything with me until the job was done, until the last interview. I tipped out the DVDs and my own notes, and opened the firm file. There were newspaper clippings marked with highlighter, letters from the police and, finally, the form with Frank's address on it. Hakea Crescent, Chapel Hill.

Hayley was dressed and holding her car keys when I walked back into the lounge room.

'This would best be done with pants,' she said.

★ ★ ★

ON THE HIGHWAY, we switched between radio stations and tried to talk ourselves into believing it would all be okay. That Ben would change his mind and call, or turn around, or pull off the road to sleep.

At the same time, as our headlights lit up the empty road, and white concrete bridges and green exit signs flashed by, I kept staring ahead, fearing that I would see my car somewhere off the edge of the bitumen, crumpled and caught by the barriers.

'It's different, late at night, isn't it?' Hayley said. 'What they play on the radio. I've had nights when I've worked till about now, so I hear it a bit.'

'Me too. The gonzo life. I'm up late, high on something.'

She laughed. 'Turns out it's fortune cookies. That's not quite the same.' She checked our speed, eased back a little.

The song playing was Charlene's I've Never Been to Me. Years had passed since I'd heard it, but only a week since it had last come up in conversation, with Max Visser. He had been talking himself into singing it that night, and now I was driving an hour before dawn on a highway with the stripper we had seen instead.

'Oh God,' Hayley said. 'My mother does this. At karaoke. That's what she tells me. She thinks it's about a woman who's never had a real orgasm. Which I'm afraid is probably her, but by that bit of the story I've got my fingers in my ears and I'm screaming, so I can't really say.' There was a car ahead of us. Not an Echo. Hayley changed lanes and we passed it. 'Where do you think he is? What do you think's happening?'

'I wish I knew.' I tried to call Ben again, but his phone was switched off.

'Turn your phone on, bugger you,' I said to him, because it felt better to say something. 'What are you doing?' Charlene was singing about sipping champagne on a yacht. I shut my phone and put it back in my pocket. 'I'm sorry for dragging you into this.'

'Come on, what would I be doing if I was at home now?' she said. 'Five am would be completely going to waste.'

At the Sunshine Coast, my father would be up already out of habit. It was closer to five-thirty, in fact, so he would be on his way to the newsagency. He walked to work and he appreciated the silence. He liked that the only noise he could hear was the sound of his feet on the damp grass. It was his favourite time of day, though it wasn't, by my reckoning, day at all. Soon he would be selling papers to early dog-walkers, the same people, day after day, each conversation refloating the same entrenched view of world events and the ills of change.

We reached the outskirts of Brisbane. I tried Ben's phone again, but there was still no answer. I wondered how fast he was driving, how much of a lead he might have. I wondered if he was close to Frank Ainsworth's house.

We passed Mount Gravatt and came up the rise that showed the city skyline laid out ahead of us. At five twenty-eight by the car clock, Hayley's phone rang.

'No one calls me now,' she said. 'No one.' Her phone had the jangling-bell sound of the classic olde-phone ring tone. 'It's in my bag. Could you answer it?'

I was already reaching behind her seat to pull the bag through to the front. The phone was lit up and easy to find. The word 'work' was scrolling across the screen. I answered. It was Melanie.

Once she had adjusted to me not being Hayley, Melanie said, 'Look, Josh, there's a guy here. He got backstage somehow. He said he was a friend of Hayley's. He's in Ross's office. Something's going on in there.'

'Okay, his name's Ben,' I told her. 'I've been working with him. Let him know you've got me on the phone and I want to talk to him. We're coming into town now on the southeast freeway. We can be with you in —'

There was a shout at the other end of the line, and a clattering sound. The phone went dead.

I wasn't getting it. Frank Ainsworth would be nowhere near the Silver Spur. What was Ben fixing? What was he doing? I wondered if I had it completely wrong.

I called back twice, but the phone line rang and rang.

'I've got Mel's mobile in there,' Hayley said. 'Call her on that if you can't get through to the club. What's happening?'

'No idea. Ben's with Ross. I got cut off.'

I found Mel's number and called it. She answered by the second ring.

'He's gone,' she said. 'He pulled the phone out of the wall on the way past. He's got Ross's gun. I don't know how . . .'

'Are we going to the club?' Hayley said. We were still too far from town, barely at Holland Park.

I put my hand over the phone. 'No. We're going to Chapel Hill.' Then I got back to Mel. 'I think I know where he's heading.'

'We can't let the police know about the gun,' she said. 'Ross'll go down for it. I've told him a million times . . . What's this guy going to do?'

'If I can stop him, nothing.'

I didn't know if he had taken it to threaten Frank, or to use it. I didn't know if we could get there first, or a close enough second. I put the phone back in Hayley's bag. I called Ben again on mine, just in case, but there was still no answer.

'So?' Hayley said. 'What's happening?'

'He's left the club with Ross's gun.'

'What? How did he . . .' It took her a second or two. 'You told him about the gun? What were you thinking telling him about the gun?'

'Well not this, obviously. Fuck . . . I need Frank Ainsworth's number. That's got to be where he's going.'

I felt like an idiot, like the fool he had played me for. In the bottom drawer with a box of ammo, I had said. And Ben had stored it away. Then there had been the chianti in the restaurant, and all the talk about the club –

the spa, the gym, the ways of getting from front to back. It had seemed at the time like the intense but purposeless microscopic focus of the pissed. I had felt sorry for him. And he had been playing us both.

I found Frank's mobile number below his address on the award nomination form. I called it, but it was off. I could imagine the phone, charging silently on his bedside table as Chapel Hill slept. I put the number in again, in case I'd got it wrong, but it was still off.

I called directory assistance.

I gave Frank's name and the address, and the voice at the other end said, 'That's a silent number. I'm sorry.'

'But I really need it,' I said, as if I was the first person in history to try that. 'I've got his mobile number, but it's turned off.'

'Hopefully he'll turn it on soon. He's decided his landline's a silent number, though. He pays for that service.'

'If I give you his mobile number, can you give me the landline?'

'No.'

We were over the river on the Captain Cook Bridge with the city buildings right in front of us. Ahead in the left lane, a street-sweeping truck was at work, its lights flashing.

'How about the number of anyone nearby in Hakea Crescent?'

'We don't give that kind of assistance,' she said. And then, in case I was still in any doubt, 'It's not that kind of service. We can't give out numbers near things, or of people you don't actually want to contact, or of people who have chosen to pay for silent numbers. I'm sorry if that means we can't help you at this time.' It was a line that had all the empathy of voice-activated software. It meant we were done.

'I've got nothing,' I said to Hayley. 'Ben's on his way to Frank's place with Ross's gun, and I've got nothing. At least I assume that's where he's going.'

I didn't want to think that there were alternatives, that he might be driving to the edge of the bush or to his neatly kept apartment with other plans for the gun, recalling the burst of Rob Mueller's head, like a melon. Frank's house was our best and only bet.

'So what do we do?' Hayley said. We were sweeping left onto Coronation Drive. The first hints of daylight were coming into the sky. 'Do we call the police? There'd be hell to pay with Ross and the gun, but . . .'

'No. He's not rational. Ben, I mean. It'd all go bad.'

I could see it. I could see exactly how badly it might go, Ben cut down by a hail of bullets in a suburban street, or holed up in the house in a siege, the last of his plans unthreading as he took shots at the bushes, working his way through Ross's box of ammo.

'We've got to do better,' I said to her, with no idea of what better might be. 'We've got to be able to do better than that. And we can get there as quickly as they can now. I think we had our chance to call the police.'

We kept driving west, with the traffic lights running our way. I had the street directory open on my lap at map 177, with my finger on Hakea Crescent.

'You stay in the car when we get there,' I told her. 'There's no point both of us getting out.' That was my whole plan, I realised. I had nothing but the first two seconds covered.

'This isn't your fault,' Hayley said after a long silence, a silence that I had spent making a list in my head of the ways in which it was my fault.

It had been almost twenty minutes since Ben had left the Silver Spur. Any time now, he would be driving down Hakea Crescent, looking for Frank's place. And we were five minutes away, or not much more. That had to be enough. There had to be more than five minutes talking before any shooting started. Or maybe the gun wasn't about that. Maybe it was about making Frank weep and piss his pants and recant, with the feel of the cold barrel against his temple and the siege back in his head. Or maybe Ben would sneak in quietly and put a bullet in Frank's skull while he slept, blow his brain across his bedhead, and we would be far too late.

I called directory assistance again. The same operator answered. I gave her Max's name and spelled Visser, and said that he lived at West End.

'Do you have a street address?' She was already keying letters, searching for him.

'Just West End.'

She stopped keying. 'I'm afraid that's a silent number,' she said. 'The only Visser at West End. And I can't give you the number of anyone nearby either.'

I hung up. I stared at my phone, at the glowing picture of Darius and Aphrodite on the screen. They were covered in paint, and laughing.

I checked our progress in the street directory. We had made it to map 178. I counted the sets of lights ahead of us. There were sixteen.

I scrolled down my contacts. There was one landline number I didn't have to ask for. I called it.

It rang and rang, and then a voice – fuzzily, crankily – said, 'Hello.'

'Fran, it's Josh,' I said. 'I've got to talk to Brett. It's urgent.'

'Do you know what time –'

'It's urgent.' People always know what time it is when they're making stupid urgent calls at dawn. When it's all gone to shit and they've got no choice. 'Just get him, please.'

I heard a sigh, and then her voice, some distance from the phone, saying, 'Guess.'

There was a clattering sound and Brett said, 'Yeah? Um, who . . .'

'It's Josh. It's urgent. Do you have Frank's or Max's home numbers?'

I heard him sniff as he thought about it. 'Don't think so. Let me check.' Francesca said something in the background and he said, 'It's urgent. I've got to check something.' He came back to me. 'Just going to the office. What's up?'

'There's an issue with Ben and Frank. Ben's on his way to Frank's with a gun.'

'What? A gun? What the fuck?' There was a thump. He was probably on the stairs.

'I'll tell you all about it later. I'm on my way there now.'

'Okay, okay, let me just . . . I'm in the office. I can get into our electronic address book from here. It's a . . .' He stopped explaining it to me, and searched. 'No. No home number. I've got Frank's mobile.'

'It's off.'

'It's Chapel Hill, yeah? Where he lives? Or

Kenmore? I can be there in five minutes. What's the address?' There was a noise in the background, a small unhappy voice. It was Aphrodite. 'It's okay, darling,' he said. 'Everything's okay. You just go back to bed.'

'I'll be there sooner,' I told him. 'Sooner than you could be. Or the police. And I know Ben. I've got the best chance of fixing this.' I still had no idea how I would fix it. 'Stay away, please. I'm not waking you up to put you in the line of fire.'

Lights flashed ahead of us, orange lights, roadworks. I told Brett I had to go.

'There's got to be another way,' he said, and I told him I'd been through them all.

'It'll be okay,' I said, because it's what you're supposed to say. 'I'll call you when it's sorted out.'

A burly guy in a sleeveless fluoro jacket stepped out in front of us and planted a 'stop' sign in the road. I wound the window down as Hayley pulled up.

'It's an emergency,' I shouted out to him. 'We've really got to get through.'

'Yeah, no worries,' he said, but not quickly. He took a look behind him. 'We've just got to shift the bulldozer round. It'll be off the road in a tick.'

'But it's an emergency.'

The bulldozer chugged along, spouting blue smoke. It filled the whole road.

'Yeah, I get that,' the guy said. 'But he won't hear me anyway unless he turns the engine off, and it'll just take longer then. The quickest way is to let him do it.'

It couldn't have taken more than thirty seconds, but every move looked like it was happening in slow motion, deliberately slowed down. It was after six o'clock. The sun was rising.

Finally, the bulldozer was almost off the road, and the guy swivelled his sign around to the yellow 'slow' side and stepped out of our way, ushering us through with a sweep of his arm. Hayley accelerated and the car skidded across the graded surface before getting traction.

I took a look at the street directory. We were a hand span away from Hakea Crescent on the map, but eleven sets of lights. Hayley kept us right on the speed limit, and almost every one was green when we hit it. The streetlights were going out as we reached the Kenmore Tavern and turned right.

I don't know what I expected in Hakea Crescent – roadblocks, police cars parked at angles, mayhem, Frank Ainsworth dead in the road – but as we drove along it, it looked very ordinary. I was counting the house numbers as we closed in on the address. We came around a bend, and I knew the house was ahead of us on the right.

My car was parked outside an opulent two-storey place that I assumed was Frank's. It was facing our way. Hayley slowed down.

'He must be in the house,' I said. There were flyers in the mailbox, and a brown palm frond had fallen onto the middle of the well-maintained lawn.

Then I saw Ben in the car, slumped forward over the steering wheel. I had never seen a dead person before, never seen someone shot, never even been near a gun.

Hayley pulled up opposite. There was no sign of damage, none of the carnage that the movies show when a gun goes off at close range in a car. I wondered if he had shot himself through the chest, and hit the seat with enough force to bring him forward again.

I opened the car door, and it creaked loudly. It seemed as if it was the only sound in Chapel Hill. I stepped out onto the dewy, well-kept grass and I looked across to my car again. There was no movement, nothing. I wanted not to go over there. I wanted to drive away, to be anywhere else.

I was about halfway across the road when Ben sat up. The movement stopped me. I had braced myself for something ghastly and forensic. He looked at me as if I might be some unnamed threat, and then worked out who I was.

I took the two steps to the car door, and I opened it. He was sitting with the gun in his right hand and his silver star in his left, its ribbon scrunched up, its seven points pressing hard into his palm.

'I thought this is what would take courage,' he said. 'Coming here and finishing it.'

'I thought you were dead.' I had imagined the siege pictures of Rob Mueller, but with Ben's face, a different wound but just as scrambled.

'I got into the house. I was going to kill him. Maybe. I got in through a downstairs room. It was a kid's bedroom. There was this four-year-old in Wiggles pyjamas . . . So I couldn't do it then. I just looked at the kid and I . . . Well, fucking Wiggles pyjamas, and now I'm about to . . .?' He stopped, looked down at the steering wheel. His nose started running. It ran into his mouth before he noticed it and sniffed. 'I don't even know what I was going to do. I only knew how to load this thing from TV.' He wiped his face with his sleeve.

That's when I could see the damage done – the damage Frank had done by enlisting Ben to support his lie, his fraud, cover his tracks. Not a shot had been fired, but it was as though Ben had spilled his brain across that Chapel Hill street anyway, and I didn't know if we could fit the mess back into his head.

I reached in and took the gun carefully from his hand. He relaxed his grip on his Star of Courage and looked at his palm and the uneven star shape pressed into it as the points went from a bloodless white to red.

'If I'd gone into a different room that bastard might be dead by now,' he said. 'And nothing would be any better.'

'Yeah, I know. But you didn't.' I was holding the gun by its butt with my thumb and index finger, as though I was taking it away for prints. We had all watched too many of the same TV shows. It seemed like a safe way to hold it, as if nothing could go wrong.

I turned around to Hayley, who had her window down.

She was about to speak, but something stopped her. She was looking behind me. As I turned, I heard a door shut. Frank Ainsworth was standing at the entrance to his house, in running clothes.

He had a hand up to his eyes to block out the sun, and he was squinting at us, looking down the slope of his lawn at our two cars, and me standing on the street. The sun was directly behind us and just above the trees, casting my shadow across my car and onto the edge of the lawn.

He walked down towards us, his keys in his hand. He was watching where he put his feet on the damp grass, glancing up at us to see if there was any sign of what we had planned. He knew the secret was out. I heard Hayley get out of her car and shut the door. I stood a little straighter, and changed my grip on the gun, taking the butt of it in my palm and resting my finger near the trigger. I wanted to look as if I had held one before.

Frank saw the gun as he came closer. The look registered on his face before he could stop it. He almost lost his footing but then kept coming. In a few more steps he reached the property line where his driveway crossed the kerbside grass. He looked through the windscreen at Ben, and then at me with the gun.

'Frank, here's what we're going to do.' I wanted to sound calm. We had all seen the movies where the guy with the gun is calm, and he lays down the terms. I would keep the gun by my side, I decided. It would never be any kind of threat, but it had rattled him to see it and that gave me my chance. 'Ben and I will come up with a figure that will compensate Miriam Mueller for her loss. It'll be a big figure and you'll pay it. I think we'd all agree no amount of money could be enough, but let's at least make her life a lot easier. I can't say right now that that'll be the end of it for her, but I'm guessing she won't want to be dragged through this in public.'

Frank didn't speak. He looked over his shoulder at the house, where nothing stirred and his family slept on.

'I'm offering you a risk-management option, Frank,' I said to him. 'Think of it that way. That's what you called me in for. And you should bear in mind that I know all I need to. I've got it fully documented, you have nothing on me and I have nothing to lose.'

(277)

He moved his keys around in his hand. He had stopped looking like someone to fear.

'Okay,' he said. 'Okay, that's what we'll do. Who knows about this?'

'You don't need to know that. What I can tell you is that you maximise your chance of keeping a lid on it if you do exactly what I say.'

'Right.'

'So you should run now.' I pointed up the street, with the gun. It wasn't intentional. I hoped it wasn't loaded. 'Run and don't look back and we'll be gone before you're home.'

'Okay,' he said, and he ran.

I wanted to see some show of fear in his gait, but he ran like any other jogger. Perhaps, after years of it, it was the only way his body knew to do it. And perhaps I shouldn't have wanted to see fear, just because I had a gun.

He ran up the street and turned at the first corner into a dead end. I figured he stayed up there somewhere, crouched behind someone's bushes or a stand of bamboo, watching for us to drive past and out of Chapel Hill.

* * *

ON THAT MORNING, I saw the start of the mending of the damage caused by the siege, and by Frank's actions that had preceded and followed it.

I called Brett and told him the crisis had passed. That it was fixed, and it was in his best interests for me to say no more than that.

Hayley and I gave the gun back to Ross, who said it might be time to retire it, at least in a tin, sealed up tight and buried under his roses.

Hayley kept quoting what she regarded as my big line to Frank, and telling me it fell well short of 'make my day'. 'I'm offering you a risk-management option, Frank,' she would say, in the most hardcore voice she could put on, and with an index finger aimed right between my eyes. I told her times had been simpler for Dirty Harry, but admitted it was the lamest threat ever made by someone with a gun in their hand.

Frank's feedback to Brett after the job was glowing. I made sure of that. I wrote it. A bonus came my way. I didn't know if it was Brett's money, or Randalls', or Frank's, and I didn't ask.

Ben never went back to Randall Hood Beckett. The lunch in his honour was cancelled. I told them he wasn't well – since I had run out of the energy that better lies take – and Frank backed me up.

I lied to Australian Story too, and got him out of that as well.

The remaining seventy-two holes of the Gold Coast mini-golf tour took a few more days to happen than I had planned. My form never improved, but Hayley's did and in the final round she beat me by three strokes.

I kept Ben involved in the settlement with Miriam Mueller, and it was at my urging that he came with me to give her the cheque. I was surprised by how different she looked from the TV interview after the siege, though I shouldn't have been. It was the first time I had seen her without that dense shock upon her, packed down with loss and awe at the way the world had opened up and swallowed her husband and spread his blood and tissue everywhere.

She took the cheque out of the envelope, studied it carefully and then slipped it back in and put the envelope in her bag. She shook our hands and thanked us. Ben hardly said a thing. He had pushed the money up. He had made Frank sell a house somewhere to raise it.

I watched her walk off down the street, no sign of her history of crisis or loss, blending perfectly with the crowd. She was taller than most of them in the heels she was wearing, and attractive enough that I saw the less subtle of the passing men pause to take a second look.

Ben took my calls at first after that, and then he started screening me. After only a few weeks I was calling less frequently and I realised it could easily taper off into nothing. In a final attempt to contact him, I went to his flat.

I had things to say about Eloise. They seemed important, though perhaps they weren't to him.

I had boxed Eloise into a corner. She slept with Ben instead of talking to me. It happens all the time, that kind of thing. It wasn't about anything particular to us. I had resented him more deeply for that than I should have, and had wanted every day we had worked together to punish him for my imperfect life. I had blamed him for the cascade of mediocre events that followed our friendship, because that had been far better than owning any of it myself. And I had pushed him and scrambled his head and sent him after Frank with a gun, to be saved only by chance, by climbing in a particular window, the window of a child's bedroom.

But he wasn't there when I arrived at his flat, so all

the rehearsing I had done in my head on the way across town was no good after all.

There were removalists at work, supervised by a small stylishly dressed Japanese woman. His mother.

'He's gone to Japan,' she said, once she had recognised me from a handful of meetings years before. She still had quite an accent. 'It happened very quickly. I have family there . . .'

She said it as though she was hanging it out for the breeze to take it. She had no more idea of what his trip might hold than I did. I noticed then that she had a box in her hands. She was gripping it firmly, and inadvertently opened it. It was his medal box, with the full-sized medal, the miniature and the lapel badge all in their places.

As I drove away, I took a final look in my rear-view mirror and saw his father's green lamp being carried into the removal truck. I googled it when I got home – Behrens plus lamp – though it took some time to work out the spelling of the designer's name. I saw pictures of the original, and its glass wasn't green at all. The green lamps were available from an absinthe website, and made to order.

A few more weeks passed before a postcard arrived from Ben. Hayley and I were both at my flat. My new oven had just been installed, and it looked shiny and almost too new next to the dated laminate of the benchtops. The camp stove was sitting nearby, back in its box, ready to be returned to my parents. Behind it on the windowsill was a new pot plant that Hayley swore I could keep alive if I put in any effort at all. So far, it was still green.

The card was a Hokusai woodblock, one of his many of Mount Fuji, and on it Ben had put, in his small neat writing, 'This place is crazy. The pachinko parlours are noise a mile high. I'm foreign here. It must be the way I walk, I don't know. I have a job interpreting for a film crew who are shooting a whiskey ad with an American star. We're all in a big hotel and I've met a girl. It hasn't worked out for her with her photographer boyfriend. We seem to have clicked.'

I told Hayley I thought it sounded great, and she said, 'Sure it does, because the girl's Scarlett Johansson and he's worked his way into the plot of Lost in Translation.'

I wanted to argue, but there was no argument to be had. He had slipped away and sent us this story, this new facade. I wondered where he was. I wondered if he might even be dead by now. I looked at the picture again, at the top of Mount Fuji covered like ice-cream, and I imagined Ben putting clear-cut Hokusai footprints in snow, trudging through it with purpose. I thought of him digging a snow cave on a mountain in Hokkaido, somewhere remote, and sealing himself in, to be found only in the spring thaw and without identity. A Japanese man, lost and never claimed, never a story here at all more than likely.

I was imagining Hokkaido, though, and the mountain. Imagining that end and any others. I had nothing else to go on. I had stopped being sure, long before, that I knew one true thing about him.

The following week, I took Hayley to the Sunshine Coast to meet my parents for the first time. We had the camp oven in the back and planned to stay the night, since it fitted with her lecture timetable and her shifts at the Silver Spur.

As we headed north, I realised we would pass close to the street where Miriam Mueller lived. I knew her address from organising the settlement. I told Hayley I wanted to check something. I think I wanted to see Miriam Mueller's house, just drive by slowly and see that all was well.

I turned left off Gympie Road, and took a right into her street. I was sure I could remember the number, but when we got there the house looked empty. I pulled up, to make certain of it. There was junk mail overflowing from the mailbox and the grass had grown long. There was no furniture on the small front verandah.

One of her neighbours was mowing his lawn, and I got out of the car and walked over to him. He stopped the mower, and wiped the sweat from his forehead with his arm. I asked him about Miriam Mueller, and he said she had gone. He told me an Asian guy had turned up one morning in a cab, and she had left with him.

'He was about your age,' he said, trying to be helpful. 'Chinese, Japanese, something like that. She had a suitcase. I don't think she's coming back. I think she came into some money.'

I thanked him, and I walked back to the car.

I wondered when it had started between Ben and Miriam. If it had been because of me, pushing him to stay involved with the settlement, pushing him to meet her. Or if it had been much earlier.

I wondered if Ben had shown me anything true, ever. I could retrace the steps as far as I liked – from the Hokusai woodblock, back to Frank Ainsworth's house and the Gold Coast and the medal, back further still into the past, to Eloise and to Tokyo Speed Ponies – but I knew I would never find the start, the point where the last allegiance to the facts was lost, where a better story broke away from the truth. And made Ben Harkin who he was, and made him rich, and gone.

ACKNOWLEDGEMENTS

I saw a movie in this story before I worked out the novel, and Rob Marsala's insightful questions about the first draft of the script helped lead me to the pieces I needed to tell it in both media.

I'm also grateful to Meredith Curnow at Random House Australia for her unwavering support, and to Sophie Ambrose for asking me for more (and sometimes less) of exactly the right things. And to Pippa Masson at Curtis Brown for her advice, for keeping so many things on track (or getting them back there) and for her tolerance of my whingeing.

More than 500 people through Twitter and Facebook volunteered their names for characters, sight unseen and despite the fine print that said I was at liberty to make the characters be/do/wear/consume/say anything. Thanks for playing the game. About twenty of you made it to the finished version, though some may consider themselves luckier than others.

Finally, I'd like to thank Sarah and Patrick for making it clear to me every day that there's a great life to be had any time I step away from this keyboard.

Also by the Author

THE TRUE STORY OF BUTTERFISH

Curtis Holland wanted to make music. Derek Frick wanted to be a rockstar. Derek won that one. Luck and sales in the millions came Butterfish's way, and Derek lived the rock dream to the max, with Curtis on keyboards, just holding on.

It was a relief, really, when the third album tanked and Butterfish imploded, letting Curtis escape back to Brisbane, to a home studio where he could produce other people's music away from the glare of the spotlight.

When Annaliese Winter walks down his driveway, Curtis is ill-prepared for a sixteen-year-old schoolgirl who's a confounding mixture of adult and child. He isn't at all ready, either, to find himself drawn to the remarkably unremarkable family next door. To Kate, Annaliese's mother, who's curvy in a way that's sometimes unfashionable and sometimes as good as it gets. Even to fourteen-year-old Mark, at war with his own surging adolescence.

But Curtis has to work himself out before he can bring anything positive to the lives of the Winter family, and Annaliese makes it all the more complicated when she begins to show too much interest in him.

Then Derek flies back into town . . .

NOW AVAILABLE AS AN EBOOK

ZIGZAG STREET

Here I am, on a work day of some importance, riding out of town in a cab with a babe I've just concussed with footwear.

Richard Derrington is twenty-eight and single. More single than he'd like to be. More single than he'd expected to be, and not coping well. Since Anna trashed him six months ago he's been trying to find his way again. He's doing his job badly, he's playing tennis badly, his renovating attempts haven't got past the verandah, and he's wondering when things are going to change.

Zigzag Street covers six weeks of Richard's life in Brisbane's Red Hill. Six weeks of rumination, chaos, poor judgement, interpersonal clumsiness . . . and, eventually, hope.

'A comic masterpiece' – *Who Weekly*

NOW AVAILABLE AS AN EBOOK